"Janna McMahan is a writer who knows how to get out of the way and let the story rip."

--*Lee Smith, New York Times* bestselling author of *On Agate Hill*

"Janna McMahan is a natural voice who gracefully walks that tightrope of being both literary and commercial."

--*Silas House, New York Times* bestselling author of *Clay's Quilt*

"The details are so real they make you shiver."

--Robert Morgan, *New York Times* bestselling author of *Gap Creek*

"Beautifully written, both funny and intensely sad, this glorious novel sparks such an escalating longing for family and the place in your heart you really call home that it is almost impossible to put down."

--*Charleston Magazine*

"Fans of Jodi Picoult's work will appreciate this novel's sparse prose, unexpected plot turns and moral complexities."

--*The Louisville Courier-Journal*

Praise for Janna McMahan and *The Ocean Inside*

"A vividly drawn love letter to coastal South Carolina. McMahan's descriptions of the Lowcountry and its unique climate and customs jump off the page."
--*Publisher's Weekly*

"The story is gripping and the characters all too real."
--*Booklist*

"A beautifully crafted, mesmerizing read I highly recommend."
--Cassandra King, author of *Queen of Broken Hearts*

"A gripping American family portrait."
--Lisa Alther, author of *Washed in the Blood*

"The Ocean Inside speaks to coastal Carolinians with a strong, familiar voice. Readers would be hard-pressed to discern that Janna McMahan is not a native."
--*The Sun News*, (Myrtle Beach, SC)

For Madison,

you always have a home.

Anonymity
by Janna McMahan

Published by

an imprint of Morgan James Publishing

5 Penn Plaza, 23rd floor
c/o Morgan James Publishing
New York, NY 10001
212-574-7939
www.koehlerbooks.com

Publisher
John Köehler

Executive Editor
Joe Coccaro

In an effort to support local communities, raise awareness and
funds, Morgan James Publishing donates a percentage of all
book sales for the life of each book to Habitat for Humanity
Peninsula and Greater Williamsburg.
Get involved today, visit www.MorganJamesBuilds.com

Acknowledgments

Research for this novel took me out of my comfort zone more than any of my previous stories. I am indebted to numerous people who gave generously of their time and expertise to help shape *Anonymity*.

I owe sincere gratitude to Steve Bewsey, the Director of Housing and Homeless Services for LifeWorks in Austin, Texas. My fictional shelter organization is loosely based on the everyday functions of LifeWorks. Steve told me stories, answered questions, shared academic studies, took me to spots where homeless youth hang and eventually read my manuscript and gave suggestions. Without his contributions this book would not have been possible.

I must also thank Jonathan Artz, director of the Columbia Family Shelter in South Carolina for letting me spend time with him. He provided me with a new perspective of the realities facing families without permanent homes.

My appreciation to Marc Klaas of the Klaas Kids Foundation for allowing me to use their Print-A-Thon project.

Thank you to Eric Michalovic and Jeremy Lewis of Devine Street Tattoo. I learned so much about the culture, history and art of tattooing from these guys. While they made good fun of me for being unwilling to get inked, Jeremy was game to give me a water tattoo so I could see what it felt like. Owwww!

A special shout out to Reece Zylstra, the real Road Dogg, for sharing his amazing stories of life as a homeless youth. I couldn't make up stuff that interesting.

Gracias to all the guys at San Jose's Restaurant for sharing their passion about Mexico's soccer leagues.

Thank you to Dan Cook and the writers at *Free Times* for allowing me to sit in on one of their editorial meetings, to Stephen Hooker, chief photojournalist at WIS-TV for his production lingo lessons and to fellow writer Ron Aiken for helping flesh out how an investigative reporter thinks.

Thank you to many friends and family who contributed to the success of this book through their assistance, inspiration and love. These folks include Dr. Laura Basile, Monica Francis, Jill Pickett Todd, Kelly Morse Jackson, Tom Bond, Dr. Joy Pierce, Edith McMahan, Shelby Miller Jones, Robin Reibold, Michele Burnette, Kristina Mandell, Trace Ballou, Lucy Hunt, Carolyn Mitchell, Kate

Moran Spurling, Doreen Sullivan, Amy Barnes, Maria Vick, Deirdre Mardon, Christian Myers, Tamara and Will Cooper and the good folks at the Richland County Public Library.

I owe an enormous debt of gratitude to my brother and sister-in-law for all the good times they've shown me in Austin. Robb and Lisa McMahan, y'all are the best.

My most heartfelt gratitude to my husband, Mark Cotterill, and our daughter, Madison. They are always supportive, understanding, and at times, sympathetic. Thank you both. You are my dream team.

Many thanks to the people of Austin. No matter whom I approached, from store clerks to UT professors, everyone was informed and eager to help. Sgt. Moss of the Austin Police was very informative about the relationship between the police force and the homeless population. Kirk Holland, manager of Barton Springs, enlightened me about the area's natural resources and park amenities. Emily Crawford, of Urban Space Realtors, guided me through the different personalities of the neighborhoods ringing Austin.

I hope my Austin readers will enjoy seeing their city through the eyes of my characters and allow me a little creative leeway when it comes to creating fictional people, places and events set in their lovely, quirky town.

This book is dedicated to the memory of Leslie Cochran who died in early 2012. He was one of Austin's most colorful personalities and his flamboyance will be greatly missed.

Finally, thank you to David Hancock of Morgan James Publishing and John Köehler of Köehler Books for seeing value in this tale. Your enthusiasm and positivity made me feel right at home. Also, my gratitude to my editor, Joe Coccaro, whose careful attention to details helped polish my story and give it light. And to my publicist, Bethany Marshall and the rest of the Morgan James/Köehler Books family, thank you for all you do.

Anonymity

Janna McMahan

NEW YORK

VIRGINIA

"Freedom's just another word for nothing left to lose."

KRIS KRISTOFFERSON

Lorelei

PASSENGERS BEGAN collecting their bags from overhead storage long before the dusty bus lurched to a stop in the terminal. Lorelei pressed her forehead against the window and peered out through the ghostly fingerprints of previous riders. People bumped into each other and apologized as they shuffled around. She followed their reflections in the smudged glass as they inched toward the exit.

Mothers caressed the damp curls of their heavy-eyed children. They planted kisses on smooth cheeks to rouse their babies. Longing drew sharp on Lorelei's heart, but she pushed it down. Emotions were the enemy.

The bus driver eyed her in his rearview, the young straggler with no one waiting for her, nowhere in particular to go. She expected him to be impatient, but he seemed content to merely watch her make her way toward the front.

"Good luck, honey," the driver said when she finally stepped off. "Girl like you, you got to be careful out there." The accordion doors hissed closed and she was left in a gas-flavored fog as the bus pulled away.

She could use a little luck. And food. She could definitely use some food.

Lorelei tried to ignore hunger, to force her body to forget the purpose of that ache. The times she was able to endure the black gnaw in her gut, she felt strong and in control.

This wasn't one of those times.

She had eaten her last Slim Jim in the Phoenix Greyhound terminal while she waited for some guy to pay her fare through to Austin. She had picked him because he seemed gentle, like he would help her when she told him about searching for her brother. She could read people now, which ones were easy targets, which ones to avoid.

For more than a year, she had been walking and hitching, cramming into rattletrap cars and vans with other worn-out travelers. She left home for Portland, then worked her way down the coast to L.A. and across the rocky flatlands of the Southwest. If she didn't have luck in Austin she'd move on to New Orleans, maybe Miami before winter. Being homeless in winter sucked.

Outside the station she spotted kindred spirits, a group with tattoos and lived-in clothes, packs and bedrolls. One had a thin dog on a frayed rope. She waited, hoping they would be cool, but one of the girls gave her a warning look, so she moved on.

Austin's heat blanketed her. The sun was low in the sky but still strong enough to force her into the shadows of buildings and trees. The sidewalk radiated heat. A digital bank sign read 107 degrees. She was parched. Her mouth, even her eyes were dehydrated. Texas was the sort of dry hot that smothered a person's spirit.

The Salvation Army was close to the terminal. She waited a block away, watching. Dozens of men were hanging around outside smoking. Some stood on the corner peering up and down the busy street as if waiting for something important to happen. But she knew they were just drunks and mentals, the usual down-on-their-luck scary losers.

The dazzling glass towers of downtown promised better opportunity, so she moved on. In a few blocks she was on the famous Sixth Street. Pubs, coffee bars and Mexican restaurants lined the sidewalks. Pulsing neon marked the clubs—guitars, tilted martini glasses, funky retro signs. Music pounded out of open doors. Light poles were plastered with hand flyers for bands. The road was blocked and happy-hour humanity flowed down the sidewalks and pooled in the wide streets, laughing, staggering along.

She stopped to admire a historic hotel with arches and a large columned balcony. It reminded her of a castle or a wedding cake. A valet jogged out to meet beautiful people emerging from a sleek black sedan.

Musicians strummed guitars and sang in front of a music store, an open instrument case at their feet littered with a few dollar bills. The tangy air outside a barbecue joint made her stomach throb. She searched the crowd for someone to help her, a mark.

Amidst the movement stood an eddy of blonde girls in short dresses and slouchy boots. Their enormous earrings brushed their shoulders. One held out her phone and her giddy friends leaned into the picture. They froze in a parody of their drunken happiness, colorful birds chirping away.

"Can you please help me?" she asked.

Four sets of coal-rimmed eyes turned her way. She saw the moment their fuzzy minds focused. Their eyes flashed up and down her dirty cargo pants, her scarred Doc Martens, her tats. She could hear their thoughts—street rat, gutter punk, trash.

Would they freak or would they help? You could never tell with college girls.

One clutched her purse tighter.

"Is there a church around here that serves food?" Lorelei asked. "Or maybe a shelter, you know, for young people?"

"Oh," one said. She snapped her fingers trying to recall. "I know that place. It's by the University Tower. What's it called?"

"It's some plant name, right?" the girl with the phone said.

"Yeah. Like Tumbleweed or something. Look it up."

The girl tapped her phone with glistening nails. "Here it is. Tumbleweed Young Adult Center. It's not far." She held the screen forward. "It's like, um, a fifteen minute walk or something. It's right by the university, along The Drag."

It seemed wrong to press for money after they had helped, so she thanked them and walked on.

Lorelei didn't bother to panhandle on the way toward campus. She was focused only on food and something to drink. As she walked, the University of Texas grew around her, pale stone buildings and walks, an important place for important people. The grounds were trimmed and impressive, although the whole city seemed to need a good watering.

To her left, pockmarked sidewalks fronted student bookstores, taco stands, churches and food co-ops. In a barren space between two buildings, a cluster of kids were hunched over paper plates. She had arrived.

The drop-in entrance was down concrete steps tucked into a corner of a church basement. She'd done this enough to know that on the other side of that weathered steel door would be a ratty couch, mismatched chairs scattered around and inspirational posters of kittens and puppies and sunsets.

And food. There would be no mouth-watering barbecue. Only foil containers of salad and pasta. Brittle cookies. Fake lemonade.

She hesitated. Going in meant revealing herself. Usually she could hang in a new place for weeks before she had to find the shelter, but once her presence was known, things had a way of changing fast. Counselors would want to talk. She never gave them her real name, never told them where she was from. Still, information would start to spread. A white girl under eighteen, alone on the streets, worried certain people. Sometimes the cops got involved, or worse, sometimes parents got found.

There were clear advantages to keeping a low profile, but the double blades of thirst and hunger had long ago carved caution from her empty hull.

Emily

SHE CHAINED her bike to the rack at the entrance to Whole Foods. It was invitingly cool inside and Emily's thin T-shirt was chilly against her skin. The market was busy and cheerful. The organic makeup section smelled like a field of lavender. Emily tried a natural lipstick. It was a little grainy, but she liked the color against her tan skin. She waved the wand from a tiny brown bottle of sweet patchouli under her nose.

At one of the food bars she loaded up a take-away box with greens and veggies. Her favorite cabernet was on sale in the wine section. She moved on to produce where memories flooded her as she reached for an avocado. Whole Foods had been her first real job after high school, and she'd spent many days stacking apples and bundles of cilantro in this store.

"Oh my God, Emily! Hey!"

On the other side of a vegetable display stood her old roommate, Beth, who had also spent a couple of years in this produce department. She looked different and it wasn't just the chunky blond streaks in her dark flat-ironed hair. She'd gained weight in her face. When Beth walked around a rack of oranges Emily understood why.

"Wow. You are amazingly pregnant."

Beth touched her stomach. "I know. I'm huge. Can you believe it?"

They both glanced around at the carrots and bean sprouts while formulating the proper things to say. It had been a long while since they'd seen each other.

"Brings back memories, doesn't it?" Beth said.

"I was just thinking that."

"Oh man, we had at good time." Beth rubbed her stomach. "And just look at me now."

"Are you moving back to the 'burbs?"

"I wish I could tell you no, but we just bought a house a few blocks from Mom and Dad."

"Wow. Back to Juniper."

She shrugged. "Good schools. Hey, you've got to come outside and eat lunch with me and my friend Kelly. We have to catch up."

"Sure. I'll be out as soon as I pay."

Emily watched Beth waddle away. She was slightly wider than Emily remembered, but overall she looked healthy and happy in her current state. They had grown up in the same neighborhood. After high school, they had both wanted to live in downtown Austin, so their parents had forced them to live together for safety. Their living arrangements had been a pairing made of parental paranoia rather than of a solid friendship.

Beth had plowed on through the University of Texas in four years and married Sam the summer after graduation. She'd had seven bridesmaids and Emily had been included in the wedding party as a courtesy.

They lost touch after Beth moved out, but Emily didn't blame her for drifting away. Apparently, she had been busy buying real estate and getting knocked up.

At a table outside, Emily found Beth and her new BFF. Both were staring at their smartphones from behind exaggerated sunglasses. They sipped smoothies and jiggled their sparkly sandals. Emily noticed they had the same pale-blue pedicures and massive handbags winking with hardware.

"Hey, Kelly. This is my friend Emily. We lived together in college in this cool little house over in Bolden Creek. It was this Spanish style, adobe-looking thing. Really cute, with a great front porch. We had some killer parties on that porch."

"Yeah, we did," Emily said. She slung her canvas bag on the table, noticing how it suddenly seemed dingy and plain.

"Are you still there?" Beth asked.

"Still there."

"This is Kelly. Sam and I bought the house next door to Beth and her husband. And that adorable thing is Megan Ray."

The sleeping toddler strapped into a jogging stroller had a head of soft, golden ringlets and plump legs. She looked like her mother.

Beth was beginning to look like Kelly too.

Kelly said, "So y'all went to college together?"

"Not exactly," Emily said as she swiped an extra chair from another table. She scraped it across the concrete patio and the racket caused the baby to start and ball her tiny fists in front of her face.

Kelly whispered, "Oh nooooooo."

They all watched, holding their breath, until the baby settled back to sleep.

"Sorry," Emily whispered as she sat down. "I'm not used to being around kids. She sure is sweet."

"I know, right? I just stare at her while she sleeps, and I can't believe she's mine. I love her so much I could just die sometimes." Kelly wiped a blue-tipped finger under her sunglasses and sniffled. "You just wait, Beth. You have no idea how much you're going to love that baby."

Kelly's rush of emotion left them silent. Somehow, even Emily felt stung by the baby's puffy pink lips and sweaty curls against her pale skin. There was an uncomfortable tug at the back of Emily's throat, a weird feeling of joy over Kelly's little cherub.

The tugging sensation traveled down to Emily's stomach, making it difficult to swallow her salad. She suddenly realized that she didn't want to talk about herself. What could she possibly say that would compete with their baby stories? It would be so much easier to just let them ramble on.

So she asked Beth, "Are you having a boy or a girl?"

Emily listened to their happy absorption in all things baby. She hadn't really given the concept much thought, but now she could see there was apparently a fountain of happiness attached to motherhood, a sense that life was filled with a profusion of possibilities. She wondered if she would ever become a mother.

But before she could think about babies, she'd have to get married—something she hoped to do, some day. Getting married had never been high on her agenda either, at least not before this moment. As she watched the assuredness of their lives, Emily saw a security that appealed to her. Could she be that girl? The one who was taken care of by a man? The one who worried about baby clothes and if her polish was chipped? A minivan driving, pinot grigio sipping, fake blonde with a toddler in tow?

What's wrong with you? Reality check, she said to herself. But this wasn't the first time Emily had experienced a twinge of envy. She had recently begun to realize that most of her high school class was moving into what seemed to be their third and fourth major life changes while she was still playing level one. It hadn't bothered her much before, but now she recognized the glare of disparity.

"We must be boring you to death with all our baby talk," Beth said. "What have you been doing the past couple of years?"

Emily chewed and thought how to phrase her lack of momentum. "I still work at Group Therapy. Frank made me bar manager."

"So you get the good schedule." Beth always looked for the kind angle.

"I enjoy it. I love the people and the money's good."

"So what about a love interest? Anybody special now?"

Emily shrugged. "You know me. I'm not into that one-guy-at-a-time thing."

"Emily likes musicians," Beth said with a wicked little smile. "We'd stay out on Sixth and Congress all night. Or we'd hang at Emo's until we ran out of money, then we'd drink beer in somebody's backyard. Emily would always end up with some musician following her home."

The more Beth elaborated on Emily's male conquests, the more Kelly's lips took on a judgmental twitch.

Anger flashed through Emily.

Beth seemed oblivious. "Our parties lasted until daylight drove us inside or the police arrived. Those were some good times."

Beth sighed and Emily imagined that if she could see her eyes that Beth would seem wistful about her past nightlife, back when she still had a waistline and a predilection for Jell-O shots. But then Beth said, "I like hitting Sixth Street, but you know, I have to admit, it was getting old. I just couldn't do it anymore."

And there it was—the point in the conversation that underscored Emily's stagnant life. Beth had a point. Really, how long could Emily continue to hang out in bars? Would she still be doing it at thirty? At thirty-five? The singles scene in Austin was smoking. Married life had always seemed lame by comparison, but maybe, just maybe if the right guy came along, Emily would entertain the idea.

It was true that her men never seemed to stick around more

than a couple of months, but often it was Emily who hastened their departure. What would it be like to make a pact with a man, to swear to the world that you would always be together for better or for worse? Maybe there was somebody out there who wouldn't eat all her food, trash her house and sleep all day. A man she wouldn't want to kick out the morning after.

"So, Emily, what was your major?" Kelly asked.

Crap, Emily thought. *Here we go.*

"I'm still undecided," she quipped. "Keeping my options open."

Kelly looked confused.

"You didn't go to UT? Where'd you go?" she asked.

"Nowhere yet," Emily said as she took a big mouthful of tasteless salad. So time had gotten away from her. So what? She didn't have to explain herself to a housewife.

There was an awkward, judgmental silence.

Kelly picked up her phone and touched the screen. "We're late for Mommy and Me classes," she said. "So sorry, but we're outie. Nice to meet you, Emily." Kelly slung her bag over her shoulder and released the brake on the bulky stroller. A curt exit.

Beth slowly maneuvered up out of her chair. "Sorry, we have to run. It was so good to see you. Facebook me. We've got our ten-year reunion coming up next summer."

Emily watched them cross the parking lot and get into a gigantic SUV. Everything about Beth and her friend seemed shiny and polished and larger than life. They pulled into traffic moving toward the highway and the sprawling suburbia beyond. Beth was as sweet as ever, but her friend had a bitchy edge.

Emily's lunch was no longer appealing. The greens were sad and wilted, like her mood. She tossed the box of salad in a trash bin. The wine bottle in her messenger bag seemed unusually heavy and Emily readjusted it on her shoulders a number of times before finally giving up and climbing onto her bike. She coasted out into the bike lane and peddled toward the Colorado. When she reached her neighborhood on the other side of the river she was grateful for the avenues of gnarly trees that cut sun's fierce grip.

At home, Emily brought her bike inside, where it lived against a wall strewn with black handlebar marks. She scooped up mail scattered across the wood floor at the front door. Skinny Cat slept in his favorite spot on the couch. Emily sat beside him and scratched his torn ears.

She switched on a couple of her funky old lamps. They threw shadows on her kitschy thrift store art. She picked through bills and coupons and a postcard solicitation from a dating service that promised to find her perfect match.

Her eyes were suddenly heavy. She needed a power nap. It was Friday, her night off from the bar. She had plans to meet friends, but that would be much later. Downtown didn't really start rocking until ten.

Lorelei

THE SIGN above the entrance read *Tumbleweed Street Outreach*. She pushed through the heavy steel door. Inside, half-a-dozen young people draped themselves over scarred furniture. One in a folding chair leaned into a computer monitor. A candle flickered from a windowsill, cloaking the room with the sting of cinnamon. Nobody looked up or even seemed to notice her.

Lorelei found the food table and heaped a paper plate with pasta salad. She bent forward and shoveled a pile into her mouth. It was creamy and cool.

"Hey."

His eyes were smiling. Genuine eyes.

"Is it okay?" she asked, the loaded fork halfway to her face again.

"Sure. Take all you want. I'm David. I'm here to help if you need anything."

He turned away. Low pressure.

She blurted out, "You got a toothbrush?"

He stopped. "Sure. You need some stuff?"

"My pack got took." She had made the mistake of stashing it in bushes in Phoenix when she went into a convenience store to buy jerky sticks. She hated to carry her things inside a store. It made her feel more homeless somehow, more vagrant, if she toted her bedroll. It made storeowners more nervous too.

"We've got all that stuff. Whatever you need, soap and

deodorant," he said.

"You got blankets?"

"Blankets and sleeping bags."

"Okay."

"You need another pack?"

"Yeah."

"Follow me."

He led the way to a back room stocked with boxes of blankets and random travel size soaps and shampoos cast off from various hotels. Canned food was arranged on metal shelves.

"Take your pick," he said, waving at a heap of used backpacks.

She stopped chewing long enough to point to the one army green bag among the reds and blues. Dark natural colors were easier to hide.

His smile was so swift she wondered if she had seen it at all. He unzipped it and tossed in a toothbrush, toothpaste, shampoo and soap. He grabbed a small towel and shoved it in. "You want a blanket or a sleeping bag?"

"Blanket. It's hot out."

"Okay. But if you're still here when it starts to get cold you need to come back because all the sleeping bags and coats go quick once the weather turns."

She continued to eat as she trailed him to another room.

"How'd you find us?" he asked as he held up food items. Lorelei nodded and he tossed them inside the pack.

"I asked around."

"What's your name?"

She hesitated, took another big mouthful of the sweet pasta and chewed. He waited patiently.

"What difference does it make?" she finally said.

He shrugged. "Everybody's got a name."

"Do I have to tell you to get that stuff?"

"No. You can come here and eat and get supplies without telling me anything. But some of the kids like to use our computer to send e-mails. They use our phone and address so they can look for work. If you use our electronics you have to give us some info. If you use the health clinic or the dental clinic, they'll want to know what to call you."

When she didn't offer more information he handed her the backpack.

"Do you need some clothes? I don't know if we have anything you'd like, but you're welcome to look."

He opened the door to a windowless storage room and the smell of stale fabric crept out. Inside, clothing hung haphazardly from wire hangers and spilled from cardboard boxes onto the floor.

"I'm afraid your options are pretty limited."

"You got any socks?"

"I doubt it. Socks go fast."

She wasn't going to wear clothes that smelled like her grandmother's attic. On the streets your style was your only cred, and she had no street cred in Austin yet. She'd have to lay low until she could use her five-finger discount to get a few things off sidewalk sale racks. It wasn't hard. Sales clerks didn't care. It was expected.

"No thanks," she said, looking into the clothing room. She'd seen the shower area, had hoped she could wash up before she left, but it would be pointless without clean clothes.

"Okay," David said and shoved the door closed. "I don't blame you. Pretty grim."

She trailed him back to the front room where kids were eating and laughing. He poured her a cup of lemonade.

"You a traveler?" he asked.

She nodded.

"Which way did you come from?"

"West."

"You here for a while?"

"Depends," she said.

"On what?" Those eyes again. As if he had all the time in the world to talk to her. It made her feel good. It made her cautious.

She tossed her empty plate in the trash, hoisted her new pack onto her shoulder.

"Thanks," she said. "You know, for the stuff."

"Anytime. That's why we're here." He handed her a small card. "This is a schedule of where you can get food. We only serve on Tuesdays and Thursdays. There are two churches that serve other days. They're both on The Drag, really just a couple of blocks down from here."

She wondered what he meant by The Drag, but decided she didn't want to give him a reason to talk more. She'd already stayed longer than she had intended.

"Thanks man," she said, and tucked the card in a pocket. "See you around."

"Sure. We're here if you need us."

Dark had fallen. She'd have to find somewhere to sack out for the night, and it was apparent from the stadium-level lighting that the city didn't want anybody sleeping in the vicinity. She needed to find a park, some spot with heavy landscaping and a water fountain. She hoped Austin didn't have mosquitoes.

She was already hungry again. She found the food card and checked to see where she could get free breakfast. Tomorrow was Wednesday, no breakfast anywhere, but University Baptist Church on Guadalupe was serving lunch. She had arrived up Guadalupe, so she headed back down that street thinking one of the churches she had passed would be the right one.

She quickly came upon an ornate stone cathedral. A couple of kids smoked on the few flat steps separating the church's entrance from the sidewalk. She read the historic marker and found the curlicued architecture was called Spanish Revival. She walked the perimeter, looking for a way into the grounds, but none appeared. A low wrought iron fence surrounded the church. She scaled it with little trouble.

Parks and alleys were risky, especially when you were alone, especially when you were a girl. But cemeteries were assured safe havens. Normal people didn't sleep in boneyards. Even gutter punks avoided sleeping with the dead.

Barbara

"SO BETH'S moving back to Juniper." Barbara's eyes fell on the red and black club stamps decorating her daughter's hands. At least they weren't permanent.

"Right down the street from her parents." Emily sighed and pinched crust from her sandwich.

"It'll be good to be close to her parents when the baby comes," Barbara said. Her e-mail dinged in the other room, but she forced herself to ignore it. This was Saturday. Her daughter was visiting. E-mail could wait.

"Did she invite you to a baby shower?" Barbara asked.

"Oh God. Don't even think that. I hate those things. Besides, I'm tired of always buying wedding gifts and baby presents and never getting anything in return."

"Well, your luck would change if you picked young men who are marrying material."

Barbara had learned not to stop by Emily's house unexpectedly. More than once she'd dropped in unannounced in the middle of the day and caught her daughter with some young man still twisted up in her bed sheets. They were always scruffy things, mostly musicians, boys with tattoos crawling their arms. Late work schedules made musicians appealing, or at least convenient, for a bartender.

"Please don't start," Emily said.

"You lack a people filter. You always have. You'll just let anybody into your life."

"Just because I don't want to live in this cookie-cutter suburb and date the khaki clan doesn't mean I'll never get married. I date nice guys."

"None of your generation actually dates. All young people seem to do now is read each other's profile online and text a few thousands times. Then suddenly, there's the hookup."

"Whatever."

"How a girl's supposed to know if a boy really likes her if all they ever do is meet at a bar? If the guy springs for a couple of beers, does that mean you sleep with him? Seems risky."

"Don't worry. I have a strict no-glove, no-love policy."

"Please. That's not the type of information a mother wants to hear."

"Well, you brought it up."

Barbara often wondered if her daughter's laissez-faire attitude was common to today's young adults. Perhaps she should have pushed Emily harder, demanded more. Isn't that what all the talk shows and magazines harped about? How her generation had ruined their children by trying to be their friends rather than parents?

"I hate all the expectations," Emily said. "Like there's some grand life plan you have to follow to reach happiness. Step one: go to college. Step two: get some big job. Step three: get married. Step four: buy a house. Step five: be a breeder. It's like, if you don't have a widescreen and a golden retriever, you're somehow less of a person. I want to know who made those rules."

"Nobody made the rules, Emily. But if you ever want to be somebody, you have to apply yourself."

"I AM somebody. I'm a person. When did *being somebody* stop meaning being an individual and start being defined by jobs and college degrees?"

"Everybody has to work. Why not do something worthwhile?"

"You don't respect what I do."

"Do you respect what you do?" Barbara swirled the ice cubes in her tea.

"Your tone implies I'm not supposed to be proud of my job."

"It was just a question."

"Right. It's just a question. Why can't you love me just the way I am?"

"It's because I love you that I want you to get past this teenage angst and grow up. Life isn't easy. You've had every possible advantage. We bought you computers, took you on nice vacations, sent you to camp, paid for lessons. I should have had such an auspicious start in life."

"Been reading your word-a-day calendar again?"

"Don't judge me for trying to improve myself. And don't change the subject."

"I'm well aware of your working-class background and how Grammy and Pops didn't help you much. Blah. Blah. Blah."

Her daughter's dismissive attitude stung. It wasn't that Barbara flaunted her childhood of diminished circumstance. It was only that she wanted Emily to understand how hard work was the only way to security in life.

"That's disrespectful."

"I'm sorry. You're right. I don't want to fight." Emily pushed away her plate. "Beth said our ten-year reunion is next summer."

"Will you go?"

"Probably not. And I know what you're going to say before you say it. I'm ashamed to go back, but I'm not. That's just it, I'm not unhappy with my life. I'm content."

"You can't bartend indefinitely."

"Really? Why not? Maybe I'll open my own place."

"With what money? Investment money? Honestly Emily, I do wonder about you sometimes."

She crinkled her nose. "It's just that I don't know what I want to do. I've never had that big goal, that one thing that I just knew I was meant to do."

"Why don't you start by picking something you'd like to study? What about architecture? You had a real interest when you were younger."

"Too much math. I'd never pass now."

"What about photography? Commercial photography pays nicely. All your old equipment is still upstairs in your closet."

"I should take that stuff. Might be fun to pick it up again."

"Put together a portfolio, even those artsy weird shots you did, and see if you can find a part-time job at a photography studio. Then you could learn the business. See if it suits you. You could still keep your job at the bar at night."

Barbara had a laundry list of things she wanted Emily to consider, but she held back. The news about Beth seemed to have loosened some contemplative place inside, but Barbara wasn't going to push. This relationship with her daughter was a delicate thing.

Gerald said to let go, that she would find herself, but he'd always been the calmer, less involved parent. Emily tried to hide that she preferred her father with his less challenging ways, but Barbara could tell. The hugs Gerald got were always a few seconds longer. Emily's smile was always brighter around him. Barbara suspected that there were times when Emily went to Gerald for money, times when they shared a secret and left her out.

While it hurt, Barbara didn't really resent Gerald. Certainly a girl should love her daddy. But sometimes it was hard being the stronger parent. Instead of the hugs and kisses, she often got the confused Emily or the depressed Emily. When things got rough, Barbara was the one she turned to.

Just like today. When Emily had called to say she was on her way home, Barbara had heard something in her voice. It was just a tiny quiver, a tone that a mother can sense.

She would deny it, but Emily came home to be reassured that she was not alone. She came home to feel safe and insulated. She came home to be loved.

And Barbara would always love her. Always help pick up the pieces. Always.

Emily

UPSTAIRS, IN the back of her old closet, Emily found a black portfolio coated with dust along the top edge. She laid it on her bed and unzipped it. A jumble of photos fell out. She fanned them around and slid one from the bottom.

It was a self-portrait, a Cindy Sherman-style shot with a constructed set and a costume, part of her experimental self-portrait phase. From the stack she pulled a simple, stark black-and-white. Dark waves of hair twisted around her skinny shoulders in the shot. Her lips were slack and her eyes, icy blue in life, looked eerily clear from the photograph, too round and lonely on her face.

For a while, she'd been absorbed by the documentary photography of women like Dorothea Lange and Diane Arbus. Their gritty shots made her want to wipe away the dirt. She loved how they made her feel uncomfortable for the humanity of their subjects.

This interest in strange photography had started with a job at a photo booth in the mall. She had liked the quiet routine. Feed the machines and they spit out images. Simple. And fascinating. For hours upon hours she looked at snapshots of other people's lives—their parties, their vacations, their secrets.

One day, while she was dumping a disposable camera onto a disc, the fragile face of a dead infant appeared. She couldn't stop looking. Eventually, the dead baby photos moved from the regular file to the late file. When she called, the number had been disconnected. The shots moved to the abandoned file and a month later Emily stole them. That packet of dead baby images was still in the back of her desk drawer.

Her mother was suddenly at her side, pulling the black-and-white portrait from the pile. She studied it.

"You look so much like me when I was younger," she said. "So pretty."

"You're still pretty."

"Oh, with this gray hair." She touched her temple.

"Geez, you've got the body of a yoga instructor. I wouldn't worry about a couple of gray hairs."

This made her smile. "Take those with you," her mother said, waving a hand over the portfolio mess. She reached into the top of the closet and came out with Emily's camera bag. "This too."

From the bottom of the portfolio, Emily pulled images of neighbors with their kids at the pool. People jogging. Dogs. There were close-ups of the jumpy anoles that clung to the sides of their house. None of these had ever satisfied her in an artistic sense. They were vanilla, just mundane snapshots of suburbia.

Barbara perused Emily's display.

"You should organize them. Put them in a form you can show somebody."

"I was never happy with most of them."

"They're nice."

"Nice?" This lukewarm endorsement showed her mother's lack of insight into art. Barbara was a practical thinker. Art for art's sake had never made sense to her.

"I don't know," Emily said. "I always felt that my work lacked that elusive element that makes you feel something when you look at it."

"Feel what?"

"An emotional response. Art should make you laugh or make you sad or disgusted or horny or angry or . . . whatever. It should make you feel something. Anything. Everything. Indifference is the worst response to art."

"These look perfectly fine to me. They show you mastered the basic skills of photography. I never was sure exactly what you were trying to accomplish."

Still don't, Emily thought. In Barbara's world, art matched the couch.

Her mother could not grasp why Emily liked the frayed edges of life, a little dirt in the cracks. Barbara felt life should be pretty and clean and efficient. She would only be happy when Emily was weighed down with a career, a husband, a baby and an enormous handbag with hardware.

"I've got to go," Emily said as she zipped the photos back inside the case. "I work tonight."

Her mother followed her downstairs and out to her car. The MINI, a sixteenth birthday gift, still got her where she needed to go.

Emily flung her portfolio in the back and got in. The windows were down, so her mother came to stand next to the driver's door.

Emily reached for the key, then she paused and looked down the street past her mother. "You know, when I was really young, I noticed that every house on this street is the same brick, that every front yard light pole is a replica. Every fourth house has identical dormers and shutters, every third house has stockade fencing around the backyard."

"So?"

"Everyone's grass is the same height because Mexicans mow on Mondays."

"Ah, your powers of observation astound me. Guess it's the artist in you. Drive safe. Love you."

On the way back downtown Emily passed big boxes—Costco and Target and Sam's. As a child, fifteen minutes of every shopping trip had been spent swimming oceanic parking lots of SUVs looking for a space. Juniper people ate in chain restaurants where neon signs called from both sides of raised super highways. They drank shocking green cocktails from the spouts of margarita machines bought at deep discount price clubs. They had theater rooms and game rooms and patios with built-in barbecues.

Everyone in her childhood had lived by the law of acquisition. She'd learned early that most of Juniper parents lived leased lives, even hers. Juniper families didn't own their homes or their cars or their children's cars. These people took alcohol-fueled Corpus Christi vacations, drove pricey, gas-guzzling vehicles, and when it came time to send their entitled children to college, they took second mortgages on their suburban homes.

Her parents would say she was unappreciative of a perfectly lovely childhood, but Emily had grown up feeling like just another one of their projects. Another task they had to manage in their hectic lives. They exhausted her with their perfection and expectations.

By the time Emily graduated from high school, all she really wanted was a way out of the pancake flat crescent of planned living that fanned the edges of Austin.

Lorelei

SHE SLEPT hard, not waking until nearly noon. Tucked into untamed shrubbery, her back against the cool stone foundation of the church, she was invisible, actually comfortable except that she had to pee. She rolled her blanket tightly and trussed it to her pack with a dirty string she kept twisted around her wrist for just such a purpose. She used another string to tie back her hair before she pulled her hood forward over her face.

A line of people had formed along the sidewalk that snaked around to the back of the church. She was relieved to see a gate open that had been closed the night before. She wouldn't have to scale the fence a second time and chance being noticed.

Although her need to urinate was painful, she walked to the end of the queue to wait. She didn't want to cut line and risk a confrontation. Inside the church, she slipped into the bathroom and found an open stall. The prickle of relief rushed her. Somebody banged on the door, but she took her time. The toilet paper dispenser was one of those irksome kinds that stopped short of a full rotation. She doggedly yanked it around and around until she had collected a thick wad of grainy paper that she shoved into her pack.

She washed her hands and face and brushed her teeth with her new toothbrush. She spit and was wiping her mouth with the back of her hand when the girl next to her met her eyes in the mirror above the sink.

"Wow. That's a wild tattoo."

Lorelei had come to expect the stares. The questions.

She raked her things off the sink's edge into her pack and pushed out the bathroom door. There was a lull in the food line. A tired looking guy plopped a large scoop of spaghetti on her paper plate. Farther down the line, she filled the rest with torn lettuce in some sort of yellowish dressing. At the end of the table she drained a glass of orange juice and picked up another to take with her.

Outside, she went around the corner of the church and sat back against a wall. An adult approached with a girl about her age. She'd been spotted. This was usually how they worked it, using another kid to break the ice. But once Lorelei saw her up close she realized that this girl was probably older.

"Hey," the girl said. "You're new."

It wouldn't get her anywhere to be rude to these people.

"Did you get enough to eat?" the man asked. He looked like Santa Claus, in shorts and sandals. He wore a T-shirt that had the Tumbleweed Young Adult Center logo over his heart.

"Name's Steve. This is Fiona."

Fiona had a nose ring and dirty white-girl dreads sticking out from under a dusty black bowler hat. A tangle of old-fashioned watches wrapped her wrists.

Lorelei liked the girl's style and the man seemed nice enough. Still, she didn't have anything to say to them.

"I don't like to eat alone." Fiona sat on the grass without waiting for an invitation.

"I got to go do something. I'll talk to you later," Steve said and walked away.

"I haven't seen you on The Drag before," Fiona said.

Lorelei hoped this girl wouldn't be an annoying motor-mouth. She decided to guide the conversation. "What's The Drag exactly?"

Fiona motioned with her fork. "This part of Guadalupe. The shopping strip down this side. See that tower? That's where that crazy dude picked off all those people with a rifle back in the sixties. Stood up there and killed like a dozen people or something, people just walking along The Drag. Real whack job. They said he had some major brain tumor or something."

"That's convenient."

Fiona looked at her quizzically. "What do you mean?"

"Just that people would think that's a legit reason for going postal. Some mega tumor would mean being crazy wasn't your fault."

"Like a free pass to off a few people?" She grinned. "I like it. You're all right."

"Where does everybody hang out around here?"

"Different places. Some people hang in the alley back here because it's close to the drop-in. There are some parks around. Most of us walk down to Pease Park on Shoal Creek. People squat down there."

"Don't the cops run you off?"

"Not so much. Not as long as nobody steals anything or tears anything up. They're pretty cool usually." She took a bite of her food and chewed. "Usually."

"What's the shelter like?"

She shrugged. "Not many beds. Hard to get into. They only want the kids who are," she made quotation marks in the air, "transitioning."

"What's that mean?"

"Getting your GED. Getting a job. Getting clean. Getting ready to go home. Getting off the streets."

"Oh."

"So, what's your story?"

"None of the above."

"Where'd you stay last night?"

She didn't want to talk about herself. Time to go.

She stood up and gathered her things.

"Hey, where you going?" Fiona asked.

"Is there a trash can around?" she asked, holding up her paper plate and cup.

"Just leave it here. I'll get it for you. Where are you going?"

"I don't know. Maybe I'll go check out that Shoal Creek place."

"That's cool. I'll go with you."

"No thanks. I've got something to do first." She needed to shoplift some clothes and find a bathroom where she could clean up and change. Afterward, she'd have to hide for a few days, just a precaution in case anybody happened to see her pinch the clothes. She couldn't afford to get picked up. You get busted, you go home.

"Will I see you back here?" Fiona asked.

Lorelei heard her, but walked away as if the question hadn't registered.

"Hey," Fiona called after her. "You didn't even tell me your name."

Emily

EMILY TAPPED the postcard for the dating site on the bar and considered the canoodling couple on the front. She had dug the postcard out of the trash a few days ago and carried it around in her pack, feeling its energy as if it were a tarot card that could foretell her future.

Maybe her mother was right. Maybe she did have a crummy people filter. But a dating website seemed so, well, so desperate. She slipped the card into a pocket and reached up to ring an old dinner bell above her head. One clang. Two.

"Last call for alcohol!" she yelled into the crowd on the other side of the bar. Saturdays were always hopping at Group Therapy. She liked the fast pace of busy nights, the heft of liquor bottles, the rattle of ice, the crack of opened beer. Men would smile and flirt. The tip jar filled. She enjoyed her different roles—DJ, psychologist, peacekeeper.

Emily cut the music and the mumbling, laughing crowd began to move. Emily kept her head down and her back turned to the customers while she counted tips. She didn't close out her register. There were always a few stragglers who waited until the last minute, insisting that the clock above the bar was fast.

"Can I still get a beer?"

She looked at the clock and saw it was clearly 2:15. She formed the word "sorry" but it melted in her mouth when she saw the lean guy across from her. He ran his fingers through a tangle of hair; a few strands flopped back down into his eyes. He had a goatee, a crooked grin, and an aura that made him seem dark around the edges. She had a vague feeling she knew him, but she couldn't say how.

"Well, I guess I can let you slide in under the wire." She smiled. "What can I get you?"

He pointed to a tap. "Lone Star, please."

She grabbed a pint glass from the cooler and pulled one with perfect foam. Napkin. Beer. No bowl of peanuts. It was late.

He took an appreciative drink.

"Nice," he said, then, "What's your name?"

"Emily." She busied herself with cleaning, trying to seem disinterested in him.

"Emily. I've liked every Emily I've ever met."

"Right."

"Seriously. Seems like a name that follows great women around."

"What's your name?"

"Travis."

"Travis Roberts?"

"Yeah."

"*That's* where I've seen you. In that tiny, little headshot on your column. I read you every week."

"That's right. *Be Here Now*, your local entertainment rag," he said sarcastically and tipped his beer toward her.

Travis Roberts wrote about city matters and things at the university. He wrote profiles of people who should be applauded... or shot. He was unapologetic about his liberal social commentary. He was controversial and witty and always interesting.

Living and working downtown in the capital city made it hard to avoid politics, so most people just embraced it. Travis Roberts was a journalistic rock star in Austin.

And he looked better in person.

"What are you working on now?" She finally gave up the disinterested ruse and leaned forward on the bar.

He mimicked her and leaned in too. "I'm kicking around a story on the gutter tribes."

"Street kids?"

"Yeah, but they don't trust anybody over thirty. I've been trying to get in good with them for a couple of weeks now."

"Maybe you can share a needle with them to show you're sincere."

He chuckled, but the smile never reached his eyes. She suddenly felt bad for having said it.

"City council's working on some new regulations. Business owners are complaining again. You ever get any gutter punks up this far?"

"Some, but nobody would come in this bar if we had a bunch of dirty kids hanging around outside. You can't really blame the businesses for being upset."

"It's not my job to assign blame. I just report the story."

He took another drink and checked out the bar, his eyes darting around, taking everything in. "I don't know. It probably won't go anywhere," he said after a while. "My editor wasn't interested in my pitch. They ran a series on homelessness years ago. He doesn't want to cover it again. Says people want to read about happier stuff."

"There's always so many of them."

"More now that the economy's tanked."

"We run a few of them off now and then. They come up to customers with take home boxes and ask for their leftovers."

"They call that a kick down."

"Really."

"If I had good images to support the story it would be an easier sell, but my editor won't assign me a photographer. You know anybody who would shoot these kids for no money?"

"I would." It came flying out of her mouth before she thought things through. She had a flash of panic after she said it.

"You a photographer?"

"Sort of." Why was she backpedaling? "I'm pretty good."

"What's your subject?"

"Mostly black-and-white portraits."

"Ever do any documentary work?"

"Nothing serious."

He shrugged, unimpressed.

"I could show you my portfolio." Could she still cobble one together from her failed high school attempt? Maybe she could go out and shoot more.

He got up off the stool. "Couldn't hurt to take a look."

"It's just a hobby," she said defensively.

He drained his beer, then patted his pocket—the universal cigarette search. He found the pack, snapped it against his hand and one popped out. He placed it in his mouth. Austin is a no-smoking city, so all her smoking customers congregated on the deck and patio. But the bar was almost empty now, so Emily leaned over with a lighter and flamed his smoke. He inhaled and twisted his lips into a devious grin.

"All right, then." Smoke curled out of him as he spoke. "So you want to be a photojournalist. Here's my card. Send me some stuff."

When he left, Emily turned to closing out the cash register. Frank sat in his favorite booth, watching the wait staff marry ketchup bottles and fill salt and pepper shakers. Emily locked the door after the last waitress left, then she poured a tall glass of orange juice and drew two beers.

"So who was that guy?" Frank asked when she joined him in the booth. Frank had never asked Emily if she wanted to be bar manager, he just kept giving her new jobs each time an employee left. People don't show, you cover their shift. It happens a few times, you're suddenly in charge.

"Just some guy."

"Really. 'Cause you didn't look at him like he was just some guy."

She smiled. "It was Travis Roberts from *Be Here Now*."

"Ah," Frank said, a noncommittal sound. No judgment, which was one of the things Emily liked about him.

Angel came from the kitchen wiping his hands on the hem of his *Keep Austin Weird* shirt. He took a seat at their booth and gulped down the orange juice. Widely considered one of the best Tex Mex chefs in Austin, Angel put Group on the map with his equally awesome beef brisket, a dish that had put ten pounds on Emily's scrawny frame over the years.

"Busy night," Angel said.

"People drink in good times and people drink in bad times. That's why I'm in the bar business," Frank said. He raised his glass and they all clinked.

Group was more than just a job to Emily. It was her comfort zone. Frank and Angel were big brothers. The bar was a community. She knew her customers and their routines. Lunch regulars were contractors, electricians and plumbers nursing hangovers with Bloody Marys. She usually got a retired group of Town Lake walkers and an array of UT professors, cops, firemen, EMS, bank workers and sales reps. Often, margarita slurping tourists would come south across the Congress Bridge looking for the SoCo shops and art galleries promoted by the "Keep Austin Weird" campaign.

Most regulars came back in the early evening to play in dart tournaments in hopes of winning enough money to cover their Lone Star and tequila shots. Late at night, Group got spillover from the thousands partying on Sixth and Congress. You never knew exactly what would walk in. Politicians, cowboys, rappers, rednecks, frat boys, punks, street performers, computer geeks, movie stars, musicians and even the occasional cluster of suburbanites in their polo shirts and pressed jeans all wandered in on occasion.

Emily was never surprised, no matter what came through her door, but this night something unexpected had happened. Travis Roberts had stumbled into her bar and offered her a strange proposition. She'd have to get her camera equipment out and take some shots. Remember how the darned thing worked. Photographing street culture was intriguing and the prospect of doing it with Travis Roberts made it all the more appealing.

Emily

A BRANCH lashed her cheek.

"Sorry," Travis said. She followed him through a wooded area along Shoal Creek. Above the fringe of trees, the tops of million dollar houses stairstepped up the hillside behind Pease Park. Traffic noise had dwindled. The most present sound was the crunch of leaves beneath their hiking boots. The creek was running low due to the summer drought. Trees had half their usual foliage; a lot of leaves had given up and fallen early.

Per instruction, she was slightly grungy. Travis had told her not to talk unless she was pulled into conversation, and she was not to show her camera until he gave her a sign.

Travis moved swiftly to where he knew a faction of the gutter tribes lived. Drag rats, gutter punks, kids on Guadalupe—just some of the terms used for the young homeless of Austin. Travis explained that the gutter tribes had further broken themselves into individual tribes, each with their own unique calling card. There were the kids who loved animals and used them to panhandle. Another group was seriously punk. The gays banded together, as did the religious kinds and the druggies.

"We're going to see some Crusties," Travis said.

"What's that mean?"

"They've been on the streets a while. They know how things work. They know the local cops. They're the seniors with all the good spots staked out and strong cred with the other kids."

"Okay."

"I like this particular group because they don't do as many drugs. They're easier to talk to. Usually, anyway. They're better than the Tweakers. Man, I tried to talk to some of those goons one time, but that was a waste of oxygen. They couldn't focus long enough to answer one question."

"Methheads?" She touched the welt on her cheek.

"Meth and heroin both. We had a wave of bad heroin last year. Found kids dead in the alley down from the drop-in. Right outside the back door of a church. Two kids crumpled up like trash beside a dumpster."

"Wow."

"And they fight over territory—where they hang out, the places they stake out to fly signs and panhandle. Some spots are apparently more lucrative than others." He stopped. "That's what we're looking for."

Ahead was a clearing where a cluster of logs and tarps made a crude encampment.

"Home sweet home," Travis said. He took a deli bag from his backpack. "You've got to ease into things with these guys." He moved forward more slowly this time and stopped a couple of yards from the camp's perimeter. Logs and broken lawn chairs encircled a struggling fire. Plastic gallon jugs of water were scattered around.

"Hey," Travis yelled. "Anybody home?"

Suddenly, three guys sat up from the ground, leaves and twigs tangled in their hair. One was a big fellow. His overalls were held together by carabineers, and a small camping headlamp held back his wild yellowish dreads. He wore black Elvis Costello glasses taped together in a couple of spots, a usual hazard of being a skater.

Travis held up both hands in surrender. "Hey, man. We come in peace."

"What do you want? You can't come down here, man," the big one said.

"Come on, Mook. You know me. I just want to talk."

Mook scorched Emily with his eyes. "Who's that?"

"My friend Emily. She's helping me. Hey, I brought you guys some sandwiches." He pitched the brown bag to him.

"Some of us are vegetarians," Mook said.

"I know, man. I remember. I brought some fancy cucumber and

tomato sandwiches for your girlfriend."

He still appeared unconvinced. Hunger washed the pimple-strewn faces of the other two.

"You got anything to drink?" He seemed irritated by Travis's kindness.

"Yeah, sure. There's juice in there."

"Hold on." Mook got up and opened a flap in a tarp strung up against a tree. He said something to somebody inside. Emily and Travis waited. A curvy girl emerged from the flap. Red slashed through her tangle of hair. She was ashy, her lips puffy from sleep, but beauty clung to her, bright green eyes against dark skin. She perched on a log and hugged her knees. Mook poked their campfire with a stick.

"Well, come on then," he finally said.

Travis didn't take a chair but moved to sit on a log, so Emily followed his lead. The smell of fallen leaves gave way to serious body odor.

"Emily, this is Mook." Travis motioned toward the girl next to him. "That's Mook's woman, Elda. Those two guys are Minion and Freestyle." They nodded a silent greeting. She wondered if they ever talked.

Mook handed the food to Elda. She went through it, peeling back plastic wrap, sniffing the clean white bread as if it might be poison.

"He says it's cucumber and tomato," Mook said.

"It's got cream cheese too," Travis said. "I mean, you're not vegan are you?"

"No," Elda said. "Just vegetarian." She took a sandwich and a juice and passed the bag back to Mook. He took a sandwich and threw the bag to the other two guys.

"So," Mook said, his mouth half full, "I've already told you we're not interested in being part of your story, so what you doing back here again?"

Travis shrugged. "Don't know. Thought maybe you'd reconsider. Tell the public that you guys aren't all thieves and drug addicts."

He laughed. "Dude, we *are* all thieves and drug addicts."

"That's not true."

"What? You want sob stories about how we got here? I told you, man, most of us are here by choice. We're not participating in that rat race. The economy's going to hell, people who chased money like it was a god are going to be shit out of luck and we'll be surviving, man.

We'll be the ones who know how to make it on nothing. You don't miss what you ain't got. We don't need rescuing." Mook suddenly leaned over Travis in a threatening way, but Travis didn't flinch.

Emily did.

"Step back," Travis said as he stood up. "Man, why you got to get all up in my face?"

Mook grinned and relaxed his threatening posture. He stepped away and took a seat in a busted lawn chair. Travis had passed his test. Mook motioned for him to sit.

Travis took a moment to let things chill again, then he said, "The city's passing more ordinances about where you guys can congregate and panhandle. Funding for services is up for discussion too. Don't you want the public to hear your side?"

The boy wiped his mouth on a filthy sleeve. "Fuck that, man. We're going to do what we do no matter what the man does. We're here to stay. We don't want to participate in the discussion."

"Some of the other kids need shelter. You can help those kids."

"I'm not into politics, man. It's no use trying to fight the machine."

"So you feel powerless."

"No. We're just under the radar, man." He moved his hand flat through the air between them. "Off the grid."

The others made agreeing sounds and nodded and kept stuffing themselves with food. Travis reached into the long pockets on his cargo pants and took out candy bars. Without a word, he pitched one to each of the kids in turn.

A rustling from up the bank made everyone freeze. In the distance stood a girl, tall and thin, a hood shadowing her face.

"There she is again," Elda said.

Everyone looked uphill, acknowledging her.

"You gonna go talk to her?" Elda said.

Mook considered, then said, "No. She needs to come on down if she wants to hang."

"Who is it?" Travis asked.

"Some new kid showed up about a month ago. Probably an Oogle. I've seen her at the drop-in. I don't know anything about her. Fiona knows her."

"She wants to join your group?"

"Looks that way. She can hang, but she's got to ask."

"She got a name?" Travis asked.

"I think," Elda said, "Fiona said her name is Lorelei."

At Halcyon Coffeehouse, they sipped soy lattes and discussed their interview attempt.

"Interesting names," Emily said.

"They don't give legitimate names," Travis said. "They don't want to be tracked. That name *Lorelei*, that's from a graphic novel."

"So, what's an Oogle?"

"A newbie. Somebody who doesn't yet know how to work the street economy. They have to learn where all the shelters are, where they can find a free feed, who to avoid, who to trust. It takes a while to learn the system. Oogles are usually younger kids, you know, fourteen to sixteen. Scared as shit. Looking for anybody to gob on to. Especially girls. Girls are always looking for the safe situation."

Indirect rosy light bounced through the front window onto their table, washing Travis in a soft glow. Emily had never worked much with natural light, but she could appreciate the effect. She took out her camera and considered shots of his hands, his strange skull ring, the whirl of foam in his coffee.

He'd never signaled that it was okay to bring out her camera when they were in the woods.

"They treat you like an unwelcome friend," she said as she raised the camera to frame his face and focused.

"Just be patient," he said. "These kids don't want their photos taken, just like they won't tell you their names. They don't want to be found. They're throwaways mostly, but some have parents looking for them."

"I can't imagine living like that. What about their parents? How can they live not knowing if their children are safe or hungry or freezing?"

He shrugged. "Some parents don't give a shit. So, don't get emotionally involved."

"I can handle it."

"I didn't imply you couldn't."

"I guess I just never really thought about how they live. I mean, I've been downtown for years, and I suppose I just sort of think of them as background noise. You know they're there, but you just tune them out."

"Well," he said, "now you know."

Travis considered his coffee. He seemed relaxed, as if hanging out with a gang of teenage squatters was just an average day. His slightly dangerous ways were attractive. He had an aggressive approach to getting a story, but she sensed something softer about him. As if his professional bravado masked a more sincere side.

"Why don't you let me take your photo? I can do better than that awful headshot you use in the paper."

He considered Emily's offer, scratched his goatee, then said, "Fine. Shoot away."

She snapped a few frames—one with his coffee to his lips, a wistful glance out of the window.

He finished his drink and motioned that he was leaving.

Outside, he lit a cigarette and stood for a minute, thinking. She snapped another picture, but he waved her camera away.

"Save it for the story," he said. Then, "You need a ride home?"

"No thanks. I got my bike." Why did that make her feel ten years old?

He nodded and walked toward uptown. She headed south for Group. Down the alley, she opened the kitchen door and stepped into the steamy wet food smell of dishwashing in action. Tino looked up and gave her a wink, then went back to blasting plates with his industrial sprayer.

Angel waved Emily over. He was slicing brisket. Reddish-brown juice flowed onto the cutting board. She thought about the Crusties and their hungry eyes.

She pinched a piece of beef and the spicy meat fell apart in her mouth. Angel's steel prep station held a dozen plates of Tex Mex in various stages of completion. He finished constructing a couple of brisket sandwiches, slung them into the service window and rang the pick-up bell. He grabbed the fry basket of sizzling chicken fingers and hooked it to the side to drain, then moved on to tossing cheese.

"Are you in the weeds?" Emily asked.

"No. Dart tournament, but we're under control."

She leaned through the window and looked into the bar to see only a normal busy night crowd. Frank was switching out a keg. The barback was hustling to dump ice. Angel was right. Everything looked under control.

"How'd your interview go?" Angel asked as he worked.

"It was kind of scary."

He stopped and gave her the fatherly, raised-eyebrow look.

"Scary weird or scary bad?"

"Scary strange. Travis was with me, and he's totally cool around them. No worries."

"Be careful. They're desperados."

"I believe you."

"Ten cuidado, Bonita."

"I am."

She grabbed her bike from the dry pantry and wheeled it out the kitchen door. She eased out of the sour alley past a kissing couple on the sidewalk and into the bike lane. Traffic was light. Night air flowed like liquid over her skin. She clicked past a couple of porch parties in her neighborhood. People waved. Raised beers.

While she waited for the kettle to heat, Emily booted up her laptop. She attached her camera and uploaded her shots of Travis. He was photogenic. The diffused light from the coffee shop's window accentuated his cheekbones. One shot was so good it needed no retouching. She wrote and rewrote the e-mail to accompany the shot. What could she write to a writer? Anything she said might sound stupid. She decided on short and sweet and e-mailed the shot to Travis at the paper.

When she hit send she let go of the breath she'd been holding.

Gone. Nothing she could do about it now.

She sipped tea and her fingers rattled across the laptop searching for the graphic novel *Lorelei*. She got a few hits and Lorelei turned out to be a character from a failed 1980s comic book, a big-busted, muscular redhead who stalks the streets of New York. Lorelei was a photographer known for controversial subject matter, but through a series of ill-fated events, she died and was resurrected as the soul-stealing incubus, Lorelei, who reduces evildoers to a withered husk. *An angel of vengeance who preys upon those who would prey on the weak.*

An avenging photographer appealed to Emily. But Lorelei didn't seem anything like her alter ego. The real Lorelei hovered at the edges, waiting for a sign of welcome. The homeless were like cautious animals, on the prowl, always watching. They grouped in the shadows of alleys, huddled in entryways during rain. Police and security constantly moved them along.

Skinny Cat wove his soft purring between her ankles. Emily reached down to scratch his ear. He had appeared on her porch five years ago. She'd fed him and fed him, but he stayed scrawny and quiet. He came to her for food and shelter and comfort, but always on his own terms. Then he disappeared for days. He led a life of mystery. Like the shrouded gaunt girl with the comic book name.

Travis

THE NEWSROOM buzzed. Phones beeped. Fax paper overflowed onto the floor. Circulation guys banged the lobby door open as they toted in stacks of the current week's issue. The art reporter's fingers snapped angrily across her keyboard, which meant she hated whatever she was reviewing. The music and food writers swapped stories, laughing too loud. The sports guy's voice traveled over the partition separating his desk from Travis's. He jawed like an old buddy with the Longhorns' coach about the possibility of a bowl game.

The receptionist dumped a five-inch stack of mail on Travis's desk.

"You look like you could use some coffee." Lily pushed out her hip in that coquettish way that always made him think of an old girlfriend he missed.

He grinned up at her. "Can't focus."

"Well, get focused. Staff meeting in ten."

She sashayed off, tossing another day's worth of crap onto the already overflowing desks of the other writers.

As she moved away, the racket of the newsroom rushed him again. He went back to poking around Facebook, looking at personal pictures of people he'd never invite out for a beer.

His editor walked through the room and Travis quickly brought up the screen that held his piece on parking meters. He needed a gripping opening, but a hook eluded him. In truth, nobody really cared about these things except for the city and the merchants. People were never interested in topics like tax accommodations and storm sewers. And the thought of all of the torpid meetings to come made him want to open a vein.

But somebody had to ask where the money goes. That was his job. To ask the questions. To find the answers. To make people care. Boo-yah.

His e-mail chimed. Another welcome distraction.

Hey Travis,
Zup? Here's my best shot of you. You look hot!
Emily

He smiled at her note and clicked the attachment. She had a good eye. He liked the contemplative nature of it. Maybe she could come up with something usable for his story if he could get inside the tribes for an interview.

Travis had mixed feelings about working with Emily before seeing this shot. This proved that she was at least adequate. But she gave off that vibe that said she was more interested in him than the project, which could become problematic. Travis was making an effort to stop tapping every young thing that thought it would be glamorous to date a writer. Theirs wasn't sincere interest anyway. Girls like that slept with musicians or artists or any guy they thought had some minor celebrity. Travis had made a vow to avoid starfuckers.

He emailed Emily a quick thank you, something noncommittal, then forwarded the headshot over to the art department.

"People!" the editor hollered from his office. "Five minutes. Conference room."

Assignment meetings were torture. If a reporter didn't have a story to pitch they got assigned something mundane nobody wanted to cover. Of course, there was no guarantee that even a good story idea would get greenlighted.

"Wow. I'd hit that." Lily stood behind him looking over his shoulder at his headshot on the monitor. She slid into the swivel chair at the desk next to him, crossed her legs and leaned back.

"You are totally inappropriate and I'm going to sue you for sexual harassment," Travis said.

"You wish. Who took that shot? It's good."

"A stringer I'm using."

People slogged toward the glassed-in meeting room.

"Better buck up," Lily said. "Game on."

"Why? Bob's just going to tell us how people want to read fluff now that the economy's in shambles. Help me out here. Tell me what I could write to get you to care about parking meters."

"Absolutely nothing." Lily twisted off to the meeting in that way that made him stare. That was another thing he had promised himself. He wouldn't sleep with anybody else from the office. That was always a disaster.

When Travis dragged himself into the conference room, his editor was already talking.

"Travis, so glad you could join us."

"My pleasure, Bob."

There were no seats, so Travis leaned against a wall.

"So, who is coming into Austin this week? Anybody good?" More and more, Bob pushed to get recognizable faces on the cover, particularly celebrities coming to town. A celebrity cover meant increased circulation, racks emptied, people coming in for extra copies. Increased circulation resulted in more advertising dollars, which meant paychecks. Entertainment sold. News, not so much. A significant news story on the cover usually meant recycling, not circulation, was what rose that week.

So maybe Travis was looking at this homeless story all wrong. Perhaps he should approach it in a more entertaining light. He could write about the talents of all of the street kids—how they can juggle and play guitar and sing. Or he could return to the tried-and-true angle featuring Leslie again. Everybody in town would pick up a copy with Austin's famous flamboyant, homeless cross-dresser on the front.

Leslie knew how to get attention—his perpetual run for mayor, his continual conflict with Austin's finest over homeless rights. He was probably the only homeless guy in America with his own Facebook fan page. It was the cheap way to approach the story, but there was no denying that Leslie's image moved papers.

Emily

BATFEST ROCKED. Every August, the city threw a massive street party to celebrate the beloved Mexican freetail bats that spent a season under the Congress Street Bridge.

The colony, mostly mothers and their pups, crammed up into the expansion joints of the bridge. At dusk, millions of bats gushed out in a black ribbon pulsing along the river corridor, devouring insects by the billions. Their extended exodus was eerie to witness, so soft, only a muffle of air unless one flew too close.

Batfest, on the other hand, was loud. The Congress Street Bridge is always blocked by a stage at one end. As the sun goes down, Austin's tinted glass skyline behind the stage mirrors the purple Texas sunset. Street vendors line one side of the bridge and people hang along the downriver side so they can watch the mass departure. People fill the walks and grassy areas along Town Lake below the bridge.

Emily walked from her house toward the river to the festival. As she approached the bridge, the crowd erupted to the high-voltage grooves of "Downtown" by Vallejo. Austin loved their homegrown bands and Vallejo's lyrics about addictions and lust and unchecked vice were always a crowd pleaser.

She wandered the party, running into friends, stopping to take photographs. Emily had started carrying her camera. Its weight against her neck gave her purpose. She felt invisible and involved at the same time. She shot a few frames of the concert, zoomed in, waited for an opportunity. Clicked off a few shots of the lead singer. Cute. Sexy.

Folks from Group had staked out a grassy hillside by the water earlier in the day, so Emily headed there to mooch a beer. She sat on a cooler and faced down toward the river walk. People below were paying attention to the action up on the bridge, swaying to the band's Latin-inspired rhythm. She scanned people through the viewfinder and that's when she saw her. It wasn't difficult to pick the hooded figure out of the crowd. She was standing still in a sea of movement. Emily trained her lens on the girl, zoomed, focused and waited.

For the longest time, the girl watched the stage. Although her jacket had a hood, it was also sleeveless and showed bands of tribal tattoos around her biceps. Emily zoomed in on her profile and focused, but the girl suddenly shifted. Emily tried to keep her in frame as the girl shoved her way through the crowd. At one point, her subject glanced to the side and Emily caught a glimpse of something on her cheek before she lowered her head and walked on.

Emily kicked over somebody's beer on her way down the hill.

"Awww! Man!"

"Sorry!" she called out behind her. "Sorry."

The girl was like mercury, sliding through the smallest openings in the crowd. Emily tried to keep up, but she found it hard to make headway against the opposing current of the festival. Emily bumped a guy carrying hot dogs and tacos. When she looked back again her street punk was gone. Emily cursed to herself and desperately scanned faces in the crowd.

In the distance, the hooded figure appeared climbing a ramp up to street level. Emily saw an opening and cut through the swarm of people. The girl paused, glancing down at those below. Emily snapped a shot, unsure if she'd focused.

Once at street level, Emily followed her for blocks, music evaporating with their every step. The girl threaded her way between people, walking rapidly, her head down. She stopped to look in a shop window. Emily saw her chance and called out.

"Lorelei?"

The girl whirled around, paused and then yanked her hood back from her face.

Emily caught her breath.

"No pictures!" the girl hissed.

Emily had forgotten the camera hanging around her neck.

"Oh, this? Okay. No problem. No pictures."

A vivid phoenix curled along one cheekbone, its frayed tail feathers touching the edge of the girl's left eye. A cascade of stars sprinkled her other cheek. A scroll design peeked from the collar of her hoodie.

"How do you know my name?" She was younger than Emily had expected for her height. Several cheap plastic barrettes held back her ratty brown hair. Blond streaks started four inches from dark roots and fell to her shoulders.

"I heard somebody call you that one day. That's your name, right? Lorelei."

She bit her lower lip, considering her answer.

"Yeah," she offered. "So?"

"I'm Emily."

"So, what do you want?"

"I just wanted to meet you."

"Why?"

"I don't know. You look interesting, I guess."

"Are you mental?"

"I don't think so."

"A lesbo?"

"No."

"So, I repeat, what do you want?"

"Can I buy you a cup of coffee or a sandwich, maybe?"

Her eyes roamed over Emily, sizing her up for weirdness.

"No thanks. Just ate." She pulled her hood back over her head and walked away.

Emily's inclination was to follow her again, but that would be no way to gain the girl's trust. She hoped Lorelei was on her way to a shelter or soup kitchen, anywhere but the alley or one of those squatter camps scattered along Shoal Creek.

Lorelei

SHE HATED the story people. You couldn't escape them. In every city there were the reporters who were so terribly interested in interviewing street surfing teenagers. Even worse were people with cameras. Being photographed was an invasion of privacy, but people just assumed if you lived on the streets that you didn't deserve any privacy.

If you were spanging, just looking for a little spare change, people wanted to take your picture with their camera phone before they gave you any money. Some people snapped pictures without asking, like you were just another stop on their sightseeing tour or an animal in a zoo.

The worst were the video peepers. Television station people usually asked before they shot. But college kids out to get a story for a school project showed no respect. They lurked around, waiting for something to happen, for some of the streets to get into a fight. They'd ask, "What's that tattoo mean?" "When's the last time you ate?" "You going to sleep in the park tonight?" They tried to incite the street punks so they could tape random reactions. They always loved a good fight.

One time, Lorelei had awakened to a video camera stuck into the hedge she was sleeping beneath. It scared her and she shouted at the guy and he ran off. She'd wondered if she was on the news that night, her feet sticking out from under shrubs.

Gutter punks knew that all reporters were liars. They portrayed the homeless as aimless party animals, addicts, or even worse, mentally unstable, pathetic people nobody would ever hire or trust. Pick a reality—partier or pathetic—apparently, there was no in-between. Simple was so much easier for most people. The truth was too complex.

Most kids hated the streets. Homelessness wasn't an adventure or a vacation. It was hunger and sleep deprivation, wet and cold. It was embarrassment and hostility and fear. Everybody had a different story, but what it all boiled down to was no safe alternative.

It didn't matter if your daddy beat you or your mama was a drunk or if you had taken off because there wasn't food at home. Everybody ended up without options. So you tried to find friends and make a little community to protect each other. You tried to blend in so nobody would run you off of a good squat or turn you over to the cops.

But there were always the really strange kids who attracted attention and ruined it for everybody. Usually it was the foster scare kids. They didn't care about anything, which was what made them so scary. They were the cutters and thieves and messed up crackheads. The ones who flung curses when they begged. Outcasts of the outcasts.

These were usually the types reporters ended up taping. The reporters all said they were looking for human interest stories, but they weren't really interested in humans. They only wanted an outrageous story, something to make people gawk. They tried to make you think they cared, but they didn't. Nobody cared. Nobody.

Lorelei never gave an interview, never let anyone have her image. She hated the cowardly stalkeratzis with their zoom lenses. There was truth in the Native American belief that photography captured a part of the soul. That part was called dignity.

Lorelei guarded what little she had left.

She wandered up Congress. Normally, she would have cut over a street to avoid the bar and club crowd, but tonight she needed something to eat and the drop-in wasn't serving. She'd have to spange.

It was both easier and harder to get money out of drunken people. During the day, she found more people gave, but it was only pocket change. At night, she got more money from fewer people. Drunks would either be rude and dismissive, or their eyes would fill with tears and they'd hand over a twenty.

Lorelei spotted a couple of girls strolling along with Starbucks cups. The way they threw their heads back when they drank meant they were finishing. She followed them and when one tossed her cup, Lorelei fished it from the trash. According to the three-second rule, the cup was practically sterile.

She walked around a corner and popped the lipstick-stained top. Sweet foam clung to the bottom and the sides. She tapped the bottom of the cup to move the foam down into her mouth. Chocolaty coffee flavor evaporated on her tongue. Her stomach growled.

Spanging by the university had dried up. All the seriously tanned students who had been so free with their money at the beginning of the school year had morphed into broke, sleep-deprived zombies by midterm. Now Lorelei was just another drag worm to the pretty, polished girls of the University of Texas.

Her favorite spot to panhandle downtown was the famous Driskill Hotel, the wedding cake building she had seen on her first day in Austin. The Driskill crowd had money, and one twenty-dollar pop was all she needed. The cute valets in their cream-colored monkey suits would run her off as soon as they saw her, but if she was lucky, the first couple of people she approached would help her, and she'd be on her way.

Outside the Driskill, a line of shiny cars snaked around the corner to the valet stand. Gentlemen in tuxedos stepped from their cars onto a red carpet and handed over their keys. Valets helped ladies in sparkling dresses from passenger seats. The couples all stopped to smooth themselves before walking through the arched-stone entryway.

The valets were too busy to pay much attention to her if she stayed around the corner out of sight. She pulled her hood close to hide her tats, pressed her back into the wall and held out her cup. Other elegant people came from down the street and Lorelei held out her empty cup. A man reached into his back pocket as he approached and her heart lifted.

"Hey!"

Lorelei turned to see an older guy in a monkey suit of a different color with a shiny gold nameplate.

"Move along," the man said. "You can't be here."

She looked back at her target and saw the man had reconsidered and was guiding his date in a wide path around her.

"I said, move along," hotel man said more forcefully. He stepped closer.

Anger flared inside Lorelei as her meal money walked past.

She jerked her hood away from her face and was pleased by his startled reaction.

"This is a public sidewalk," she said.

"And this is my hotel, so move along."

"Oh, so you own this hotel? I doubt that Mr. Monkey Suit."

"Listen, you little bitch. I'm the concierge here. Now move along or I'll call the cops."

She swung the empty cup in his direction and coffee dregs flew out staining the man's white shirt with flecks of brown.

"Goddamnit!" He grabbed at her, but she was already down the sidewalk.

She turned around, laughing and skipping backward. "Mr. Monkey Suit! Mr. Monkey Suit!" she called. "Go lick some boots, Mr. Monkey Suit!"

The man shot her the bird, threw up his hands and disappeared into the hotel.

Lorelei was suddenly mad at herself for pushing the confrontation so far. She'd never be able to spange at the Driskill again. Panic set in. The concierge was probably calling the cops now. Just like the man said, she had to move along.

David

BLACK WAS already pooling under the boy's right eye. A crust of blood ringed his nose. His posture said he was used to abuse. After fifteen years counseling homeless kids, David could spot certain indicators—the hunched stature, the hanging head, the sideways glance that never quite made eye contact.

The black eye and bloody nose would normally have been an indicator too, but apparently the boy had brought that bit of hurt upon himself voluntarily. David had seen this kid around. He ran with Mook's clan. He was one of the skaters. Everybody called him Freestyle.

David had been doing his usual rounds on The Drag, walking around outside the drop-in, talking to kids in the alley behind the churches on Guadalupe. He knew this community and it knew him. Some were local kids from destitute, dysfunctional homes, but most were transplants, children who had escaped abusive situations or foster care kids who aged out of the system and were on the streets at eighteen. They had to make money, find a place to live and something to eat. They had to deal with sex and drugs and danger. Their adolescent minds often made bad decisions about adult issues.

David spotted an Austin beat cop and a UT campus officer talking to a group of young men. Three boys stood on the sidewalk while a fourth, Freestyle, sat on the curb, holding his nose. David walked up to check out the situation.

"Officer Dance, Officer Sanchez, is there anything I can help you with here?" he asked. David knew the city police and university officers even better than the homeless youth.

Officer Dance, the cop, motioned to Freestyle. On the sidewalk beside the boy lay a hand-scrawled sign that read, "HIT ME $5."

"These individuals here thought they'd take this young fellow up on his offer." The cop turned to the students. "What the hell's wrong with you guys? This is assault."

The students had lost all bravado.

One of them whined, "It was just a game."

"To you maybe," Officer Sanchez said. "Do you think he thinks it's a game?"

Officer Dance said, "Too bad this isn't campus jurisdiction. You're in my territory now. I think we need to take a ride to the station, see if this fellow wants to press charges. Assault is a serious offense."

Horror eclipsed the students' smug faces.

"We're sorry, man," one of them said. The kid stepped forward and extended a hand, but Freestyle ignored the gesture.

Freestyle struggled to his feet on his own. David saw his chance to further defuse the situation. He handed Freestyle a wad of napkins from his pocket. The boy pressed the napkins to his face.

"Officers," David said. "Why don't you let me take this young man with me? You take care of those three, and we'll be on our way."

"Son, do you want to press charges?" Officer Dance asked.

"No harm. No foul," Freestyle said.

A knowing glance passed between the officers. It was a common enough situation—two introduced species bound to clash. Avoidance was usually the best approach. The officers nodded and David quickly guided the injured boy back toward the drop-in. As they walked away, one of the students pleaded, "Yes, sir. But he asked for it."

David slid a bottle of Coke across his desk. Freestyle drank half with a greediness the counselor had seen many times.

"Why'd you fly that sign?" David asked.

The boy shrugged. "Why not?"

"Letting people hit you is no way to make money."

He shrugged again. "I used to get hit for no money. Seemed like an improvement." He gave the mock grin that so many of the street kids had perfected. The look that said they couldn't care less what happened to them. "Sides, man. I'm a skater. I live for bruises."

"Look, you can't do that again."

"Duh."

"Dude, how can you expect other people to respect you if you don't respect yourself?"

He met David's eyes, hate simmering inside him.

"Look, man, I'm just an abortion that couldn't get paid for. That's all."

"That's not true."

"Yes, it is. My mother told me that. More than once."

Counselors had a bad habit of saying, "I understand." You're hungry? I understand. You're frightened? I understand. You've been hurt? I understand. But truly, how could anyone who grew up in a loving family ever understand that level of rejection?

Even after all these years, David could still be stunned by the wickedness in the world. His job was to take this broken soul and try to patch him together again, give him purpose and a little self-esteem.

And sometimes it was the worst of jobs. David had been spit on. Cussed out. He'd been hit. Kids had screamed at him. Cried in his arms. Slept on the floor in his office. Bled on him. Sometimes they disappeared on him. Occasionally they even died on his watch.

David had given out as many hugs and tissues as he had meals. But only occasionally did he ever get a call from someone who made it, one of his kids who had managed to escape the downward spiral and have a normal life.

David dreamed of building a huge lodge out on Lake Austin where he would feed his kids steak and baked potatoes for dinner every night. He'd enroll them in school and churn out a legion of new doctors and teachers and social workers. But the reality of limited resources always meant more demand for beds, food and services than Tumbleweed could provide. On any given night, David had only one bed for every seven kids under eighteen who showed up in need. He hated to turn anyone away, but it was something he did on a daily basis. He hoped he had a space for Freestyle.

"You got to get that eye looked at. Ever been to our clinic?"

"No."

"Our people can patch you up. You hungry?"

David opened a desk drawer and handed over the sandwich and chips he'd brought for lunch. The boy didn't bother to say thank you. He made short work of the food and then said, "Can I use your bathroom?"

"Sure, down the hall on the right. Come straight back, okay?"

Freestyle nodded and walked out gingerly, touching the bridge of his nose.

David picked up the phone and called one of his caseworkers.

"Amelia, what's our census look like for tonight? We got any beds open?"

He could hear her riffling papers on her desk.

She came back on. "One."

"Great. I need it. Hold it for me, will you?"

"Sure thing. What's the client's name?"

"Freestyle."

She laughed. "That's a good one."

"I know. They just get more and more creative, don't they?"

"Yeah. Want me to take Mr. Freestyle?"

"No. That's okay. I've got a little rapport going. I think I'll keep him for a while."

"Fine. You going to send him on to the shelter now?"

"No. I'm sending him to the clinic first. He got beat down."

"Poor thing. He get jumped?"

"Something like that."

After ten minutes, David had waited long enough to know that Freestyle had taken off. After a feed and a bathroom break, he probably decided against a visit to the clinic. David hadn't even mentioned the shelter to him. That's usually when the wilder kids bolted. Many needed help, but they split if they thought they'd have to give up information or abide by a few rules.

David could try to find him later, maybe stop by Mook's squat down by Shoal Creek and try again to convince Freestyle that he needed to have his face checked out. It was difficult to keep track of them all, but David had a long mental roster of his kids, their character, their track record and their health situations.

He pondered Freestyle's story. Maybe it was a true tale, maybe not. Homeless youth were not the most honest people. Why not lie? They had nothing to lose. They were survivalists. They would tell you what they thought you wanted to hear just to get what they needed. They all had a heartbreaking story and even after all this time, David was not immune.

He decided not to pursue Freestyle, reminding himself that he had to maintain strong professional boundaries. Freestyle would have to decide on his own to seek help. David picked up the phone and dialed Amelia.

"Hey," she said.

"That bed we talked about?"

"Yeah."

"I won't be needing it after all."

"What happened?"

"He bolted."

"Happens."

"Right," he said and sighed.

"You all right?"

"Yeah. Yeah. Sure. No worries," David said. But some days, like today, David could use a hug himself.

Lorelei

SINCE SHE stepped off the bus in Austin, the weather had been unmercifully hot and dry. Drought was wearing on the city. Municipal fountains were shut down, a water source the homeless used to spot bathe and cool their tired feet. Irrigation was restricted, so landscaping provided less shade and camouflage. Every gust of wind swept up a whorl of dust, and some of the kids had taken to wearing bandanas over their faces, making the public walk an even wider swath around them.

City beat cops had started to patrol the creeks and wooded areas of town, looking for campfires. While most days were still hot, temperatures dropped at night. Mook's squat was one of many encampments building fires to knock the four a.m. chill.

Lorelei had grown accustomed to the unexpected appearance of cops in the middle of their squat. Mook never got defensive or seemed upset by their surprise arrivals. Often, he walked away into the trees to have a conversation with them. Once, Lorelei saw them show Mook pictures. She figured he told them about other street rats and in exchange they left him alone. While other squats were broken up and forced to move, Mook maintained a steady, enviable spot and a relatively hassle-free existence. It was one of the reasons Lorelei had joined his group.

But police had been cracking down on urban campfires. Even though both camping and fires were against city ordinances, the cops usually looked the other way unless there were complaints. The drought had made it more dangerous for surrounding neighborhoods. Anybody caught with a fire would be written up, and their camp would be torn apart. Before they left, the cops made the kids use their precious jugs of water to douse the glowing remains of the previous night.

Without fire, Lorelei needed a sleeping bag. The ground was still warm, but her thin blanket wasn't enough in the middle of the night. Other kids talked about the bone-chilling Texas nights to come. She had an idea of what to expect. She had camped in California desert. Sleeping bags were bulky and heavy and hard to hide, but she had put it off as long as she could.

Lorelei made her way to the drop-in, about half an hour's walk, a gradual uphill climb from Shoal Creek. She rested on the way, stopping to watch women in bright-white tennis suits play on a court at a fenced-in club.

It was early and the drop-in was nearly empty. David was in his closet-sized office, his face creased in deep concentration. She knocked and as he looked up, his expression changed. He always seemed glad to see her. If she didn't know better, she would swear he actually cared about her. He never picked her for information. He never pushed. It seemed as if David saw her as a real person.

There was only one sleeping bag in the supply room. It had a jagged rip along the bottom panel. When she told David she could mend it, he handed her two tiny hotel sewing kits. She pocketed a couple of batteries for her flashlight. She didn't take any canned or dehydrated food since she no longer had access to fire. She'd have to spange for fast-food money instead of living on the Ramen diet.

Lorelei had learned that if she arrived early enough, she could do laundry and shower in peace. She put her clothes in to wash, then took a long shower letting hot water prickle her face and back. She never felt clean, no matter how much she lathered and rinsed. It was as if something other than dirt and body odor clung to her skin, something that tainted her from the inside.

The drop-in didn't usually serve breakfast, but when she walked back to the lobby there were miniature boxes of cheerfully colored cereal scattered on the food table. Alongside those were small squat cartons of milk. Lorelei used a plastic spoon to punch through the perforated H-cut on the front of a box. She filled it with milk and shoveled the sickeningly sweet cereal into her mouth. The taste brought a flood of school memories.

She should be a junior now, excited about prom.

Instead her days would be filled with the relentless search for food and a safe place to sleep. And boredom. Long days with nothing to do, no one worth talking to. She had thought when she left home that she would get to see the world. And in the beginning she'd had a fun group to hang with in Oregon. She'd seen some pretty phenomenal natural spots in the Pacific Northwest—massive sequoia, redwoods and rocky beaches strewn with giant elephant seals. She'd been to music festivals all down the California coast where she'd met hippies and performance artists and people dressed in Renaissance garb. She'd slept in a barn on an organic farm and once woke up on a freezing beach with pebbles pressed into her cheek.

It had been an adventure, but along the way she'd been hungry and tired and scared. Travel companions flowed in and out of her life, so she'd learned to keep to cities with youth services. At one point, she realized that she rarely saw the pretty parts of town. Shelters were never in nice areas; nobody wanted transients hanging around their neighborhood, gumming up their pretty views.

While she waited for her clothes to dry, Lorelei used the drop-in's computer. She had long ago stopped checking her Gmail. The few old friends who did know her e-mail address had stopped responding. She was left with only junk mail.

Instead, Lorelei checked her Facebook page. She always smiled when she saw the redheaded superheroine she used as her profile pic. All her Facebook friends were travelers like herself, nobody who was a risk to her anonymity. She kept up with a dozen travelers who posted sporadically. Sometimes she was able to reconnect with a friend lost to her, but nobody had posted anything to Lorelei's wall and she had no messages.

She posted, *Anybody in Austin?*

A hefty girl asked her how long she was going to be on the computer, so Lorelei logged off.

Next, she picked through the deteriorating boxes of board games. She would have enjoyed a game of Monopoly or Risk, but there was nobody around to play. Every Monday after dinner, her family had gathered to eat dessert and play board games. It was a Latter-day Saints' tradition called Family Home Evening. The sad, torn boxes of Scrabble and Yahtzee made her remember the laughter, the happiness before things spun so out of control. She used to hate

Family Home Evening, but now she couldn't really remember why.

She checked out the shabby selection of paperbacks on the drop-in's shelves.

David walked by on his way out, and she stopped him.

"Dude," she said. "Your books are all bodice rippers and lawyer stories. Where do you keep the good books?"

"That's just what people donate," David said. "The library is a short walk from here. You can use the drop-in's address and telephone to apply for a library card."

"Really?"

"Sure," he said. "Have a party."

The Austin Public Library was a beige-concrete four-story building with a couple of metal benches outside. Lorelei knew that its austere exterior was a way to discourage the homeless from hanging around, but it hadn't worked. There was an older lady sitting on a pile of backpacks and bedrolls gumming a cigarette. The woman looked up at Lorelei and held out her hand.

"Sorry, ma'am," she said and shrugged as if to say, *we're in the same boat.*

Lorelei's mother used to take her to their local library. She remembered seeing a few homeless men sleeping in the lobby. Her mother called them "the unfortunates." She never fully explained their presence, so Lorelei didn't understand homelessness. She thought that it would be the coolest thing in the world to live in a library. To her, that was the opposite of unfortunate.

At the entrance, Lorelei was confronted by a large sign that read *No Bedrolls.* She couldn't leave her new sleeping bag outside to be stolen.

"Would you like to leave some of your things here, young lady?" a kindly older woman asked her from behind a high counter. Lorelei hesitated. She'd learned never to be separated from her possessions.

"Do I have to?"

"It's library policy—no bedrolls," the lady said. "I don't usually do this, but yours looks nice and clean, so I'll keep it behind the desk with my things if you like. Otherwise you'll be asked to leave. Don't worry. I'll take good care of it. You can keep your pack."

Lorelei saw she was being offered a kindness, and she reluctantly handed over her new sleeping bag. Now she understood the lone gypsy guarding the pile of possessions outside.

She found the graphic novel section and read two in an hour. While her mother had always wanted her to read books like *Anne of Green Gables* and *Little Women*, she'd always been attracted to the action adventure panels of Manga and comic books. Her mother called them boy books, but Lorelei didn't think art of any kind had a gender bias. She just liked more contemporary story lines with situations and problems that could apply to a girl like her.

She could only add the weight of one book to her already heavy load, so she decided to reread *Twilight*. She loved the descriptions of Washington state, so much like the Oregon she had run away to. She understood clumsy, pale Bella and her emotionally clumsy parents. But what she liked most of all was the love story of Edward and Bella, love that was pure, without restrictions or conditions. That was what parents were supposed to have for their children—unconditional love. What a joke. Parental love came with nothing but conditions.

Lorelei found a large paperback edition of *Twilight* and approached the front desk. A different volunteer was behind the circulation desk. The new woman slid her a library card application. Lorelei quickly filled it out and handed it back. The woman began to enter information into the computer. Her eyes fell upon the address and she stopped typing and gave Lorelei a quick disapproving glance.

With clipped efficiency, the woman scanned Lorelei's new library card. The volunteer printed out a return sheet, slid it inside the book and snapped the cover closed.

"This book is due back in two weeks," the woman said. "It's a high demand book, so please return it so others can enjoy it as well."

Lorelei thanked her and headed to retrieve her bedroll from the other desk. As she walked away she heard the woman say to no one in particular, "Well, we'll never see that book again."

That night, after mending the sleeping bag, Lorelei propped up against a log, switched on her flashlight and began to read. This would be her third time reading *Twilight*. At home, she had borrowed a girlfriend's copy and hidden it under her bed. She knew her parents wouldn't approve, even though Stephanie Meyer was LDS too. Mormons were a diverse group, a confusing thing for a kid.

Mook and Elda were gone somewhere, probably somewhere warm, but the others had set up camp again. Freestyle was slumped in a rotten lawn chair, one of his eyes ringed like a raccoon. College boys had jumped him.

Minion picked out Green Day's *Good Riddance* on the strings of an old guitar.

He sang, "I hope you had the time of your life."

Lorelei always liked the song, particularly the part about tattoos of memories.

When she felt the tug of sleep, she snuggled down into the comforting confinement of the sleeping bag. One advantage to sleeping bags was she could stuff her things into the bottom and not worry that someone would steal them while she slept.

She was soon dreaming about walking to school through powdery snow a foot deep. Above her, slate-gray mountains pushed against a blue, blue sky. Her breath grew short, and she struggled through deeper and deeper drifts. Snowbanks rose around her ten feet high. She fell. She got up and trudged on. She fell again. She hurt her hand.

She jolted awake. Pain seared her fingers and up her arm. She screamed and kicked, struggling to free herself from the sleeping bag. Another hot poker pierced her skin. She screamed again and fought the confines of the fabric.

Then, somehow, Mook was there, unzipping her sleeping bag, rolling her out onto the hard ground. Flashlight beams scraped the night. Mook cursed and crushed something under his boot.

She shrieked and slapped hysterically at her hand.

"Calm down." Elda tried to wrap her arms around her. "It's gone. He killed it."

"Get it off! Get it off!" Lorelei screamed. The pain streaked up past her wrist. She swatted at her stinging arm.

Mook grabbed her and gave her a solid shake. "Shit, girl. It's just a big bug. You're okay. Calm down."

Her terror broke and she came to her senses.

"Look," Mook said as he lifted a six-inch centipede with the end of his knife. He held the black bug out in front of him. Its yellow pinchers slowly opened and closed; a few of its many red legs twitched in agony.

"Yuck," Elda said.

"Texas centipede," he said. "Hurts like a mother, but it won't kill you."

"Unless you're allergic to bee stings," Elda said. "You aren't allergic, are you?"

"No," Lorelei whimpered. "I don't think so."

"It was just looking for a little warmth." Mook flung the bug into the woods. "We've all been stung by some big nasty Texas bug. Just be glad it wasn't a scorpion. Comes with the territory. You're official now."

He walked back into the lean-to. The others scanned around them before they lay down again.

"You should go to the clinic in the morning," Elda whispered. "Just to be safe."

Lorelei sat alone on a log for the rest of the night, holding her injured hand out in front of her. Tears rolled out of her for a long while after she had calmed down. She was embarrassed by her inability to regain full control, and she tried to be quiet so she wouldn't wake the others again.

The pain settled in her arm and started a throb in her shoulder. She grew cold but couldn't bear to get inside her sleeping bag again. She rocked herself, weeping softly, as she waited for daybreak.

Barbara

TEXAS HAD four seasons: drought, flood, blizzard and twister. Austin was usually horribly humid, but all of Central Texas had been parched for months and Barbara missed the sticky, moist air. This morning brought more clear skies, but the temperature had finally dropped to nonlethal.

Barbara cranked up the air conditioning in her SUV and blended with the traffic flowing toward downtown. Her phone rang and she could see on her dashboard that it was one of her PR interns from UT. She hit the talk button on her steering column.

"Hey, what's up?"

"Are you on your way in?" the girl asked.

"A few minutes out, but I've got to stop and set up something before I come in. Is everything under control?"

"Yes, but they're driving me nuts dragging ass."

"Apparently, nonprofits move slow." Barbara had been hired to manage Keep Austin Cleared, the city's annual litter clean-up program. "How's media looking? This is a one hundred percent positive client. We won't have any protestors or crisis management today, no angry letters to editors tomorrow."

"No media yet. Shouldn't they be here by now?"

"They'll show. Give them another hour. Then we'll start making calls. How do the shirts look?"

"It's a sea of green around here."

"I picked up another 10,000 cups. The logos are crisp this time. They look much better. I'm going to make the printer eat the cost for the first batch. Banner for the after-party?"

"Got it."

"Can you handle things until I get there?"

"No problem. People are trickling in, but it's still early."

"Call me if you need me."

Traffic was fierce on the tangled highway system. She cut around slow cars and old trucks filled with produce. As she waited for a light, Barbara couldn't help but read bumper stickers. It seemed the majority of vehicles in Austin were held together by adhesive slogans. There were vegans and soccer moms and alternative bands. Plenty of people wanted peace and many had strong opinions about the former president from Texas. Austin gave new meaning to the term information superhighway.

The city gleamed in the distance. It didn't look in need of a polish. Barbara suspected that Austin's litter problem came from tourists and transplants and the homeless, but that would be a very un-PC thing to express. Truly, she should be thanking whoever was mucking up the city because it meant she had a job.

Since being downsized from a corporate public relations position, Barbara had struck out on her own. Businesses of all types were scrambling for attention in a tight market. Newspapers and television stations had cut nearly half of their reporters. Those who were left were overwhelmed with work, so getting them to appreciate a story was harder than ever. Oddly, being a small, reasonably priced PR firm seemed to be a growth opportunity in a bad economy.

She parked in front of Group Therapy. Inside smelled of sour beer, but the hardwood floors were clean and the tables tidy and ready for the lunch crowd. Emily waved a giant knife in Barbara's direction. Fruit wobbled on a scarred cutting board in front of her daughter.

"Hi, sweetheart," Barbara said as she wiggled onto a barstool.

"Hi."

"I don't have long. My assistant's taking care of things for me this morning."

"Can you eat?"

"I'd love some of Angel's beef brisket if he's got any made this early."

"I'll check." Emily opened the swinging door to the kitchen, spoke to someone and then came back. "No problem. So what's up? What are you doing downtown today?"

"Working for the big cleanup, you know, Keep Austin Cleared? I did all the media and branding this year. We're handling the closing ceremonies and the party after. Why don't you come on down and help with the clean up efforts?"

Emily gathered her hair behind her, twisted it up and stuck a pencil through the mass of curls. This was her way of thinking before speaking.

"I'd like to, but I can't. One of my bartenders called in sick. I have to pull a double today."

She was probably lying, but Barbara couldn't blame her. Over the years, Barbara had made her family volunteer to do everything from handing out water at marathons to pretending to be happy customers for commercials. Why would Emily be eager to pick up trash?

"So this is your new client?" Emily asked. "How's it going?"

"Great so far. I did the volunteer media release and we got tons of people. I was surprised. Community organizations, business and social clubs, churches, bowling leagues and softball teams. Lots of UT students. Apparently, sororities and fraternities use Keep Austin Cleared as part of their social service requirements."

Emily set a Diet Coke in front of her mother and Barbara took a sip.

"Thank you. So, I spent last week shooting b-roll of litter-packed areas of the city. I had that delivered with the media release a couple of days ago to all the TV stations. I'm hoping they'll use it as before and after shots."

"Smart."

"Hey, I'd like to hire you to help me. Can you go to the dump with me in the morning and take some shots? I made these bright-green branded garbage bags for the event and I found out where the city is taking them all. I'm hoping to get shots of a mountain of those bags. There will be literally thousands. Pictures like that will help me get the job again next year."

Emily pondered the offer, then she said, "Sure. Why not?"

"I'll pay."

"Even better."

The kitchen door swung open, and Angel came out with a basket of food.

"Hola, Senora Barbara."

"How you doing, Angel?"

"Can't complain, but I still do."

Barbara had always liked Angel. She could felt his protectiveness toward Emily, which gave her some comfort about her daughter working in a bar.

Barbara's iPhone chirped.

"My assistant," she said. Then, "Hey, what's going on?"

"Where are you?"

"I'm downtown. Just a few minutes away. Why? You need me?"

"I think so. I've got some reporter being an asshole."

"Really? What's his deal?"

"Apparently there's some standoff between gutter punks and frat boys down here in the alley by the drop-in. Students say the area is theirs to clean. Youth ministries had some of the street kids cleaning it. They got into a disagreement and wouldn't you know it, some reporter shows up right when things start to go down. Can you come?"

"Fifteen minutes."

So much for no drama. Crisis management first thing. Damn.

Barbara looked longingly at Angel's glorious sandwich.

"Could you?" she asked.

He smiled. "No hay problema. I wrap it up for you." He took the basket back to the kitchen.

Barbara parked in a no parking zone and attached a media pass to the rearview mirror. She didn't qualify for a media pass, but she had managed to pinch one from a political campaign she was involved in once. It always worked. People never messed with reporters.

Down the urine-tinged alley behind a church she found the unhappy standoff. On one side of the alley, young men wore the bright-green protective gloves Barbara had ordered for the event. A couple had on her T-shirts. On the other side, boys were dressed in drab sweatshirts and pants. They seemed overly dressed for the warm weather.

Barbara's fidgety assistant was standing next to a guy with a skinny notebook in his hand, a messenger bag slung over one shoulder—obviously the reporter.

As Barbara approached, she heard the reporter say, "I heard that one of the street kids was assaulted by a student last week. You know anything about that?"

"That's not really why we are here today," Barbara interjected. "Hi, I'm Barbara Bryce. I'm helping with this event."

He looked perturbed. He didn't bother to shake her offered hand.

"And can I ask your name?" She smiled her most sincere smile.

"Travis Roberts. I'm with *Be Here Now*."

Great. The town's liberal rag would usually be a big supporter of this event. Were they suddenly hostile?

"Let's focus on the positive aspect of this, shall we?" Barbara said.

"I'm not here to report on the litter event," he said. "I'm following up on a report that one of the street kids got punched in the nose. I just stumbled up on this fresh conflict."

"They're harshing our vibe." This boy had black disks the size of quarters in his ears. Emily called those ugly things *gauges*, but Barbara always thought of them as tiny hockey pucks. His friends had hardware in their eyebrows and various orifices. "We're just trying to help and these dudes come along and move in on our territory."

"It's not like we want to be in this piss-soaked shit hole," one of the students said.

When she spoke, Barbara directed her words toward the frat boys, thinking it more likely she could reason with the students.

"Hey, guys. What's the problem? There's more than enough trash to go around."

"Huh, I'll say," remarked the student who seemed to be the leader. Like his friends, he had gelled hair and perfect white teeth.

"Why don't you just pick another spot?" she suggested.

"We were told to clean up this area. This particular spot is ours every year. Why can't they move?" the student asked.

"Why can't you work together? Look, you guys take this side of the alley." Barbara swept her arm past the street kids and then in the other direction past the students. "And you guys take this side. It's half the work for both of you."

Less work seemed to strike an acceptable accord with both sides. As they thought it over, a disheveled man in his thirties sauntered up the alley, his hands shoved deep into the pockets of his camo pants.

He stopped and took in the situation.

"Hey, David Simpson," he said. "I'm the director at the Tumbleweed Center. Is there something I can do to help here?"

The angry demeanor of the street kids immediately cooled.

"Are you in charge of these boys?" Barbara asked.

"Not for this event," he said. "That would be the Street Youth Ministry. Is there a problem?"

"I don't know," she said. "Is there a problem here, boys?"

They all shook their heads and mumbled.

"Great. Then let's all get back to doing our thing. How about it? We're all happy, right? Can't wait for the big party tonight, right?" she said.

"Like we'd be welcome at your stupid party," one of the punks said under his breath.

"Of course you guys are welcome to come. We'll have hot dogs and popcorn and all sorts of goodies. I'll give you some shirts."

"Like those?" One of the street kids pointed to the frat boys in Barbara's bright-green creations. "No thanks." His group snickered and the students bristled.

"Guys, stop it," David said. He had a strong masculine voice that got their attention. Trash bags rustled open and both sides turned to their tasks.

"Barbara Bryce, and this is," she said, motioning to Travis.

"We know each other," Travis said. "What's up, David? I guess you're the person I really should ask about this. I heard about an altercation between some UT students and a Drag kid last week. Said a boy ended up with a bloody nose. You know anything about that?"

"It was no big deal. We diffused the situation."

"Was it students bum hunting?"

"No. That's not the case and don't write that."

"Look, man. We're on the same side here. People should know what it's like to live like these kids do. Face the things they have to face every day just to survive."

"I'll let you two talk," Barbara said. She handed the reporter her card. "If you want to discuss the cleanup, give me a call."

"Yeah, okay. I got all your releases and stuff already," he said, dismissing her. Sometimes it was easy to hate reporters.

"Great, then," she chirped. "Maybe I'll see you at the afterparty."

Lorelei

EXHAUSTION OVERTOOK Lorelei just after daybreak, so weary she forgot her fear of giant insects. She had crawled back into her sleeping bag and cinched the opening around her face.

The voices started far away. Was she dreaming? She could hear people stomping through the underbrush like awkward animals. Without warning, three adults, all in the same DayGlo shirts and gloves, stepped into her fuzzy vision.

"Oh," one of the women said. "People are living here."

"This must be a hobo camp," another said. No apology. They just stood and stared, obviously unsure how to react.

They held garish green garbage bags and sticks with metal ends for collecting trash. The man gripped his stick tightly, but the women held theirs loosely at their sides.

Lorelei's head felt as if it would split down the middle, and she pulled her hood tightly around her face. She longed for dark glasses to cut the flash of sun through the trees. She could hear other people moving through the woods, apparently stumbling upon other camps. She heard Mook.

"Hey folks. How y'all doing?" he drawled cordially.

"Oh." They were startled and obviously a little frightened.

"This must be cleanup day, huh?" Mook said.

"That's right," the man said.

"That's so nice of y'all to help keep the city clean. How about we take care of this spot right here and you can find somewhere else to clean up? As you can see, some of us are still sleeping."

Lorelei moved to get up, but when she pushed up on her arm, pain seared her right side. She collapsed to the ground in a whimper.

"What's wrong with her?" one of the women asked. "Is she drunk?"

"Centipede sting," Mook said.

They looked as if they didn't believe him. He crouched next to Lorelei.

"Let's see that hand," he said.

She could barley move her arm away from her body. Mook pushed up her sweatshirt sleeve and there was a collective gasp.

He gave a concerned whistle. "Man, her arm is hot."

Red streaks ran the length of her arm and a stab of pain coursed through her each time she moved.

"Child, you need to go to the doctor," one woman said.

The woman bent down and slowly pushed back Lorelei's hood. She caught her breath when she saw the tattoos. She hesitated, and then laid her hand against Lorelei's cheek the way mothers check their babies for fever.

"This child is burning up. She needs to see a doctor right now."

"We could take her to the clinic," Elda said from somewhere behind them. "I think they're open on Saturday."

"Lorelei, can you walk?" Mook asked.

"I think so." He helped her to her feet, but Lorelei's head felt stuffed with cotton and her balance was off. She bent double and again collapsed to the ground. She began to cry and rock, cradling her arm against her chest.

"I'll take her," the man said. "My car is up by the bridge. Can you help get her to my car?"

"I can carry her," Mook said. "She can't weigh anything."

He worked his arms underneath her legs, stood and clutched her to him. She whimpered, then put her head on his shoulder.

"Lead the way," Mook said.

"My stuff," Lorelei mumbled. "My things."

"We'll keep it, Lorelei. I'll keep it all safe for you," Elda said.

"No," Lorelei said. "No. I need it."

"We should go. Why can't she leave her things?" the man said.

"You wouldn't understand," Elda said as she rolled up the sleeping bag with all of Lorelei's pack inside. "Go on. I'll carry this."

Mook followed the man, picking his way through the underbrush. The women held branches out of the way. Mook struggled to climb an embankment and the women both grabbed one of his arms and helped. He recovered, and soon he eased Lorelei into the backseat of a sedan. The man got behind the wheel and one woman got into the front.

Mook gave directions to the clinic. Elda shoved the sleeping bag bundle into the floorboard of the backseat.

The kind woman got into the back and nestled Lorelei's head on her lap. "Poor child," she said as she brushed stray hair from the girl's face.

The woman's soft touch made Lorelei long for her mother. Lorelei's thoughts roamed and merged—children on the bus ride into Austin, their sweaty curls and slack lips. A centipede, black and menacing. Her mother, worried, always so worried. A boy she knew once, a dark boy with kind eyes that felt like love. She needed to sleep. If only she could sleep. It felt so good to lie down, to be comforted.

"Why?" the woman asked her friends as they wove through Austin's flurry of traffic. "She's such a lovely girl. Why would she mark herself up like this?"

Lorelei wanted to reiterate Elda's words, but she couldn't force them from her mouth. *You wouldn't understand.*

They parked outside a nondescript brick building tucked away on a side street. The man came around and opened the back door.

"Do you think you can walk now?" he asked gently. She could hear the hope in his voice. The old fellow couldn't carry her the way Mook had. She mustered strength and wobbled her way in the front door with their assistance.

They entered a waiting room filled with wan people and Lorelei's heart sank. She knew it could be hours before she was seen. The kind woman rapped lightly on the intake window.

Taped to the sliding glass was a poster that listed all the tests the clinic provided including HEP and HIV screenings. They offered safe sex kits and needle cleaning bleach kits. There was a poster about unwanted pregnancy and another about lice and scabies.

A nurse with an irritated look came to the window, but as soon as she saw Lorelei her expression changed. She slid the window open quickly.

"What's wrong with her?" the nurse asked.

"She was apparently stung by a centipede. I think she's having an allergic reaction."

"Is she having trouble breathing?"

Lorelei recognized this as a sure way to the front of the line. She nodded and grasped her throat.

The nurse jumped to action. "Meet me at the door. Bring her on back."

In the exam room, the nurse helped ease her up onto a bed with a crackly green mattress that reminded Lorelei of fracturing ice on frozen puddles. She closed her eyes against the droning fluorescents. The florid disinfectant smell increased her headache.

"Open up," the nurse commanded. She stuck a thermometer under Lorelei's tongue. She slid a blood pressure cuff up on her good arm. The thermometer beeped and the nurse removed it.

"One hundred," she said with clipped efficiency.

Lorelei was familiar with the white pulse ox clip with the red light that the nurse clipped to her finger.

"This is to check your oxygen level," the nurse said.

Lorelei nodded.

"Did you really get stung by a centipede or is this a track mark infection?"

"Bug bite," Lorelei said.

"Okay." The nurse crinkled her nose, then scribbled on a chart. When the oxygen results started to register she said, "You're doing okay. High nineties. You say you're having trouble breathing?"

"I feel better now," Lorelei said.

"Right. You been smoking anything? Weed, crack, meth?"

"I don't smoke."

The nurse looked doubtful again, but she secured an oxygen mask over Lorelei's nose.

"A man brought this," someone standing outside the curtain said. "I think it belongs to your patient."

"Is this your stuff?" the nurse asked.

Lorelei nodded. She scanned the room for the kind woman who had helped her, but she was gone. Lorelei knew she would never see her again.

A jagged pain raced through her when the nurse straightened her arm. She touched the inside of Lorelei's elbow, looking for track marks. Her arm and her shoulder crawled with fire, but she didn't dare ask for pain meds.

"What sort of drugs do you take?" the nurse asked.

"Nothing." The mask muffled her voice, but her frustration with the line of questioning communicated well enough.

"Look, no judgment here. I just need to know so I can help you." The nurse looked tired. She had gentle brown eyes and a wig that was much too shiny and straight to be her own hair. She wore a pilled sweater over a smiley face smock that looked so soft it must have been washed a thousand times.

A doctor came in, and the nurse reeled off all the symptoms she had collected on her chart—trouble breathing, slight temp, headache, nausea, swelling and redness in the arm.

"How long ago did you get these stings?" the doctor asked.

"I don't know. Early this morning, I guess."

"So about six hours ago? Well, that's actually good news young lady. If you were going to go into anaphylactic shock you would have already done it. Still," he whistled, "this is one of the nastiest centipede attacks I've ever seen." To the nurse he said, "She's definitely sensitive. Let's hook her up with an IV just to be safe. Let's give her epinephrine and a steroid to calm her skin reaction. Put her in a bed and let her sleep it off."

Within minutes of the shots, Lorelei was feeling better, and she drifted off into a black and dreamless sleep. When she awoke it was dark outside, and she heard coughing and a faint cry from a distant bed.

"About time you woke up. I've been waiting for somebody to talk to all day."

She looked over at the next bed to see a cute boy about her age. His hair was bright orange. His clothes said *street*. He rolled his eyes toward a pregnant girl in the next bed, crying into a pillow. Behind her, a guy was passed out and snoring loudly. Even from three beds away, Lorelei could smell the sickly-sweet stench of alcohol. At the end of the long room a woman rocked a child in her arms.

"They're not much for conversation, if you know what I mean," he said.

A smile crossed her lips, and she realized that she felt better.

The boy said, "My friends call me Cargo. What's your name?"

She tried to say Lorelei, but her mouth was too dry to form words.

"Here." He reached a plastic pitcher on the table between them and poured her a cup of water. She sipped the tepid water slowly.

"Lorelei," she finally croaked.

Another nurse, in another pilled sweater, came by to hand him a tiny white cup with a couple of pills rattling around in it.

Cargo held it out to the nurse as if giving her a toast. "Bottoms up," he said, and threw back the pills. He washed them down with water and opened his mouth for her to check inside. Satisfied, she moved on.

"You here for meds?" she asked him.

"Yeah. Had to get back on them. I was getting a little crazy, you know?" He wiggled his fingers by his face and rolled his eyes and whistled two notes. "Manic shit. Haven't slept in days. What about you?"

"Centipede bite." She held up her hand, happy to see that no pain shot through her this time.

"Gnarly."

"What do you take? I mean for manic stage?" she asked.

"Lamictal."

"That one make you itch?"

"Like little squiggly creatures crawling under my skin. How'd you know?"

"My brother used to take that. He'd scratch like he was going to tear his arm off. They're probably giving you generic. You've got to take the brand name. It won't make you itch so much."

"Like I have a choice." He smiled. "What all stuff did your brother take?"

"All kinds—Lithium, Seroquel. Stuff that made his muscles spasm. Some that made him lose his appetite. He got really skinny."

"Fun with side effects, huh? How's your brother now?"

"I don't know. I haven't seen him in a while."

"Did he get better?"

She shrugged. "I don't know. Like I said, haven't seen him."

The nurse returned.

"How you feeling?" she asked Lorelei.

"Better."

"That's good. Those steroids will fix you right up. Here, let me take your pulse." The woman went through the routine of checking vitals. It was amazing how much attention doctors and nurses gave when they could see a physical problem—how little when they could not. It was the things people couldn't see or touch that made them turn away. Cargo was lucky to get any help since his problems were inside his head.

"I'm hungry," Lorelei said.

"Well, honey, food is scarce around here. I can bring you some Nabs and a soda. That's about all you're going to get this late. We don't generally feed folks and I hate to tell you this, but nobody stays overnight."

"I have to leave?"

"Everybody does."

She noticed the pregnant girl gathering her things.

"You got somewhere to go?" the nurse asked hopefully.

"Yeah. Sure. Of course."

The woman looked at her as if she knew the truth, but didn't push the subject. She had her own problems, probably a hungry family waiting at home.

With the help of her orange-haired new friend, Lorelei loaded her pack. He tethered her sleeping bag to the pack for her, but she decided it was easier to balance the load if she carried it. The nurse had warned her that it had turned unusually cold, so she wore all her warm clothes, the most obvious sign of homelessness. Outside, the temperature was dropping. She got her bearings. She was a long way from the park, too far to walk in her condition.

Cargo suggested that she come with him, but the last thing she wanted was to hang around with some guy who would talk her ear off all night.

She considered her plight. Even if she made it back to Shoal Creek, the probability was high that her group had been run out of camp like everybody else. Of course, they would come back. They always did. Still, she wasn't going to walk all that way to find nobody there. It was too late to get into a shelter. She'd have to find somewhere to sleep, a cemetery or school grounds.

But first she had to get something to eat and she wasn't going to spange tonight. It was too cold, and she still felt weak. She walked toward South Congress, the area the town called SoCo. It was a long shot, but with her bandaged hand she was more likely to solicit some serious sympathy.

Emily

EMILY DRAGGED the black spongy bar mats through the kitchen, past the heated ballgame banter. To Angel and his sous-chef Tino, futbol was religion. Frank had bought the guys a television for the kitchen and mounted it to the wall above the food prep station. He'd gotten them Telemundo so they could watch la Liga Mexicana.

Angel and Tino quarreled and shouted, shaking their fists at the TV and spewing Spanish. Angel had polished his kitchen skills and his English in the resorts of Cancun, but Spanish was always the language of futbol. At times, the kitchen crew's shouts could be heard above the music in the bar, always some disagreement over which team was superior. Angel liked the dominating Atlante from his hometown of Cancun. Tino criticized Atlante for being a glamour team that imported talent. Tino, apparently a purist, liked the all-national Mexico City team Cruz Azul.

Emily paused to watch them rant.

"No, that's okay, guys. I got it," she said, propping the door open with her butt. "I don't need any help. Thanks anyway. Really. I'm fine." They didn't bother to look her way.

Emily leaned the heavy mats against a wall and turned the hose on them.

Someone stepped from the shadows. Emily gasped at the looming figure. She thought it was a hefty guy, but then she realized it was the tall homeless girl with a big pack strapped to her back. She clutched a sleeping bag. One of her hands was wrapped in bright-white gauze.

"Hey," Emily said.

"Hey."

Emily waited.

"So, you got any food you don't need?" the girl finally asked.

Emily finished dragging the last mat up against a wall to drain while she stalled. She brushed her hands off on her pants.

"How'd you know I work here?"

Lorelei shrugged. "You followed me, so one day I followed you."

"I didn't really follow you. I just saw you at Batfest."

"Whatever. You got any food or not?"

Emily waited a moment, trying to give the impression that she was deciding if she wanted to help. Then, "Sure, there's just me and the cooks here right now. They're cool. Come on in."

Lorelei trailed Emily inside. Tino's hands were down in the industrial sink, but his eyes were on the TV. He flung soapsuds in the air and cried, "Que idiotas!"

Angel laughed and dried knives.

"Excuse me, guys," Emily said. "This is Lorelei."

Tino only nodded, but Angel extended his hand.

"Hola, Miss. I'm Angel and this is my cousin, Tino."

She started to shake and then remembered her injury and pulled back.

"What happened to you?" Angel asked.

"Centipede," she said. She pouted like a little girl, an unexpected change in demeanor.

Angel grimaced and sucked air through his teeth. "I have felt the scorpion's sting, but not the centipede. Did it hurt?"

"A lot!"

"Ay, caramba!"

This made her smile, and her stance became less guarded.

"Hey, are you hungry?" Angel asked. "I was about to make myself a sandwich. How about you, Emily? You hungry?"

Emily looked around at his clean kitchen.

"Sure, man," she said. "I'd love a grilled cheese."

"What about you? You want a grilled cheese or maybe turkey sandwich?" he asked Lorelei. He lifted a skillet down from its high hook.

"Could I have turkey *and* cheese?" the girl asked in a childish way. Emily thought Angel must seem fatherly to her. She probably missed having someone to feed her and protect her.

"Si! Turkey and cheese! What about my orange juice, Emily?" Angel was a recovering alcoholic and juice was all he ever drank.

"Lorelei, you want anything?" Emily heaved open the steel door to the walk-in.

"Juice is good."

"Tino?"

He shook his head and continued to clean without taking his eyes from the game.

The walk-in cooler smelled like Emily's grandparents' basement cellar, earthy and weird. She found the jug of juice. She grabbed a giant jar of pickles and slammed the door with a metallic thud. She wiggled up onto a countertop and began fishing for pickles with a giant serving fork.

"Pickle?" she asked, holding out the big fork with one skewered to the end.

Lorelei grabbed it and crunched it down in three bites.

Angel slapped a slab of butter into a frying pan. He chattered on about his new baby, pointing with a spatula to a photo of his wife and baby girl. There was another of his whole family—Angel, his wife, their baby and both of their sons.

Lorelei studied the photos with genuine interest, but her eyes kept drifting back to the frying pan.

Angel slipped the toasty sandwiches onto a plate and cut each in half. He piled the plates high with salty potato chips. Emily poured glasses of OJ. Angel crammed his mouth full and patted his stomach.

"Cochino," Tino said, and snickered.

"I know, I know," Angel said rubbing his round gut. He winked at Lorelei. "He just called me a pig."

She smiled again and ate as if she hadn't eaten in a week.

"Lorelei, I like that name. She's a superhero. Right?" Angel asked.

She stopped eating for a second. "Wow, how'd you know that?" she asked, her mouth full of bread and cheese.

"Yeah, how *did* you know that?" Emily asked.

"I have teenage sons. They read comic books. I like them too," Angel said. "And tattoos." He pushed up his sleeves, revealing tats on his forearms. One was a snapping banner that read, *Familia*, another the Atlante team brand emblazoned across a soccer ball. A small scroll on the inside of his arm read *Easy Does It*. Another was Speedy Gonzales, his floppy feet accelerating, air puffs shooting out behind him.

Lorelei touched the cartoon. "Why do you have that?"

"Because I'm the fastest cook in Austin."

She studied his work but didn't offer to elaborate on her own ink.

Tino scrubbed the skillet Angel had used, then pulled the plug. Water gurgled and burped down the drain.

"So, where you going to stay tonight?" Emily asked. "It's supposed to turn cold."

Wrong move.

"Don't worry about it," Lorelei snapped in an icy voice.

"I'm not worried. Just asking."

"Don't ask. I can take care of myself."

"Hey, I'm not gonna hassle you."

"I gotta split." Lorelei shoved the rest of her sandwich into her bag. She took the glass of juice with her.

Emily followed her to the back door. The girl shoved outside and started down the alley.

"You're welcome," Emily called after her.

"Whatever," Lorelei said over her shoulder. Then she stopped and said, "Look, don't think this means we're friends or anything."

"Why would I think that?"

"Because people think if they give you something that you owe them. I don't owe you anything."

"No. You don't owe me anything."

"I hate charity. Charity's never free." She jerked her hood over her head, her breath a pale cloud in the alley's last light.

Lorelei

SHE COULD have played the sympathy card and probably ended up couch surfing at Emily's. But Lorelei had reacted before she thought things through. Sometimes she had low impulse control, or so she'd been told.

Now she would have to find a place to sleep. She scanned the unfamiliar street in this unfamiliar part of town. Town Lake was close, but she didn't know that terrain or who might be hanging there. While considering her options, the lights flickered out inside the bar. Lorelei watched from the shadows of an alley across the street as Emily, Angel and Tino came outside into the alley. Emily pushed a bike. They walked up to a rattletrap truck, one her father would have called a rice burner. Tino hefted the bike into the back. All three got into the little truck and drove away.

Lorelei made her way back down the bar's alley and assessed the wooden fence. She'd been rock climbing, so the fence wouldn't ordinarily present a problem, but her hand was beginning to hurt again. She needed something to stand on.

She walked to the dumpster, took a deep breath and wrestled open the corroded square access door. A putrid reek hit her in the face. Inside she found an enormous refried bean can and thanked God not everyone in Austin recycled. She shoved the door shut to cover her tracks.

The can added more than a foot to her height. She'd always

been tall, nearly five ten, which had helped her pass as older on the streets. Standing on the can, she could easily get a grip and swing a leg up and over. Bars never opened early, so she was sure she could be gone before anybody showed up in the morning. She'd have to remember to hide the can when she left.

She threw her bedroll and pack over the fence. *Man up*, she whispered. Three agonizing tries later, she dangled inside the fence. Her feet touched a wooden bench, and she dropped down.

It wasn't a large area, just big enough for half-a-dozen tables. Flea market chairs were scattered around a fire dish. Her heart leapt! A fire! In a corner lived a poorly stacked rick of wood and a pile of kindling. She used a long, thin piece of firewood to poke at the ashes gathered in the bottom of the metal saucer. A glimmer of orange hope appeared.

She needed to stoke the coals. She searched for newspaper to no avail. She opened her pack and pawed through her things with her uninjured hand. She could feel her heart pulsing in her other hand. It was painful, but she could live with it.

She poked through her pack but found nothing. She rarely carried anything that wasn't absolutely necessary. She could go through the dumpster or take stacks of local papers that always lived in racks along the sidewalk, but climbing back out sounded painful. Then her fingers touched her library book.

Survival instincts told her to sacrifice the book, but her heart told her that it would be worse than stealing, worse than lying. Books had been her closest companions, her escape from misery. And she knew if she burned it that she would never be allowed to check out another.

Besides, if she burned *Twilight* what would she use to entertain herself tonight? Reading held her rapid thoughts at bay until she could fall asleep. Without a good story to follow, her own tumbling, twisting thoughts kept her awake all night, leaving her exhausted and depressed the next day.

Depression was like an ugly uninvited friend that came for an extended visit, familiar but unwanted. Depression allowed her to finally sleep, but it wasn't the type of sleep that nourished. It was a sucking black hole that made her forget to eat, made her immobile until somebody literally forced her to move along.

So she tried to stay happy, to focus on the positive, like when she had a good group of friends to hang with, when somebody gave her a real meal, or she found an animal buddy for a while. Lorelei didn't worry about her moods. She had come to realize that hers was a common cycle of the destitute—hopefulness, frenzied restlessness, depression. Nobody was in control of their emotions all the time.

At the moment, Lorelei was content with her situation. She had found an ideal setup—a private spot where she wouldn't have to sleep on the ground. She decided not to burn the library book. She could make fire from far less than she had to work with here. She'd built fires from practically nothing at that brat camp her parents had sent her to.

Lorelei found a Naugahyde chair with a hole in the seat. She picked at the cushion stuffing and out came a wad of curly fibers perfect for growing a fire. She gathered all the stuffing she could without it showing. The last thing she wanted was to ruin a sweet spot by calling attention to her presence.

She decided to use one of her soiled shirts for fuel too, just in case the fibers didn't have enough burn life. She gathered kindling, then a handful of larger pieces of wood, and finally a couple of logs from the stack in the corner. She stuffed her shirt and the fibers in the bottom of the fire dish, added the kindling, then a few larger pieces of wood. She built the embers into a flame that spread their healthy glow to the dry wood, and finally, she arranged the logs on top.

Soon, she had a blaze that she feared might call attention from neighbors, but a quick look around revealed only one-story businesses. There were no second-story apartments to look down on her. She felt confident that the flames weren't visible from the street.

Lorelei pulled a bench close to the fire and spread her sleeping bag out. She fed the blaze and ate the rest of her sandwich. From a water hose, she filled the red plastic glass she'd taken. It was a good glass. She'd keep it.

The fire was reassuring, and she made a mental note to acquire the needed equipment for a new tinderbox. Her tinderbox from camp had been in the pack that was taken in Phoenix. Making fire was one of the survival skills she had learned at Nez Perce, the wilderness camp her parents had sent her to when she was fifteen.

Adults called it wilderness therapy, but all the kids recognized it as their desperate parents' attempts to reprogram them. The idea was to make a child so miserable, so hungry and cold and tired, that they developed a renewed desire for home. What are a few chores and an early curfew compared to eating twigs and sleeping on bitter ground?

Only sometimes, it backfired. Sometimes, instead of resulting in a child's submission, the camps served to stoke the fires of willfulness and defiance. Or, as in Lorelei's case, it made the children realize their ability to survive on their own.

Living in hard circumstances had given her confidence and cunning. The camp taught her how to make temporary shelters and tell time from the sun. She learned there were many edible things that a person didn't have to buy. She learned about hypothermia and sun exposure and first aid.

They'd dropped her group in the middle of the woods with a compass and told them to find their way out. She'd learned to navigate on foot, how to walk her way out of a situation. She'd never been independent before, had always been driven by her harried mother from home to car to school to car to mall to car and back to home for so many years that she felt as if her feet rarely touched actual ground.

She discovered that she liked to walk. Getting around through her own physical efforts felt *good*.

Camp made her realize she was strong. Not just strong-willed like her parents insisted, but durable. She'd always lived a cushy life filled with television and Twinkies and temple. But once she went long stretches without eating or sleeping, she realized she was tough. She learned that she didn't cry easily and that she rarely got sick.

The most significant thing she learned at camp was that she wasn't alone. Nez Perce was filled with other kids just like her—not the popular, not the athletes, not the scholars—kids with parents disappointed in their offspring.

Back home, she'd kept in touch with her camp companions. Even though Lorelei's father had taken away her cell phone and computer privileges, she'd gotten around that problem with an online account at the library. Her mother was always happy to drop her there.

For more than a year, she'd written to her Nez Perce friends. Eventually somebody suggested they form a clan to travel around. One boy had an older cousin who lived in a community house in Oregon. He suggested they could all live there and share the rent. One by one, e-mails started to contain stories of adventure. One by one, her camp friends left home and made their way to Oregon.

As tension mounted at home, Lorelei planned her own escape.

She saved money and stocked her travel pack.

She left in the middle of the night, a note on her bedside table.

Don't worry, Mommy. I'll come back. I just have to do this. I'm searching. I hope you understand.

But the road had transformed her, both mentally and physically. She couldn't go back now, even if she wanted to.

Travis

EVERY DAY, reporters consider dozens of media releases, everything from nonprofit fundraisers to local politicians announcing candidacies. Most reporters have a love/hate relationship with mass releases. Travis had spent the last hour going through e-mails and three days' worth of snail mail. He read the agendas of upcoming municipal meetings. He checked the minutes of the last University of Texas board meeting.

The public had a romanticized idea of reporters as always doing the investigative thing. The truth was so much more boring. Of course, early in his career, Travis had thought he would be the next Woodward or Bernstein. Politicians would quake at the mention of his name.

He had broken some important stories, won a few journalism awards over the years. Those things didn't go to fluff reporters, not to the sound bite people, but to the real reporters asking the hard questions.

On occasion, there would be the proverbial manila envelope in the mail (usually from some disgruntled state employee) or hand delivered over a beer with a "you didn't get this from me" caveat. But usually, he'd start checking his Google alerts, and then some minor bureaucrat's background would look interesting. He'd check more and end up discovering a past violation. Travis would follow the electronic paper trail. Other things always appeared. He would request documents, file Freedom of Information Act requests. Information officers, who'd been up his ass when they had a story to sell, suddenly became unavailable when questions got tough.

Today, his Google search of "Texas" and "homeless" produced a congressional story on new laws that would change the way police and social workers track runaways. It would provide improved social services like extended outreach and shelters. The proposed legislation would allow more time for youth shelters to win kids' trust before the police entered their names into a national database.

Travis laughed at that. He doubted David Simpson ever reported any of his kids. Word gets around that you're in the business of ratting out and the kids stop coming.

A Texas senator sponsored another bill that would provide transportation to school for homeless youth who wanted to continue their education. This could be the hook for his story. Still, he'd need to know its effect on Austin before pitching to his editor.

"Bob says five minutes, people," Lily called through the office. "Assignment meeting."

Travis made it to the conference room in time to see Bob fling his editorial calendar onto the table.

"This is every cover for the foreseeable future. It's sparse. All ideas are up for discussion. No reoccurring events, please. Special sections are coming up."

There was a collective groan. Writers hated special advertising sections—fashion, home, sports, summer activities issues.

"All right, folks. Shut up. I don't hear you groaning when you get your paychecks."

"Where's interns when we need them?" somebody said from the back of the room to a round of halfhearted laughter.

"No sloughing off on the interns," Bob said. "Resources are slim. I need everybody to be willing to cover things outside their normal beat." He paused, then said, "So, ideas, please. Lead stories and covers."

"What about the renovations to the skate park?" the sports reporter suggested. "They've got twelve-foot bank ramps and seven-foot quarters, a ninety-foot pool with a waterfall. And they added new rails, mini-ramps and wedges. All built with private donations."

"We just covered their fundraising efforts last summer.

Remember? We even ran the skate terrain master plan," Bob said.

"What about the baby koala at the animal park? That would make a cute cover," Kristen, the annoyingly perky social writer, suggested.

Bob looked to be considering it, and Travis couldn't help but interject. "We've done a lot of light covers lately—Oktoberfest and that Dracula ballet. It's been a really airy month."

"That's true," Bob said. "We have been a little light lately."

Others nodded.

Kristen shot Travis a scowl. Travis smiled back. Too bad. So sad.

"We haven't covered the drought," Bob said. "Water management's a hot topic right now. What about it, Travis? You up for it?"

"Sure. City's still rationing. Gentrified areas are whining about their lawns. Charity car washes are banned. Fountains are off around town. I'll take it."

"It might not be cover material, but it'll be substantial," Bob said.

Damn, Travis thought. He hadn't had a cover he cared about in six months.

One of the associate editors piped up. "I was watching the Weather Channel last night. It said we might actually get some rain from that tropical storm that's moving through the Gulf."

"That's good to know," Bob said. "But even if it rains, we'll probably still have a water deficit the rest of the year. Travis, find out about the repercussions of this drought. What's the water level in the lakes? How's it affecting business, tourism? You know the drill."

"Sure thing."

Back at his desk Travis made a list of questions about what the National Weather Service was calling "an exceptional drought." He started with the city's website where revised water restrictions would be posted. Austin residents and businesses were limited to watering with sprinklers once a week and would face stiff fines for violations. Golf courses could water fairways once a week and tees and greens every other day. Restaurants could serve water only to customers who requested it. The city was limiting water use, including cutting back on spray park times. Due to wildfire threat, outdoor burning was banned throughout the county.

Travis made a note to call the assistant director for environmental affairs at the Austin Water Utility to see how much the levels had dwindled in the two nearby lakes that supplied the city's water. He'd have to call the city manager to check how many employees the city would add to enforce the new water regs.

The story was shaping up. Travis decided to take lunch and go over his notes. Outside, it was day two hundred and ten without a drop of rain. The force of the Texas sun had bleached color from the world, leaving everything depleted and seared to the bone.

Travis grabbed a hot dog from a corner vendor and headed to the walking path around Town Lake. The earth was hard-packed, dusty fissures under his feet. Weather.com had said that Tropical Storm Gordon had blown by Cuba, inflicting only minor damage. If it stayed on course, Gordon could make landfall somewhere between Brownsville and Galveston. The storm wasn't expected to develop into a hurricane.

A hurricane would make for a better story and probably dump a ton of water on Central Texas. Travis envisioned a tornado-like cover image, buildings caught up in the vortex. Readers were always interested in severe weather. He realized the bad karma of wishing a hurricane on your hometown, but it was guaranteed to move papers.

Lorelei

RAINDROPS EXPLODED in hard plops. They smacked against the plastic tarp she had draped over a rope between two trees. Lorelei had enough experience living outside to know that big drops meant a lot of rain was on the way. She repositioned her tarp to buffer against the sudden wind and used rocks to anchor the bottom where water might run in. She figured she'd have to pack up, but she didn't want to be premature about it.

She lay there listening to the random patter against her flimsy shelter. She could see the engorged sky, low and gray and disgruntled. There was no lightning or thunder, but the clouds were vast, bold inflations ready to unload their burden on the world.

The SoCo area hadn't been accommodating to her homeless status. She had always prided herself on never dumpster diving or eating out of trash cans, but in SoCo she'd been reduced to both. Scraping old refried beans out of jagged cans a couple of nights was enough to send her back to Mook's clan by the creek.

The rain picked up and her friends began to wake. They seemed confused at first, as if rain were a part of life wiped from their memory banks.

Mook walked out of his lean-to, his arms extended skyward.

"Thank you," he said to the clouds. "Thank you, Mother Nature. Bring it on."

Elda came out and began to twirl, raindrops plunking into the parched dirt under her bare feet.

They froze when two police officers stepped through the underbrush into their space. Mook's face washed with recognition and he relaxed.

"What's up?" he said. "What can I do for you, officers?"

"Sorry, Mook. You guys have to evacuate. This rain is supposed to come down hard, and you guys could get trapped down here if a flash flood comes through. You've got to move to one of the shelters."

"I'll just go to my mom's."

"That's okay. What about Elda?"

"Her too."

"Okay. The rest of your bunch can go to University Baptist. They're opening up their basement."

Lorelei slipped away as they were talking.

"Miss, Miss, come back here, please." One of the officers caught her up by her arm. She winced at his touch, her arm still sensitive. He let go. "Miss, I need to see some identification."

"I have a friend I can go stay with," she said. "But she lives over in Bouldin Creek. If I'm going to make it, I've got to go. Can I go?"

"Bouldin Creek's being evacuated too."

"Then I'd better hurry. She won't leave without me."

She could see him calculating her age. She also knew he had a job to do today, and running her through the system would take a long time. All she needed was a persuasive argument.

"I swear," she said. "She's like a sister to me. Family friend." Then for good measure she added, "She lets me stay with her all the time. I even know where her keys are."

"She's telling the truth," Mook said. "She can call her." He held up a trac phone.

Lorelei knew there were no minutes on that phone. Lots of kids had phones, but they never had minutes.

"What do you think?" the first officer asked.

The other uniform shrugged. "Long as she's nowhere around here."

Lorelei made a show of gathering her things.

"We'll be back to make sure you guys are out of here." They walked deeper into the wooded area of the park.

"Man, first they tell us we're a hazard with our campfire," Minion said. "Now they're telling us we're going to get washed away. What a bunch of crap."

Mook and Elda slung packs over their shoulders and headed out. They didn't bother to take their tarp or any of the chairs or water jugs.

"Hey, can we go with you?" Freestyle asked. There was a certain pleading tone to his voice that was embarrassing. The street was no place for crybabies.

"Look, dude. My old lady's been really sick. She can't have a bunch of assholes sitting around eating her food and blasting her television all day. You should go on to the shelter."

"Fuck that, man," Freestyle said.

Mook shrugged. He and Elda walked away.

Lorelei didn't bother to ask to go with them. She'd never been invited. She sat under her tarp, neatly packing her things. She didn't rush. She had nowhere to go.

Minion and Freestyle trudged off, heads down like two soggy soldiers. Minion's guitar was wrapped in two bright-green garbage bags. She didn't ask where they were going. She had a hunch they wouldn't go far, only to one of the round drug hole culverts where they smoked whatever they had managed to get their hands on that day. They might even try to walk to their drug dealer's, where they could hang out and use. She'd gone with them once and she had no desire to return.

Lorelei sat under her makeshift tarp wondering what she should do. Yesterday, when she stopped at a newspaper stand to check what day it was, a headline had screamed, "Gordon Expected to Slam Coastline." She'd tried to read the article through the scratched plastic door. A tropical storm had turned into a coast ripper hurricane. She figured this weather was leftovers.

Lorelei dreaded trudging up the hill to the drop-in. The storm began to pick up force and she quickly decided the drop-in was too far away. Her tarp sagged with water weight. She had to move. The only sturdy shelter she knew of nearby was a covered picnic area. She pulled the tarp over her head and took off that way.

Under the picnic shelter, dozens of others were crowded together atop scarred wooden tables. The downpour had arrived, pounding the metal roof of the shelter. It was impossible to hold a conversation. The sodden figures huddled like animals.

Perched on a table, Lorelei watched Shoal Creek. In only minutes, it had gone from a trickle to a full creek bed. Water pushed again the banks, then rushed their direction like tentacles reaching for prey.

Lorelei thought of Minion and Freestyle. They couldn't possibly be in the culvert.

The dry, hard-packed land refused to absorb the torrent thrust upon it. As Lorelei watched, deep pools formed in low-lying spots, then merged. Water rose in the swollen creek until there were no boundaries. Creek water rushed into the shelter and under picnic tables. Trash and debris swirled beneath them.

"Oh my God!" a girl said.

"Let's get out of here," someone on a far table shouted.

Lorelei watched a group wade toward the road, their packs on their heads like refugees. Lorelei held her position, watching to see how the others fared. It would take another couple of feet before the water reached the top of the table. She doubted it would rise that high.

The deluge reminded her of the story of the great flood and Noah's Ark. That flood had taken forty days and forty nights to cover the earth, but this storm had taken only forty minutes to invade everything.

Two girls stepped off of her table to make their getaway. The table lifted slightly under Lorelei. One girl fell and washed yards away where she caught hold of a Frisbee golf pole. She grappled with the mesh basket, trying to hook an arm through the chains. The current pinned her friend against a bricked barbecue grill. Neither girl could move. A boy waded into the brown, churning water to attempt a rescue. He fought to keep his footing. Lorelei didn't wait to see the outcome of his heroic efforts. She jumped from table to table until she was close as possible to the bank.

She stepped into the chilly current. The rain grew harder, pelting her face. Rising water moved like a predatory animal through the trees, but Lorelei could read the flow. She had kayaked enough at camp to recognize dangerous spots. She laboriously picked her way up the hillside toward the road.

By the time she reached the park's edge she was frantic. The violent sky puked its guts into her mouth and eyes. Several times, she clawed her way up an embankment only to slide down into the greasy mud at the bottom again. Finally, she stumbled up and onto the side of the road. She waved her arms against oncoming headlights. Cars rushed by, pounding sheets of water onto her.

"Stop!" she screamed. "Please, stop! Please, stop!"

Over and over, sheets of water pummeled her until she thought she would dissolve in her boots. She shivered. Her teeth snapped. Her weakness made her angry. Against her resolve she began to cry out.

"Stop! Please, stop!" She fell to her knees, exhausted.

Then, like a ship from outer space, bright lights cut through the rain and illuminated her. A van crawled to a stop along the road shoulder. A figure in a raincoat got out and came toward her.

"Can you walk?" the man yelled as he approached.

She grabbed his arm and tried to pull herself up, but her saturated pack was too heavy. He helped her to her feet and picked up her sleeping bag. She leaned against him. They made their way to the white panel van. He opened the sliding door. She crawled inside. There were no seats in the back, only neatly hung walls of tools.

Rain thrummed the shuddering van.

"Just sit on the floor."

She collapsed and water squished out of her onto the thick rubber mats. The man slung her pack beside her. He climbed in and slammed the door shut behind them.

"Shit, girl," he said. "What are you doing out in this storm?"

"I . . . because I . . ."

"Here." He handed her a small towel. "It looks dirty, but my wife just washed it."

Lorelei tried to wipe her face, but she was shaking too hard.

"Ccc . . . cold," she stammered.

"Oh, right." The man moved to the front of the van and turned the heater to full blast. He came back to her and said, "Can you move up to the front seat or do you want to stay here? It'll be warmer up front."

He helped her into the passenger seat. The warm air coming from the vents made pinpricks dance on her numb hands.

"You got somewhere you need to go?" he asked. "They're evacuating the city along the river. I'm on my way to get my wife and get out."

"Can you take me to Bouldin Creek?" Lorelei asked. It was the only thing that made sense to her.

"Sure thing. That's right on my way," the man said. "Let's just hope the bridges are still open."

Emily

EMILY'S MOBILE rang much too early. She didn't answer. None of her friends would call so early. Next she heard her text alert. Her e-mail chimed in another room. Somebody really wanted her attention.

On voicemail, a somber sounding man warned Emily that she lived in a flood-prone area. She was advised to evacuate. The evacuation wasn't mandatory, but Emily knew enough about Austin's flood history that she wasn't going to risk it.

She made tea and checked the weather outside her front door. It was windy and pouring so hard that she was instantly covered in a fine mist from the blow. The flood in her street was deep enough for a small boat to navigate. That got her attention.

Emily had to move fast to get out of the city in her tiny car. Outbound lanes would be open, but bridges going downtown were always closed during flood warnings. Every year some yahoo tried to cross a closed bridge and ended up with his car swept away, usually while he was still in it.

Emily called her parents. Her father answered on the first ring.
"Hey, sweetheart."
"I'm coming home. They're suggesting people evacuate the city."
"Well, come on then. Your mother's making chili."
Her mother came on. "Emily, you be careful in that little car."
"I will."

"And don't forget that rain slicker and those boots I got you."

"Oh, yeah. Those. Okay. I'm packing now. I'll see you in about an hour."

"Take some water and a few granola bars. You know, in case you get stranded or something."

"Should I take a jar to pee in too?"

"Well, Miss Smarty. That might not be a bad idea."

Emily grabbed the cat carrier out of the hall closet and set it by the back door. Skinny Cat wasn't on the front porch. He didn't come when she called. While she waited for him, Emily moved things to higher ground. Important papers and photo albums went in the top of a closet. She hoped her shelves were tall enough that her books wouldn't suffer.

She packed clothes, jewelry, laptop and camera equipment—anything looters would steal. In no time, Emily had a good-sized pile of duffle bags, backpacks and organic grocery bags filled with precious things.

She grabbed a flashlight and batteries. She stuffed a favorite pillow and a blanket into a garbage bag and threw it by the back door. Dressed in her raincoat and rubber boots, Emily tromped across the backyard to the MINI. It was only a short distance away, but it was hard to make out in the squall. Puddles were already six inches deep in places. Emily squeezed into her car, her slick coat squeaking against the seat. She backed up to the kitchen door where the awning covered the stoop to the cargo area of her car.

As she loaded the back of the MINI, she called and called for Skinny Cat. When the weather got rough he'd always come for an extended stay. Emily saw movement in the storm and waited for him to show. A phantom shape appeared at the edge of the road.

Emily watched a figure materialize, tall and lanky, in no hurry to get out of the drenching rain. As the person came closer she recognized the girl from the streets. How had she found her?

Tino had suspected somebody of making fires in Group's patio dish after he found six charred buttons. They had all figured it was Lorelei. And now it seemed she had followed Emily home at some point too.

The drenched figure walked with her head hung, braced against the downpour and wind. When the girl reached the back door, she stopped and stood in the rain.

"Lorelei?"

She turned her face up. She was pale, her lips waxy.

"What are you doing here?"

"All the shelters are full. I got nowhere else to go."

Water dripped from her nose and trembling chin.

"Well, don't just stand there. Come inside."

She left her wet things outside the door. Water dribbled off her onto the kitchen floor.

Her hair was plastered against her skull. Her skin was nearly colorless and the most prominent part of her was the swirl of inky tattoo that slashed the side of her face. She was otherworldly.

"I was just leaving," Emily said.

"I got no place else."

"Yeah, you said that. What about the shelter, the drop-in?"

"They're full."

"What about the churches downtown? They almost always open up for extreme weather like this."

Emily couldn't, absolutely wouldn't take this girl to her parents' house. But she couldn't leave her here, either. It might become a danger zone. She couldn't put her back out in the rain.

"What do you want me to do?" Emily asked her.

"I'm cold."

Emily's tea had gone forgotten in her haste. She stuck it in the microwave and thought about her options while she watched the mug on its slow rotation. The machine's merry ding was disconcerting. She handed Lorelei the mug.

The girl took an appreciative sip.

"Thank you."

"I have to leave. They're evacuating the areas around the river."

"I heard."

Her mother always hated it when Emily brought Skinny Cat with her. She was going to flip out when she saw this stray.

"Let's go," Emily said.

"What?"

"Get in the car. We're going to my parents' house."

"Can't I just stay here?"

"No. You can't. You can either come with me or you're on your own. I can't take you downtown. I'm sure all the neighborhood bridges are closed and probably the big ones are all outbound by now. We have to leave."

Emily grabbed two garbage bags from under the sink.

"Here, sit on this. This one's for your pack and stuff. They're too wet just to throw in."

Lorelei bagged her things and shoved them in among Emily's stuff. She spread the plastic bag on the passenger seat and climbed in. Emily took one last look around for Skinny Cat, but he was still at large.

"Good luck," she whispered. "To both of us."

David

AUSTIN CHANGED after Katrina laid waste to New Orleans. Like a lot of urban areas within driving distance, Austin got thousands of hurricane evacuees. When the clouds lifted over Louisiana, there was, as they say, no "there" there, so people stayed where they were. But low-income housing was scarce, and once FEMA terminated rental assistance, Austin's homeless population hit crisis proportions.

This time the bad weather was on the Texas coast and a new wave of weather refugees swept Austin mere hours ahead of Gordon. Motels filled, even the skanky low-priced ones. People without rooms were taken in by the city's emergency shelters in churches, rec centers and in various buildings and gyms on campus.

Gordon flushed street kids from the urban creeks and filled the Tumbleweed Center's facilities quickly. The drop-in and emergency housing were beyond capacity. The clinic stayed open for the night. David had kids doubled up in transitional housing. When there was no more room, David tried to send the needy to various churches, but he soon got texts that there was no room anywhere.

Food and blankets ran out, but nobody complained. Volunteers had showed up with supplies earlier, but not enough. Once the storm passed, the inventory of basic supplies would have to be replenished, which would be difficult.

The kids had been quick to stake out space in the drop-in. Sleeping bags were scattered where different groups clustered—the animal lovers in one area, the gay kids in another. The Emo kids gathered around the computers. David had heard that Goth was out and Emo was in, but he couldn't yet tell the nuances of their undead looks. Druggies huddled in a corner. The drop-in had a strict no-using policy, but half the kids came in already altered.

They were a unique bunch—lip rings, choppy hair, tats, gauges, dreadlocks, bleached cut-offs, Argyle socks, frayed coveralls, fedoras, plaid chucks, ripped skirts, ratty knitted hats and flannel shirts. Their lives hung from carabineers hooked through belt loops and packs. Most of the kids had acne. The boys had all manner of struggling facial hair. Some wore cheap aviator sunglasses that boasted dirty glamour, like young Hollywood gone to seed. They were a wet and smelly bunch, but they had style.

David picked his way across the sea of sleeping bags, stopping to talk, taking inventory, looking for some of the younger ones. A few kept up a persistent cough. David made note of infected piercings. One kid cupped his hand to his cheek, a sure sign of a toothache.

"Hey, Mr. D. Zup?"

"Looking good, Mr. D."

Freestyle was kicked back on the couch next to Minion. His eye seemed to have healed. He used a Sharpie to draw on his skateboard—skeletons and flames.

The last time David saw Minion he was busking on the front steps of University Baptist, strumming his guitar with his hat on the sidewalk. He'd propped up a cardboard sign that read *Need money for new strings*. David didn't usually give out cash, but he'd slipped him a five. He figured Mook and Elda had gone to Mook's mother's apartment. David looked around for Lorelei, the new addition to that tribe.

"Hey, how you guys doing?" he asked them.

Freestyle didn't answer.

Minion said, "Everything's cool."

"You seen Lorelei around?"

"Nah. We left her at the creek. She was going to some friend's house."

He doubted that.

Minion picked a few notes on his guitar. "Hey, man, thanks for the fiver. Got new strings. Listen." He launched into The Cure's *Boys Don't Cry*. The room grew quiet. David surveyed the kids while he played. People sang low. The drop-in's windows rattled and lights flickered. David had been through similar situations, and he figured that at some point the power would fail.

In the entryway, behind a baby gate, a scraggly yellow dog slept next to a matted collie-mix. The yellow dog raised his head and stared vacantly at the guitar player before lowering himself back down. David scratched each dog in turn, but they both seemed too exhausted to be appreciative.

The drop-in was one of the few shelters that welcomed pets. Homeless animals were usually well-socialized and sweet-natured. Some were family pets kids didn't want to leave behind to be abused. Others were strays taken in by empathetic hearts. Animal friends provide warmth, protection and unconditional love in a cruel and uncertain world. Why leave them out in the rain?

Travis scratched the dogs' ears again, then he went on outside to check on a faulty drainpipe by the door. The drop-in was at a high spot in the county, a whopping eight hundred feet above sea level, so the water flooding the entrance posed little danger. He'd meant to fix the broken downspout, but that project always got moved down his to-do list.

After a few tries, David jury-rigged the downspout to reroute the water away from the steps. He stood looking out at vacant, flooded streets. It was odd to see no traffic or pedestrians.

The city had gone more than half the year without a drop and now this deluge of destruction would be ruinous. Pease Park down on Shoal Creek would be a mud pit. Lots of the urban camping spots would be unusable. The drop-in would be swamped with increased demand for services for weeks.

The storm would shake up the kids' fragile social structure and make them scramble for resources. There would be fights over squatting rights, over blankets and clothes and food.

When it stopped raining and the water receded, Austin would have visible wounds—millions in real estate damages, business closings and infrastructure issues.

But the real tragedy in such violent weather was death.

It wouldn't be the students in their campus dorms or the business people who had fled to the suburbs who died. It wouldn't be the folks in Penbrooke, the fancy neighborhood uphill from Shoal Creek, or those in downtown apartments with sunset views who were swept away. It would be the homeless who vanished, washed out of their hovels and drainpipes and camps. Nobody would even notice when these people were gone.

Emily

SHE EASED the MINI onto the main road. Vehicles crawled along in the middle lanes. She avoided the outside lanes where solid streams rushed past them down toward the Colorado. Storm sewers bubbled with brown water and trash.

They passed Bouldin Creek Coffeehouse and Emily's favorite Mexican bakery. She saw a flash of hunger in Lorelei's eyes.

"Here, have an energy bar and a bottle of water," she said.

Emily struggled to find the correct gear to forge ahead against the water's force. Lorelei shivered and Emily turned on the heat. She cursed herself for not suggesting Lorelei change into dry clothing before they left.

The exit onto MoPac was clogged with traffic, but they inched forward until they made it on. Her tiny car weaved and wobbled against the maelstrom on the raised highway.

"How far is it?" Lorelei asked.

"On a good day I can get there in twenty minutes. Today, who knows?"

Traffic thinned as they moved away from downtown. The windshield fogged with moisture and body heat. Emily handed Lorelei an old shirt from the back.

"Can you wipe the condensation away?"

She leaned forward and erased the fog, but it formed again, mirroring her swipes. The rain came in waves, so hard it was possible to see past the headlamps. Between the fogged windows and the rain and the gale force winds, Emily's nerves were frayed. She decided to pull over on the shoulder and wait for a break in the storm.

"Pray somebody doesn't rear end us," she said as she set the hazard lights flashing.

Lorelei seemed unfazed. Emily was suddenly glad the girl was with her. She was calm and Emily realized that she'd probably seen a lot more difficult situations than this.

They sat in the quivering car, looking out at the taillights of vehicles creeping past. Even at slow speeds their rooster tails of water engulfed the MINI.

"This is some crazy storm," Lorelei said.

"I hope my cat's okay."

"He'll be fine. Cats are tough."

Water thrummed against the driver's side.

"Maybe I should call my mother," Emily said. "She's probably worried."

Lorelei pursed her lips and rolled her eyes slightly.

Emily's face burned. She realized that the tone of her voice had made her sound weak. Sure, Barbara would be worried, but Emily decided not to call.

Emily squeaked as she tried to shed the raincoat.

Lorelei gave her another strange look.

"A gift from my mother. Attractive, right?"

The girl grinned.

"Can you help me?"

Lorelei yanked on one sleeve until Emily could pull herself free.

"Thanks. It's like a freaking sauna in here," she said.

"Got any music?" Lorelei asked.

"How about some Stevie Ray?"

"Why does everybody in this whole town listen to that lame stuff?"

"Stevie Ray's a god."

"To you maybe. You got any Radiohead or Beck or Green Day?"

All musicians who provided anthems for displaced, disgruntled youth.

"Or Pink maybe?" she suggested.

"Sure. Pink's cool. I've got her on my iPod, but I only have a CD player in my car."

"Do you like I'm Not Dead? I like that song on it called *Dear Mr. President*. It's about homelessness and politics and stuff."

"How about something a little more relaxing, considering our situation? Maybe some Regina Spektor?"

"She's a little whiney, but okay."

"It's in the glove box."

Lorelei found the CD and pushed it into the player. A mellow voice warbled out, but it was hard to hear over the rain. Emily couldn't take both and was glad when Lorelei gave up and abandoned the music.

As if she were reading Emily's mind, Lorelei said, "I'm sorry I smell so bad."

Emily was unsure how to respond, so she said nothing.

"I know I stink."

"That's okay. I'm guessing you can't help it."

"I go to the drop-in and shower a couple of times a week, but this week I've only had a McBath."

"A what?"

"You know. At McDonald's."

Emily found that amusing, but she didn't dare laugh.

Looking back over her shoulder, Lorelei said, "You can pull out now. Don't be a wuss. Nobody's going to hit you."

"If they did, we'd be toast. All those massive SUVs would run right over my little car."

"Sometimes you've got to take chances. We can't sit here forever."

"This car's really old."

"Why don't you get a new one?"

"Because it runs fine. Besides, I don't have any money for a new one."

"Aren't your parents rich?"

"No. Why would you think that?"

Lorelei didn't answer. She was studying the traffic situation behind them.

"Go now," she said. "Nothing's coming."

With caution lights flashing, Emily eased back onto the highway. An hour later, they arrived at Gerald and Barbara's house.

"I thought you said your parents aren't rich."

How could she explain that her parents were not congenitally wealthy like the Texas oil families and the celebrities and dot-comers who lived in lavish Mediterranean homes on the limestone bluffs that ringed the lakes? That her father hadn't had a good job in nearly five years, and that she feared money problems would eventually destroy her parents' marriage?

"They're not rich. They're in debt."

"Then why do they live in such a big house and drive such nice cars?"

"That's what keeps them in debt. It's called 'living above your means.'"

Emily gripped the steering wheel and considered her childhood home. She knew it would be a relentless undercurrent of tension inside. Either Lorelei would diffuse the situation or make it unbearable.

"You don't want to go in," Lorelei surmised.

"Not really."

"Why not?"

"I suspect for many of the same reasons you don't want to go home. I don't get along with my parents that well. Not my mom anyway."

"So why come home?"

Emily chewed her lip and wondered why herself.

"It's not like that. I don't hate them. They're not bad people. They're just so . . . Republican."

Lorelei nodded understanding. "I hear you."

"It's better now that I'm an adult, but my mother still tries to tell me what I should do. How I should live."

"Bet it's not as bad as when you're a kid. Eat this. Eat that. Go to bed. Do your homework. Show some respect."

The girl had a point. "No. You're right," Emily said. "It's not like being a kid."

Emily could see Lorelei bracing for this new situation. The tattoo coiled up the side of her smooth cheek pulsed when she tightened her jaws.

"How long are we staying?" she asked.

"Until they say it's safe to go back downtown or until I can't stand it any longer. Whichever comes first."

The front door opened and Barbara appeared. She held her arms crossed in front of her and even through the rain Emily could see her expectant look. She should have called her.

"That your mom?"

"That's her."

"She's kind of intimidating."

"You got that right. Leave your stuff in the car. We can get it all later."

This seemed to make Lorelei uneasy.

"Your stuff's safe. Believe me. It's better this way."

"Okay."

"You ready?"

"I guess. This is going to be weird."

Emily put her hand on the door's handle and prepared for the deluge.

"You have no idea."

Barbara

SHE WAS surprised to see another person step from the passenger side of Emily's car. Her daughter was never a child to bring home unexpected guests. While other mothers in the neighborhood complained that their refrigerators were always raided by a swarm of kids, Barbara had been left wondering if Emily had any friends at all.

The girls ran through the rain, dodging washed out spots on the brick walk. They stepped into the entryway, water dripping down onto the terrazzo.

"Careful," Barbara warned. "These tiles get really slick when they're wet."

"Yes, ma'am," the girl said.

Emily shed her rain jacket and waited to be told what to do with it.

"Laundry room," Barbara said.

"Okay," Emily said.

"And why don't you give me your sweatshirt and I'll fling it in the dryer," Barbara said to her young visitor. "I have a cardigan you can put on."

"No thank you," Lorelei said.

"But you must be freezing."

"I'm fine."

There was something genuine about the girl's shabby appearance, as if the fade of her clothes was earned. No artfully ripped jeans or distressed designer T-shirts for this child. She held her head in such a way that Barbara couldn't see her face beneath her hood. The smell of the child hit her then and reality set in. Emily had brought home a street urchin.

"This is Lorelei," Emily said. "This is my mom. You can call her Barbara."

Gerald appeared from around the corner and gathered Emily in a bear hug.

"So good to see you. What an awful day, huh? Who is this?" Gerald said.

"This is Lorelei. This is my dad. You can call him Gerald."

"Nice to meet you," the girl said.

"We were just about to sit down to some chili. I'll set another place," Barbara said. "Gerald, why don't you and Lorelei go check the Weather Channel and I'll have things ready in ten minutes."

"Can I take your coat?" Gerald asked the girl.

"She's fine," Emily said.

"But she's all wet."

"Really. She's okay. Let it go."

Gerald seemed unsure. He was trying to be gracious, but this girl wasn't receptive.

From the kitchen, Barbara said, "Emily, could you please come and help me?"

"Sure, Mom." By Emily's tone, Barbara knew what was coming. When she rounded the corner by the wine rack, Emily was already on the defensive.

"So who is she?" Barbara whispered.

"Just a girl. I'm trying to be her friend."

"Why?"

"Because . . . I don't know. Lots of reasons. Because she needs a friend."

"Is she homeless?"

"What difference does it make?"

"It makes no difference at all. I was just asking."

"Uh-huh."

"She smells awful."

"I'm well aware of that. I drove all the way out here in the MINI with her."

"Would she be offended if we offered to let her take a bath? You have some old things upstairs she could wear while we wash her clothes."

"She doesn't like to accept help."

"Then why is she here?"

"Geez, Mom. Do you want us to leave?"

A crack of thunder rattled the house.

"No, of course not. Don't be accusatory. I'm just wondering how you . . . oh, never mind."

"She showed up at my house while I was packing to come here. I couldn't very well leave her standing there in the rain with nowhere to go. I mean, my God, they're evacuating the city."

Barbara peeked into the den. She could see Gerald's profile in his chair and the back of the girl's head.

"Why won't she take off that hood?"

"She has tattoos. They're off-putting to some people."

"Is she going to wear that hood up while we eat?"

"I don't know. Probably. Please, don't act like a dork."

Barbara bristled. "I most certainly will not 'act like a dork.'"

"Just don't give her the third degree."

"I think I should get a little credit here. You did spring this on me."

She could see Emily reconsidering her words.

"You're right," she said. "What do we need to do to get ready for dinner?"

Barbara decided if the child wouldn't change her wet clothing, then they would eat on the wooden chairs in the kitchen. No way was she ruining her dining room cushions.

When the table was set, Barbara said, "Let's eat. Lorelei, if you'd like to wash your hands before we start, our powder room is in the hall."

They sat at the table waiting for Lorelei. Ten minutes ticked by, their food growing cold.

"Do you think you should check on her?" Barbara asked Emily. "No."

They waited silently, hands in their laps. Finally, the bathroom door opened, and a few moments later, the girl reappeared. She had taken off her grungy sweatshirt and tried to brush her violently streaked brown hair back into a ponytail. Tacky plastic hair clasps gripped above her ears. Barbara wondered if she had used her brush and made a mental note to throw it away. The tattoos were strange and large, but Barbara had seen worse.

"I left my sweatshirt on the bathroom door. Would you mind if I borrowed that sweater?"

"No, of course not," Barbara said. She went to the closet and selected an older brown one that seemed more the girl's morose style. "Here. Feel free to keep it. I haven't worn it in years."

Emily glared at Barbara from her end of the table, but Barbara failed to see how the offer of a nice cardigan could be offensive.

"Thank you." The girl pulled the sweater on and buttoned it up. She unfolded her napkin onto her lap and waited. Barbara raised her spoon and began to eat and the others followed suit. But that was where Lorelei's manners ended. She must have been starving because she finished her first bowl of chili and asked for more before anybody else had eaten half of theirs.

"Thank you," she said when Barbara set another full bowl in front of her. "You're a totally awesome cook."

When they had all finished, Barbara said to Emily, "Why don't you and your father clean the dishes while Lorelei and I go make up the guest bed?"

Emily seemed nervous about leaving them alone, but Barbara was going to prove her daughter's bad assumptions wrong. In the upstairs linen closet, Barbara selected her oldest sheets and towels.

When Barbara began to make the guest bed, the girl stepped opposite of her. The rhythm of Lorelei's movements showed that she knew the routine.

Barbara smoothed the edges and laid towels at the foot of the bed.

"Thanks for your help," she said.

"I'm sorry to put you out."

"Honey, I'm the one who's sorry. If I had known you were coming I would have had things ready. Here are some towels. The guest bath is through that door. There should be plenty of soap and shampoo. There's a new toothbrush and some paste in the medicine cabinet. Oh, and here, I grabbed the hairbrush from downstairs. You're welcome to keep that and the toothbrush if you need them."

"Okay," she said meekly. "Thank you."

"Emily still has some clothes and pajamas here. I can leave them outside the door while you bathe."

The girl nodded, but didn't meet Barbara's eyes. Maybe Emily was right. Maybe she was stepping on the girl's pride.

As Barbara picked though the drawers in Emily's room, she heard the shower turn on. She selected a warm pair of pajama bottoms and a faded UT shirt that had actually been hers in college. Barbara also selected a faded cotton camisole with a shelf bra and a pair of underwear. These items she laid neatly folded on the floor outside the bathroom door.

When she came downstairs, Emily and her father were watching local storm coverage.

"Emily, why don't you ask your friend if she'd like to launder her clothes?"

"Okay. I bet she has a bunch of dirty stuff in that backpack in my car. And her sleeping bag looks like a rat's nest. Could we wash that too?"

"Of course, just make sure you use hot water."

Emily went up the stairs and knocked at the guest room door. There were muffled voices. She came back down with her arms full of clothes, her nose crinkled at the smell. She went into the laundry room connected to the garage by an access door. The garage door screeched up.

"How bad is the weather report?" Barbara asked Gerald.

"Bad. They say this may be a five-hundred-year-flood."

According to the animated weather girl, Austin was known as Flash Flood Alley, one of the most flood-prone areas in the nation.

"That bit of media attention is going to be bad for tourism, not to mention downtown development," Barbara said.

"Doubt it," he said. "You can't keep Austin down. This city will grow no matter what."

The garage door scraped back down and Emily banged into the laundry. Barbara fought the urge to ask if she needed help. The washing machine dial made its scratchy metal grind and then there was water running.

Gerald pushed up the volume on the television. News reports from the coast were better than expected. Offshore oil refineries that were slammed during previous hurricanes were spared this time. Residential damage was bad but not insurmountable. People were already trickling back to their homes and businesses. There were shots of residents taking plywood down and stripping the giant X marks of tape from windows.

"It seems Gordon decided to hold most of its water until South Central Texas and then unload on us," Gerald said.

"We always get that. We needed rain, but this is ridiculous."

Emily plopped on the sofa next to her mother.

"She's asleep," Emily said, looking back up the stairs as if to make sure of this.

"I don't like the tattoos," Barbara said.

"I know. It takes some getting used to."

"It's sick. Nobody should have their face tattooed."

"Maybe the tattoos were to make her look tough, less approachable, if you know what I mean."

"Nobody is ever going to hire her with a face like that. She's going to have to get those removed before she'll get anywhere in life."

Barbara recognized the defiant flash in her daughter's eyes and braced for impact.

"So," Emily snapped, "let me get this straight. It's fine for you and your friends to get Botox injections and facelifts and have eyebrows and lips permanently tattooed on. It's okay to get the fat sucked out of your hips and injected into your cheeks and have your eyelids sliced off and bags of silicon stuffed under your chest muscles, but a pretty design on somebody's face makes them a horrible person?"

"Tattoos aren't pretty. They're a distasteful sign of lower class."

"Other cultures find them beautiful."

"But honey, this isn't other cultures."

"She's right, you know," Gerald said. "It's not just bikers and criminals and military anymore. Lots of people get them now."

"I can't believe you're taking Emily's side. Thank you very much, Gerald. How about I just run right out and get one? How'd you like it if I had a big old dragon tattooed up my arm?"

"I don't know, hon. Seems kind of kinky to me."

Emily laughed.

"Very funny," Barbara said.

"You don't have any tattoos, do you?" he asked Emily.

"No."

"Okay," he said.

"But I was thinking about getting one. A great big bird on my lower back."

"What the kids call a *tramp stamp*?" Gerald laughed and turned back to the weather.

"Gerald, this isn't funny. Do you want your beautiful daughter to have a tramp stamp?"

"Leave me out of this."

"Would you think of me any differently if I had artwork on my back?" Emily asked.

"I don't know," Barbara said, but her thoughts were more truthful. She knew that she wouldn't be as eager to claim Emily if she marked herself that way. Piercings could close; crazy-colored hair grew out. But tattoos were a commitment.

Still, she dared not protest too much.

Emily

THE WHINE of the treadmill carried up the stairs and through Emily's old bedroom door. Her mother's steps a soft punctuating rhythm, Emily listened as her mother ran and ran and ran.

"That woman needs a bike," Emily said out loud to the room.

Emily switched on the tiny television on the bureau. She twisted her hair up. The polished local newscaster said Austin was in shambles and Emily stopped, toothbrush in mouth, to watch brown churning ribbons of water pushed high against the banks of an unidentified river. A house was wedged under a bridge. Parking lots were lakes of mud. People cried. A man waded into a flooded area to rescue a dog on a floating pile of wreckage.

Downstairs, her father was watching the same thing on the plasma while he flipped pancakes. He had bacon and eggs already arranged on a platter and orange juice on the table.

"Smells good, I'm so hungry," she said, filching a piece of bacon. She wandered over to the coffeepot.

"Emily," Dad said. "I want to talk to you about something."

"Sure, Dad. What's up?"

"Not now. I thought maybe we could go to lunch. You know, just you and me."

Emily's phone beeped. It was a text from Travis.

Need photographer 4 BHN flood story. Interested? Will pay.

"Hold that thought, Dad."

She texted back.

Yes. In burbs. When? Where?

Another beep.

ASAP. Come to the office w camera.

K. Meet you at noon?

Beep.

K.

Emily went to the laundry room to fold the rest of Lorelei's clothes. The sleeping bag came out clean with the scent of fresh linen fabric softener that was the smell of Emily's childhood. She stuck her head into the garage where her mother was pounding out three miles on her gerbil wheel.

"Morning," Emily said.

"Tell your father not to eat eggs," Barbara said as she huffed along. "His cholesterol is sky high."

"Okay. I will." She hesitated. "I need to ask a favor."

"Ask away."

"Can I borrow your SUV?"

"Why?"

"I need to go downtown."

"Why? It looks like a war zone. You probably shouldn't go home for a couple of days."

"It's a job."

She paused the treadmill.

"Okay. I'm all ears."

"So, I know this reporter, and he works for *Be Here Now,* and he asked me to shoot a story he's working on."

"Which reporter?"

"Travis Roberts."

"Ugh. He's an asshole."

"No he's not. Anyway, I have to go right now."

"Do they pay?"

"Yes. So, can I borrow your vehicle?"

"For how long?"

"I don't know. A day or two."

"And I'd have to drive the MINI?"

"I guess. Unless you could get Gerald to drive it. The tires are kind of bald."

Her mother considered this, then said, "There's a press pass in the glove compartment. Hang it on the rearview and you can park anywhere."

"Thank you. I really appreciate this."

"Wait. There's a condition."

There was always a condition with Barbara.

"You have to take that girl with you. No leaving her here."

"I wasn't going to leave her."

"So what are you going to do with her? You just going to let her out downtown and say 'see ya later, have a nice life?'"

Emily hadn't thought that far ahead.

Barbara moved to the heavy bag. Before she landed her first punch she said, "She's not all together, all together, if you catch my drift."

"I know she's damaged."

"And there's another condition."

"What?"

"You can't let her live with you. I mean, what do you know about this girl? If you let her live with you she's going to need her drugs one day and just take your purse or your television or something."

"I'm not going to let her live with me."

"Promise me."

"Okay. I promise."

An hour later Emily and Lorelei were in Barbara's Acadia on their way downtown. Like the majority of cars in Austin, her mother's vehicle was bright white. There was no telling what color it would be after today.

"You don't look like you come from a place like this," Lorelei said as she watched the commercial signage whip by.

"Everybody's got to be from somewhere. Where are you from?"

She didn't answer, so Emily just left that line of thought open. "You're right. My parents belonged to the country club, but I never liked the plaid polo crowd."

"Yeah. I knew some of those kids."

"How about alternative rockers? The ones around here are pretty sad," Emily said, trying to connect. "Posers." She'd hung around with a few of those types in high school, but most of them never got past the first few riffs of *Smells Like Teen Spirit* on their thousand-dollar Fender birthday presents.

Lorelei stared out the window and chewed a fingernail.

After a few minutes of lull, Emily said, "So, I got a photography job today for a newspaper. You ever read *Be Here Now*?"

"Sure. You can get it all over the place for free."

"Do you read the column by Travis Roberts?"

"Yeah. I read the whole paper. That guy, he's pretty smart."

"Yeah. He is smart. That's what I like about him."

A pause.

"Do you *like* like him?"

"I don't know. Maybe."

"Does he like you back?"

Emily shrugged. "I don't know. I'm betting he'll come around."

"You have a lot of boyfriends?"

"I wouldn't say that. I date a lot."

"So you have sex a lot."

"Well." Why did this embarrass her? "Well, I guess that's true."

"God, don't wig out. I've had sex."

"Really."

"Everybody my age has had sex. Especially gutter punks."

"Why?"

"That's just how things roll. I used to do it with a guy who was like, thirty or thirty-five."

"That's gross."

"Why? Because you think I'm jailbait?"

"There's no way you're eighteen."

"Maybe I am, maybe not."

She jiggled her foot. She seemed eager to get back into town. Maybe she had taken something that had her jacked up. If she'd smoked crack in her parents' bathroom, Emily would never hear the end of it.

The southern part of town was a mess. Stalled cars were abandoned in giant pools of water right in the road. Gutters were clogged with fast-food cups and plastic toys. One intake drain was clogged with a Virgin Mary and a tiny donkey cart filled with flowers, popular Austin lawn ornaments.

Every so often, Lorelei would whisper, "Wow. Look at that."

The SUV plowed through standing pools and rubble, water raking the undercarriage, monster sprays of water pluming from both sides. There was no way the MINI would have made it.

As the road gradually descended toward the river, the drama increased. Downtown damage would be worse around the creeks and the low-lying parks. There would be nowhere for the homeless to camp and all the shelters would be filled. Emily knew when she promised her mother that Lorelei wouldn't stay that it was probably a lie.

Still, her mother's warnings rang in Emily's head. It was true. Lorelei could take advantage of her, but if Emily wanted to gain her trust she would have to trust first. But even with this thought, when they pulled up outside of her house, Emily chose to leave her important things in the vehicle. No need to unpack just yet.

The yard was a pit. The front porch stained clay-red. All around her house was a ring of sienna about a foot high. The first few steps leading to the back door were slimed.

"Just grab what you need and leave the rest here. I'll be back later."

Lorelei had only two things, and she took them both. She slipped her boots off when she reached the top step and left them outside.

"I have some house shoes you can wear. You can sleep on the futon in the spare room." Emily pointed down the short hall. "Just throw your stuff in there."

She went to the spare room. Water came on in the bathroom.

Emily tried the television. It was dead. When Lorelei came back, Emily said, "Sorry to tell you this, but there's no TV. I don't have a house phone and I'm taking my computer with me, so you don't have much to entertain you here."

Lorelei looked at Emily's bookshelf. "Are you kidding? You have all these books."

"Knock yourself out."

"Sweet," she said absentmindedly, already absorbed in the titles on the spines. Emily suddenly realized that Lorelei always lived without phones and televisions and computers. A book was most likely the height of entertainment to her.

"There's not much food. I'll bring a pizza when I come back, but I have no idea when that will be. You can eat anything you can find."

"Whatever. I'm not hungry."

Back in her mother's vehicle, Emily slowly picked her way downtown toward her meeting with Travis. He was a mystery. He seemed indifferent to her charms, but she was determined she'd get his attention.

She cut through her neighborhood over to the Congress Street Bridge, a strong high structure that was a main artery into the city. If any of the bridges into downtown were open, this would be the one.

As she drove it occurred to her that there was beer in the fridge and a cheap bottle of wine already open on the counter. If Lorelei took a mind to get drunk there was plenty of alcohol around. She could have a cell phone tucked away somewhere. What if she called some of her friends and invited them over to the house? Maybe her mother was right. What did Emily really know about this girl? And why did she feel compelled to help her?

Maybe she did have a crummy people filter. This could really come back to bite her in the ass.

Travis

HIS ASSIGNMENT had gone from the dry subject of drought to the juicy job of writing about the aftermath of a major flood.

The last great flood ripped through Austin back in 1981. That event took Shoal Creek from ninety gallons of water per minute to six million. Just like then, thunderstorms had ringed Austin for miles, and the city had gotten ten inches of rain in four hours. Dark purple clouds spun out tornadoes that eviscerated the area. The capital city was a raw sore waiting to be examined.

Like rescue workers and the military, reporters and photographers ran toward events and places everybody else tried to escape—fires, war zones, natural disasters.

If it bleeds it leads. Loss of life is always first on the agenda, followed by the number of people forced to flee. Next is the dollar amount of property damage.

Travis needed a photographer, but their chief photojournalist was trapped outside of the city with his family in a flooded house. The other *BHN* photographer was in the hospital delivering her first child. None of the stringers were answering calls.

"Bob," Travis said as he flung himself into the editor's office chair, "I'm getting nowhere with photographers. I got my own stringer. Mind if I bring her on board?"

"Just get me a cover shot."

"Will do."

"Do whatever you have to do. Deadline is three on Tuesday."

He'd just finished packing his reporter paraphernalia when in walked Emily. She said she had wheels for the situation, so Travis had agreed to let her drive.

She stopped at the front desk and talked to Lily, who looked back at Travis, a little frown on her face that made him smile. She pointed Emily toward his desk.

"Hey," she said. "I'm ready. Let's do this thing."

"Did you just drink a triple espresso or are you an adrenaline junky?" he asked.

"Both," she said.

He followed her outside to an enormous SUV.

"Whose wheels?" he asked as they got in.

"My mom's."

"The dashboard looks like the cockpit of a 787."

"I know, right?"

A press pass dangled from the rearview.

"Where'd you get credentials?"

"Those are my mom's too."

"She a reporter?"

"Public relations."

Travis wondered where the woman had snagged a precious press pass, but there was no reason to bring this up to Emily.

"So? Where to?" she asked

All business. He liked this side of her.

"Drive down to the waterways. Pease Park first. You know, down by Shoal Creek."

"Where we went that first day?"

"Exactly."

"Bet it's all underwater."

"Guess we'll find out. Things will probably go by fast, so if you don't mind, I'm going to talk into my recorder while you drive."

"Fine by me."

Travis grabbed a digital recorder from his pack. Within a mile, he had clicked it on.

"Too much water," he said. "In all the wrong places."

Emily

BARBARA'S SUV plowed through deep pools awash with debris that would have thwarted a lesser vehicle. At the top of a rise, Emily abruptly halted. The slope was steep and the road below ended in dirty coffee-colored river roiling with plastic bottles, clothing, lawn furniture and general yuck.

"Whoa," she said.

"Can you make it?" Travis asked.

Emily swallowed hard and gripped the steering wheel when she realized where he meant.

Stranded at the bottom of the hill, two guys and a girl huddled on the roof of a car. Water spiraled above the tires.

She checked to make sure the all-wheel drive was engaged and then slowly plowed on.

"Where's your camera?" Travis asked.

"In the back, in my bag."

He took it out and began shooting the marooned storm victims as they approached. Something about his actions seemed callous, but Emily shook it off. There was no reason he couldn't get his story at the same time they helped the kids.

The SUV shuttered in the current. She fought to keep a straight path.

"Shit," Emily said. "Shit. Shit. Shit."

"You're doing fine. Just keep moving."

She maneuvered up next to the car. Water was forced into the wedge between the two vehicles and rushed over the hood of the stranded car.

"Back up. This won't work," Travis said.

"If I get parallel can they climb in the back window? If we open the door water will come in."

"I think that'll work," Travis said.

Emily repositioned the SUV. When they were in a solid spot, Travis thrust the camera at Emily.

"Take pictures."

"Now?"

"That's your job. Do it."

He crawled behind the driver's seat and let the back window down on the side near the car. Suddenly, the SUV lurched with the full of force of the water against its side.

"Come on!" he yelled. "You have to crawl through! I'll help you."

Cold and in shock, the three marooned kids moved like arthritic old people. The boys held on to the shaking girl as she straddled the distance between the car's roof and the SUV's back window. Travis grabbed her, and she fell inside on top of him.

"Get in the back," he said.

She moved back to the third row of seats. Travis turned to the window in time to see the first boy's grip fail on the window's lip. He had jumped and missed. Travis grabbed his forearms, but the crush of water pushed the boy under the vehicles.

"Pull him up for God's sake, Travis!" Emily cried. She had been getting a few shots, but she flung the camera up on the dash, reached out the driver's window, grabbed a handful of pants and yanked as hard as she could. That raised the boy out of the swirling suck enough that he could wedge his feet against the outside mirror. Travis let go and Emily pulled the boy inside. Water rushed in with him and filled the floorboards.

They sat panting, dripping water.

"My mother . . . my mother's . . . going to kill me," Emily said, looking at the sludge and water everywhere.

"Just tell her you're a hero," Travis said. He turned back to the last boy on the car's roof. "Come slowly. Put your hand on the roof, then your foot on the window ledge," he yelled. "Don't dive."

The last boy was tall and lanky, and he made it inside with little effort. They had a hard time moving around so that the three kids were in the back and Travis was back up front with Emily.

"Are you guys okay?" Travis asked when they had finally settled.

"Thank you so much," one boy said. "We've been sitting there for like, a day or something."

"Surely not that long," Travis said.

"No, really man. First we were down there where those picnic tables are, and then we, like, waited for the water to go down and we came up here, and then, like, this big whoosh of water came through again and we were lucky to get on that car. They stopped traffic on this road yesterday. There's been nobody down here."

"Anybody need a drink?" Emily handed them a bottle from her mother's stash in the console.

"Yes, oh thank you," the girl said, coming from the back seat to grab the bottle. She drank and then passed it to one of the boys.

"I'm Emily. This is Travis."

"I'm Star. That's Monkey and Skittles."

One boy finished the water and handed the empty bottle back to Emily.

"So where do you guys need to go?" Travis asked.

None of them seemed to have a plan of action. They looked at each other for a good proposal. Finally, Monkey said, "I guess the drop-in."

"Okay." Emily put the Acadia in reverse and pushed back against the current until she could turn around and be somewhat confident that the brown creepy water didn't mask a ditch.

They held a collective breath as Emily maneuvered up out of the chewed up creek corridor. She thought of the crazy people with four-wheel drives who think they're invincible. Those were the people rescue workers would find dead in their vehicles.

In only a few minutes they reached Guadalupe, but by then the rain had returned with conviction. They sat on the street, nobody wanting to brave the downpour. It occurred to Emily that she could park wherever she wanted with the press pass.

She pulled onto the sidewalk and crept along the wall of the plaza outside of the drop-in.

"Think I'll get a ticket?" Emily said.

"In this rain? I doubt it," Travis said.

When they stopped, he said, "Come on, I'll help you guys get inside." The kids ran for the entrance. Travis grabbed the camera bag and gave Emily a wink.

"Jackpot," he said.

She had no choice but to follow. They sprinted down a few concrete steps to a door. Inside, she was surprised by a couple of scraggly dogs in a playpen. Off the entryway a main room opened up, and as she stepped farther inside the body odor hit. Every inch of floor and every piece of furniture was taken. All eyes turned to the new refugees.

Star, Monkey and Skittles vanished into the room.

Travis tried to hand the camera to Emily. "Here."

"No," she said, and pushed it away.

"Do it," he hissed. "I'll do the talking. You get the shots."

A man came toward them. He had the beginnings of a beard and his brown hair curled down inside the collar of his biker jacket. He extended a hand to Travis.

"Hey, man. What's up?" he said.

"Hey David. This is Emily."

"Hello," she said and shook his hand.

"David's the director here," Travis said.

"Thank you for rescuing the kids. They told me what you guys did. I'm grateful for your help," he said.

"Absolutely," Travis said. "No problem."

"I'd offer you a cup of coffee, but we're fresh out."

Somehow, Emily didn't believe that. She suddenly sensed tension between the two.

"So, if there isn't anything else I can do for you," David said.

"Can I talk to a few of the kids? Find out about their experiences with the weather?"

"Not now. They're pretty shaken."

"Come on, man. Just a quick interview. I'm on deadline," Travis said.

Emily doubted that too.

"Maybe you can come back tomorrow when we've got things sorted out. Right now, we just have to get everybody fed. You understand, right?"

"Sure. I understand, man. I'll come back later."

"Nice to meet you," David said.

"Yes. Nice to meet you." That's when Emily heard a shout and turned to see Travis snapping pictures of the room.

"Hey! I asked you nicely," David said. He stepped between Travis and the room, blocking further attempts at photos.

"Yeah, you tell him, Mr. D.," a kid shouted.

Travis put up his hands and backed away.

"I changed my mind. Don't come back tomorrow," David said. "Stay away from my kids."

"All right," Travis said. "All right, man. I'm just trying to do my job."

David gave Emily a look that implied she was guilty by association. She opened her mouth to protest, but there was nothing to say in her defense. She had known Travis's intentions.

Outside, the rain had eased. The interior of the SUV grew clammy with their damp body heat. Their breath clung to the windows.

"Well, that went well," she quipped.

"Don't worry about David," Travis said, undaunted. "He's overly protective of his kids. I can find us plenty of places to shoot storm damage. Hopefully, we'll scare up some other people to interview."

Emily had intended to tell him about Lorelei, but the day had clicked by so rapidly that she hadn't had a chance. Now she knew it was good he didn't know. She couldn't allow Travis to descend on Lorelei like he had those kids. She had to protect her a while longer.

Lorelei

A LAYER of mud covered the concrete porch to Emily's house. Her welcome mat would never recover, but the flowerpots could be saved. Lorelei found a rotted garden hose coiled in the mud beside the house and a ratty scrub brush in the mildewed shower.

She threw out the welcome mat. With clothing detergent and elbow grease, she scoured the concrete. She cleaned all the pots and the two tiny steps, and by midday, the porch looked presentable again.

She never stopped for lunch. Lorelei cleaned the entire house from the kitchen floor to the bathroom shower.

While she cleaned, Lorelei opened the occasional drawer without finding anything the least bit racy or verboten. No giant dildos or bongs hidden in a corner. Emily had beer and wine and a couple of ashtrays, but it didn't look as if she smoked. In the back of a drawer Lorelei found rolling papers, but no weed.

There were a few family photos scattered around, one of Emily's parents and another of a really old couple Lorelei took to be grandparents. There was even a snapshot of a thin cat stuck to the mirror in her bedroom, but there was nothing to indicate she had a boyfriend. No clunky man shoes under the bed. No oversized sweatshirts. The bathroom was a wreck, but there were no telltale bits of man hair stuck to the sink. Emily seemed to be a loner. That was good for Lorelei.

It was after five and dark was closing in when the big white
SUV pulled around behind the house. Lorelei almost laughed when
she saw the shape it was in. Mud stuck like thick chocolate to the
undercarriage and splashed in wide swaths down the sides. The
windshield was opaque except for the arching paths of the wipers,
and even that space was streaked with muck.

Emily took a few minutes to get out and cautiously pick her way
through the bog of a yard. She toted the camera bag and balanced a
giant pizza box. Lorelei relieved her of the pizza at the door.

"Thanks," Emily said as she pushed past. "I'm exhausted."

Emily kicked off shoes and stripped off dirty clothes, shedding
them into a pile by the back door.

"Oh my God, I'm so tired I could pass out," she said. "I really
need to take a shower. I'll be out in a few minutes. Help yourself to
the pizza. Don't wait on me."

Lorelei heard the shower turn on. She found plates, forks and
paper napkins. In the refrigerator she found a couple of cold Cokes
and a shaker of Parmesan, and in a cabinet, some hot pepper flakes.

A few minutes later, Emily emerged, a towel wrapped around
her head. She wore a thin white nightshirt, her breasts moving
freely underneath. She rubbed the towel against her hair, and thong
underwear peeked from beneath the shirt. Lorelei didn't see any
tattoos or piercings.

"Lorelei," she said. "I can't believe you cleaned my house."

"I was bored."

"Really? Thank you, but you didn't have to."

"It needed it."

She grinned. "Yeah, the bathroom was nasty."

"I've seen worse."

"Guess you think I'm a total slob. Hey, want to see my shots?"

While her images loaded into the computer, Emily shoved pizza
into her mouth. "Wow. I took five hundred," she said around a wad
of dough. Her eyes scanned the laptop. "Look," she said, and slid
the monitor around. "This was freaky. That's somebody's shirt." A
man's white dress shirt was twisted around a pile of driftwood, but
it looked like somebody was still inside.

"That *is* weird."

Emily hit *slideshow* and suddenly the story unfolded. Shot after
shot of a contorted world.

"Wow. You're wicked good."

"Thanks."

"You see people. You really see them."

"I can't wait to show these to Travis. Help me pick a couple dozen good ones."

An hour later, thirty possibilities were e-mailed to Travis at the paper. When she hit the send button, Emily took a deep cleansing breath and let it out slowly.

"All right then," she said.

She took the flashcard out of the reader and inserted it back into her camera. She picked up the Canon and pointed it at Lorelei, but the girl put her hand up to block the shot.

"Come on. Why don't you want to have your photo taken? You're such an interesting person." She adjusted the lens and a red light winked at Lorelei.

"I have my reasons."

"But what if I never showed anybody. What if I just took them for me? For us to see."

"People always want to take pictures of the homeless. It's exploitive."

Emily lowered the camera. "I'd never exploit you. I want these for art's sake. Look, it's true that Travis wants to write about the homeless and I'm working for him, but I'd never show them to him or anybody else. I spent all day with him, and I never mentioned you."

"Really?"

"Look, we can even erase any shots you don't like right after I take them. Don't you at least want to see what you look like?"

"You'll erase them if I say so?"

"Yes."

"Promise."

"I promise."

She hesitated, considering.

"Well, I guess it would be okay."

Emily slowly raised her camera. "Look out the window."

Lorelei turned her cheek to the camera. Emily clicked and the camera whirred. Emily considered the camera's tiny screen and said, "Check this out. You look awesome."

Lorelei studied her image, then she handed the camera back. She unzipped her sweatshirt, and underneath she wore a stained sleeveless tee. Emily now had a chance to study the girl's arm tattoos up close. She had railroad tracks, an owl, tribal armbands, a silly little dog.

"So you'd never show these to anybody?" Lorelei asked.

"Never."

Emily raised her camera again. "Just relax. Be yourself."

Lorelei leaned her shoulders against the kitchen's stucco wall. She raised her shirt to reveal a tiny yin and yang peeking from her jeans. Emily turned her camera vertically and adjusted a setting.

"Let's try you in black-and-white."

Lorelei let her unruly hair fall forward. "Okay" she said. "Take it."

The camera whirred again and Emily checked the LED.

"Wow. Black-and-white really makes your tats pop. Look."

"That's cool."

"Okay, ready?" Emily said.

She snapped off a couple more and Lorelei stared into the lens, her pupils wide and empty.

Emily lowered her camera to consider a different angle.

"You're so skinny, I can see your ribs."

She reached up to move a stray piece of hair when Lorelei stepped forward and kissed her. The kiss was firm but gentle, and long enough to raise her heart rate. The girl didn't back away, but ran her hands up and down Emily's arms.

"Lorelei," Emily said, their breath mingling. "I think you have the wrong idea."

"Isn't this what you want?"

"No. I just want to take your picture."

"There's usually a price."

"For what?"

"If somebody helps you."

"I told you before. You don't owe me anything."

"I like you. It would be okay."

Finally, it was Emily who stepped back. "Look, I'm not a lesbian and I'm certainly not into kids, so no offense, but I prefer dudes my own age."

"I've had sex with lots of people. I want to."

"Sorry. I don't do girls."

"So . . . pictures are really all you want?"

"Look. Let's forget about the photos for now. I'm going to make some tea. Why don't you tell me why you got those tattoos?" Emily busied herself with the teapot. Lorelei, amused, could tell she had rattled her.

Lorelei stood against the wall, rolling her shoulders from side to side in a sexy way, twirling her hair. It was a while before she answered. How much should she tell her? How much could she reveal and still be safe?

"People take your stuff," she said. "Things get lost. But you can never lose your body art. Nobody can take it away from you."

"That makes sense."

"They help me remember. See, I'm a storyboard, like a comic book, like *The Illustrated Man*. You ever read that? It's about this dude covered in tattoos, and his tats move and each one tells a different story. That's sort of how I feel. Every one of these is something about me."

"Like what?"

"Okay, like this owl." She turned her right arm toward Emily. "That's my name from a camp I went to once. I was 'Whispering Owl Running.'"

The bird was a stark geometric graphic in black with dark-red details. It was upright with its wings open to each side in a perfectly balanced design. Fat tail feathers anchored the bottom. Large eyes studied you.

"I like it. Really unusual. I recognize that style. Isn't it Indian?"

"Haida. His tribe is from Canada. He was sort of my boyfriend, for a while. Then he took off."

"What's that one?"

"My little dog."

"Cute."

"Yeah. He's cool. I swear sometimes he'll move around on my skin and make me think about home. I know it sounds crazy, but I can feel them sometimes. Like they're trying to tell me something."

"What's that?" Emily asked, pointing to a skinny one that ran down her left forearm.

"Railroad tracks."

"You hopped trains?"

"I've done it. The tracks mean I'm a traveler. All travelers get one."

It had started at the community house in Oregon, a foreboding old structure outside of Portland where she had met up with friends. There were living spaces on the first floor and men and women's floors above. It had been fun at first. She was from a big family and had grown up in a house filled with loud older brothers eating everything and being gross.

But after a week, the kids she knew from camp had developed a darker side. Lorelei watched in fascination and horror as drugs and alcohol morphed them. Some grew twitchy, while others became morose. Some were energetic, while others slept all day. There was dejection and anger, punctuated by runs of happiness and friendship.

On one nice mellow night, they were all sitting around the big den downstairs. Somebody had scored some wood and the fireplace was roaring. Girls were braiding each other's hair. A blunt was being passed around. A guy said, "Who wants a tat?" His own body was littered with ink. A couple of kids raised their hands.

The guy sterilized a sewing needle and metal soda cap with a lighter. Somebody produced a bottle of India ink. He wrapped the needle in dental floss and bunched it to the end to hold the black dye.

Under her right eye he had scraped her first stick and poke, ten connected lines that formed an open star. Four others got the same design that night.

She hadn't known it at the time, but once your face was tattooed, nothing held you back from decorating the rest of your body. Later, Lorelei had let the guy scrape an armband into her, but she immediately regretted the poor design.

That was when her Haida wolf boy showed up and fixed everything. A tribal artist, he was traveling down from his native land, exploring the world. He had amazing animals inked on his arms and chest, each one significant to his people.

When he saw Lorelei's botched arm art, he asked if he could make it right. With his face bent to fixing her arm, she had fallen in love with his raven hair and his smooth brown skin—like the wolf boy's in her favorite novel. Later, as her arm tingled as if from sunburn, she gave herself to him. She had been with boys at home, but it had never been good. The first time she truly made love was on a dirty bed in a community house with the boy of her dreams.

His name was Joe, and he didn't like living at the house, so she had followed him into the realm of giant trees cloaked in green velvet moss. They lived on the berries and mushrooms from the Columbia River Gorge outside of Mount Hood. They zipped their sleeping bags together and were so warm they paid no attention to the cold that enveloped their dank Oregon woodland. It was here, one starry night, that he broke her heart.

"You need to go home," he'd whispered to her. "You're too young for this life. It's dangerous. Go home while your parents will still take you back. Finish school."

The next morning, she awoke to find her wolf boy gone.

"He gave me my owl. It's my favorite."

"Did your Haida artist do your phoenix too?" Emily asked.

Lorelei touched her baby smooth cheek. Like switching off a light, her mood shifted dark.

"This tat. The guy that did it. He's looking for me."

"Really?"

"I thought he was cool at first. I thought he loved me. But we were drinking one night and had a fight, and the next thing I know I wake up with an outline of this bird on my face. He said I begged him to do it, but he's a liar."

"Oh, man."

"I tried to run away, but you know, Phoenix isn't that big of a city. He found me."

"He gave you a phoenix because you were in Phoenix?"

"Yeah, something like that. Anyway, I ended up living with him for a year. So see, that's why you can't take my picture. He might see it. He'd come looking for me. That's why you can't ever let anybody see those photographs."

"I promise. But he's in Arizona. That's a long way away from Austin."

"Not far enough."

"Why didn't you go to the cops if you were afraid of him?"

She twisted her lips in a way that said Emily was naive.

"Because cops send runaways home. Duh."

"You can't go home?"

She rubbed her face roughly with both her hands and gave a weary sigh. "No. I can't. I can never, ever go back."

"Why?"

The past clouded her eyes. "You know that camp that I told you about?"

"Uh-huh."

Emily waited.

Finally, the girl said, "That's where they send kids that are problems."

Lorelei watched Emily's eyes for a reaction.

"You know," she continued. "Kids who do things they aren't supposed to do."

"Like what?"

Lorelei's bottom lip quivered. "Stuff."

"Drugs?"

She nodded. "Some kids."

"Sex?"

"It doesn't matter why. Look, I'm sorry I even brought it up. Everybody's got something wrong with them. My parents just don't like me is all."

"Oh, Lorelei, what would make you say that?"

"Trust me. You know when your parents wish you'd just disappear."

David

EVERY DAY had been turmoil since the flood. His staff was stressed to the point that David was concerned for their health. He'd tried to send a couple of people home, but they refused.

The Red Cross arrived once a day to distribute water bottles and blankets, but there was a paucity of food. David was on his way to a city council meeting to request emergency funding for staples, but a young woman in crisis waylaid him in the hall.

The girl's hands trembled and she nearly dropped her trac phone.

"Mom, Mom, can you hear me? Mom? MOM?"

Tears rimmed her eyes.

"You probably just ran out of minutes," David said. "I bet she didn't hang up on you."

The girl checked the tiny screen and caught her breath when she saw he was right. She seemed relieved, but then her voice began to hick with emotion.

"I want to go home. I want to go home and . . . I . . . don't . . . have any . . . money."

"Let me take you to Amelia," David reassured her. "She helps girls who want to go home."

On occasion, a kid decided home wasn't that bad after all. The return rate had definitely gone up since the flood. Others simply moved on to places with more resources. Phoenix and Santa Fe were the next stops to the west. It was New Orleans going east, but since Katrina, demand for services had outstripped the city's resources tenfold. David tried to persuade his kids that New Orleans had nothing to offer, but they still headed there drunk on just the idea of Mardi Gras.

After David introduced the freaked out young lady to Amelia, he tried to make his escape again. This time, another staff member waved a phone at him.

"No time," David said.

"Searching parent." That was all she had to say. David never passed up a chance to reconnect families.

"I've given up and started calling morgues," the woman said. She didn't sound upset, her tone was almost deadpan, perhaps dulled with pain or antidepressants. "The Austin morgue said you know all the kids. Said you might be able to help me find her if she's still alive. Which I doubt, but anyway, can you help me?"

"I'll try. What's her name? What does she look like?"

She described Fiona, with different colored hair, a small heart tattoo on her hand—the only real description needed.

"She was in Austin two nights ago," David told her. "I saw her myself."

"Can you get her to call me?"

"I'll ask her if I see her. How old is she?"

"Nineteen."

"She's an adult. I can't force her to do anything she doesn't want to do. You understand that, right?"

"Oh. No. You can't? Can I call the police to find her?"

"Not unless she's committed a crime. And being homeless isn't a crime."

"So she *is* homeless."

"Without a doubt."

She was silent. Then, "Well, what should I do?"

She could come to Austin and she'd most likely find her daughter, but if Fiona didn't want to go home, there was nothing her mother could do to force her.

"I'll pass along the message. Do my best to get her to call you." David scribbled down the woman's contact information. After they hung up, he stuck the slip of paper into his wallet so he would have it with him.

He sprinted to his motorcycle, sure he would be late to the

council meeting. A touch and the engine of his 883 Iron Black Denim hummed to life. It was a wicked ride that scored serious cred with the kids.

He'd had an old car when he started working at Tumbleweed, but he soon learned that he would be forever giving rides if he didn't draw strong boundaries. One day, his girlfriend was driving and a kid recognized his car, banged on the window and scared her to tears. So David got a bike. The girlfriend eventually left, but the Harley stayed.

He zipped through traffic trying to make up for lost time. One of the things he liked most about riding was the concentration required. He had to focus, which meant he didn't have time to consider problems like girls crying to go home and parents searching for corpses instead of children.

David parked and walked past the giant gleaming guitar sculpture outside of Austin's futuristic city hall. He had brought a stack of files to review while he waited for his turn to speak. He didn't have to wait long. He walked into chambers just in time to hear a council member addressing the city's homeless situation.

"I propose we buy these folks bus tickets out of Austin back to where they came from." The key term in his statement being "out of Austin."

"Lots of cities are doing it," the councilman said.

David searched the room until he locked eyes with the director of the Salvation Army. David could see his counterpart was seething.

"Like what cities?" another council member asked.

"New York's doing it. It's been proposed in a lot of larger cities."

The council member's ignorance of the situation astounded David. He walked forward toward the microphone stand, positioned in the middle of the aisle in front of the dais. The council chairwoman nodded acknowledgement. She waited for an opportunity, then said, "I see Mr. Simpson is here from the Tumbleweed Young Adult Center. Mr. Simpson, according to my notes you are later on the agenda. Do you have something you'd like to contribute to this particular conversation?"

"Yes, Madam Chairwoman. I do. I think the idea of shipping the homeless out of Austin is an uninformed and insensitive proposal."

The council member who put forth the proposal openly scoffed.

"Of course you do," he snapped.

"Mr. Simpson has the floor. Go on, Mr. Simpson. Give us your opinion," the chairwoman said.

David swallowed a lump of dread. Public speaking was the part of his job he hated the most. He took in a large breath and held it while he pulled his thoughts together.

"I can't speak on behalf of the other shelter organizations represented here, but I can tell you about the homeless youth in Austin. Half of my kids have no home to return to. Period. No parents, no grandparents, no relatives, nobody who can provide a home. Most of these young adults have aged out of the foster care system and they have nowhere to go."

"What about public housing?" the chairwoman asked.

"The waiting list for public housing is about two years, so that creates a gap between the time the state releases them as adults and the time housing becomes available. And then there are the younger ones. I've got a least five hundred every night under eighteen. These kids don't even qualify for public housing."

"Five hundred? Every night?" The chairwoman seemed surprised.

"Tens of thousands of homeless youth come through Austin every year. Most of these kids have no home and it's *not their fault*. Children are not in control of these situations. They are at the mercy of the communities where they land. A lot of them happen to land in Austin. They're our children now."

The council members looked at each other. Public officials were pragmatists. They viewed the homeless problem as a costly burden, a truth that couldn't be denied. It was hard to drum up sympathy for the tattooed, scraggly-haired children their constituents shooed away from their business doorsteps. Taxpayers didn't vote for representatives who handed out money to shiftless people.

"We hear your reasoning, Mr. Simpson, but there is only so much the city can do. Only so much money can be allocated to this particular problem. Do you have any suggestions to help us deal with this in a more sensitive and effective way?"

He stammered. There was no denying Austin already committed very generous resources to the homeless.

David had spoken passionately and made his point, but the council's point was made as well.

They all knew the truth. He had come today with his hand out yet again. He was a beggar, just like those he served.

Travis

HE LOVED working late in the newsroom. There were fewer people around. No ringing phones or sexy co-eds to distract him.

Travis banged out the flood story, his writer's block gone. No boring screed on parking meters or city council meetings. He'd decided to open with a scene that would put readers right in the action.

"Giant swirling walls of water," was how Ava Torres described what she saw coming at her as she drove over the Winsor Street Bridge in Pease Park. Torres, a domestic worker in the Penbrooke neighborhood, was on her way home when she crossed the usually reliable bridge and was suddenly in the clutches of savage rushing water.

"I shouldn't have stopped my car, but I panicked," Torres said. "As soon as I stopped I knew I'd done the wrong thing." Water invaded her car and Torres ended up on the roof where an off-duty police officer rescued her in the pouring rain with a rope and the help of two citizens.

Torres was almost a casualty, but luck was on her side. Others were not as fortunate. Torrential rains took two lives and swept away many millions of dollars of property in Austin during the aftermath of Hurricane Gordon. Cars were pushed around like floating beer cans. In places, the city remains a crumpled mass of mangled sewer lines pushed above ground, street signs, broken concrete and structural steel.

Surviving handbills and posters formed a high water mark on buildings. In the floodplain, thick fingers of brown water pushed out into neighborhoods, natural areas and parking lots. Cars were stalled and abandoned all over Austin. People were stranded on roofs in low-lying areas.

As Austinites are painfully aware, hurricanes from the Gulf of Mexico tend to unleash on Central Texas. This time, county water stations registered a rise of eight feet in twenty minutes. There is no way to prepare for that.

It was a good start. There were so many ways the story could go, but he liked leading with an individual crisis instead of generalities about property damage and local government reaction.

His e-mail chimed for attention. It was from Emily. She had sent images and the release he needed to publish her photographs.

Travis opened the attachments. The shots were interesting and well-done, if a little on the artsy side. He wondered if she had retouched a few. Travis had forgotten to tell her that legit news sources didn't manipulate images.

She'd caught a woman crying out as she watched her house wash away. Another of a boy holding a dog, both covered in mud, the whites of their eyes the only clean spot on the pair. There were people kayaking down city streets and piles of debris caught on the upstream side of a bridge. His mind was already spinning captions.

The last one he opened was the money shot. Emily seemed to have a steady hand under pressure. The image was the two stranded boys, blanched, drenched, huddled on a car's roof. Water lapped up and over the hood below them. Their eyes were averted out of the frame, watching their friend climb into the back of the SUV. The emptiness in their eyes said it all. They were part of the damage.

All the pieces of a front page article were there, but time was short. Still, he wasn't worried. He liked working against deadline. He responded well to pressure.

Emily

THE MORNING was robin egg-blue. The air had a brisk edge. Fall had arrived on the wake of the rains. The city was in ruins and Emily needed a latte.

Lorelei was awake and sitting on the back stoop, cleaning mud from her Doc Martens when Emily got up. The girl had been with her for a few days.

"You hungry?" Emily asked.

Lorelei shrugged.

"Let me throw on my sweatshirt and we can walk to get some coffee."

Mud had dried to chalky crust in unexpected spots along the streets. A certain strange stench wafted by at times, making Emily aware of the earth.

Above the entrance to Bouldin Creek Coffee hung a sign: *Our mission is to inspire community action, intellectual foment and people-watching.* On the side of the register: *Slacker special: Regular coffee $1. You know who you are.*

They ordered. Emily paid.

While they waited, Emily took a *Be Here Now* from a metal rack. She held the magazine toward Lorelei. "Look!"

"That's so cool."

Her stranded street punks stared out from the cover.

She grabbed a short stack of papers. They found a patio table outside and began to read. Emily immediately regretted that she hadn't suggested captions for her photos. Did photographers get to do that? She didn't know. She'd have to ask Barbara.

Emily let the first sip of latte burn its way down her throat, hardly noticing the heat or the approach of her friend Leslie, Austin's icon of weirdness. He was winding his way between tables, talking to people. One table stopped him for a group photo. A visor that read *A positive voice in Austin* held back his wild gray hair. Like always, he smoked as if his life depended on it.

A vagrant cross-dresser, Leslie was one of Austin's most loved citizens. He hung around Sixth and Congress during business hours, often with a lengthy message scrawled on plywood railing against what he viewed as the Austin police force's mistreatment of the homeless.

Like many people around town, Emily had bought Leslie a cup of coffee. Leslie leaned in to give her a hug.

"Hey, Em. What's going on? I haven't seen you in a while, sugar."

"Leslie, hey. Look, I took this picture."

"Girl, that is good. I've seen those two around."

"This is my friend, Lorelei."

"I'm Leslie. Nice to meet you, sweetheart."

"Leslie!" somebody yelled from another table. His attention was pulled away, and he teetered over to the other table in his heels.

"He's a trip," Lorelei said.

"Leslie runs for mayor all the time." Emily pointed to a Leslie for Mayor bumper sticker on the wall among the jumble of other oddities.

Leslie high-fived and knuckle bumped a table of young guys.

One of them said, "Fight the power."

"Everybody thinks he's a scream," Emily said.

"Does he always have a beard and wear a bra?"

"Yeah, and a thong in the summer. He's like Austin's human weather gauge. People say you can tell the temperature by what Leslie wears."

This day, Leslie sported hot pink bellbottoms ringed with white flowers at the hem and a matching pink halter top with peep toe platforms. He wore a cropped zebra print coat.

"For a homeless guy he sure can dress up."

"Yes. He must be resourceful."

Where *did* Leslie keep his stash of costumes and signs?

"He's been in rehab, got beat up a couple of weeks ago. Says he was trying to convince some kids not to do drugs."

"Yeah," Lorelei snorted. "Good luck with that."

"You know what they say, 'Crack is whack.'"

"Don't make me gag."

They watched Leslie work the room.

"I have a brother," Lorelei said softly. She sipped her coffee and waited for a reaction to her casual announcement.

Emily tried to seem disinterested. "What's his name?"

"Noah. He's sick."

"In what way?"

"Schizophrenic. When he's on his meds he does fine, but he needs somebody to make sure he takes them like he's supposed to." She took another sip of coffee and paused to gather her words. "He ran away from home. But I guess when you're twenty-two you can't technically run away from home. My parents are tired of trying to take care of him. He was a drain on them. An embarrassment, I guess."

"So, where is he now?"

"Who knows? I keep looking for him, but so far, no luck."

"That why you came to Austin?"

"Yeah. He stays in the adult shelters. That makes it harder for me to find him. But he moves a lot. He's probably not here."

"We could ask Leslie if he's seen him. He knows about everybody."

"Maybe. I don't know."

"Have your parents filed a missing persons report?"

"I doubt it."

"You don't talk to them?"

"No. They don't care about me either. Plus, they'd hate these," she said pointing to her face.

There were probably plenty of parents who would reject their children over something as superficial as tattoos. Emily wondered if her parents would be like that. A tramp stamp or something she could easily hide would be one thing, but Barbara wouldn't be able to handle a facial tattoo. Emily was still considering this as they walked back to her house.

"So, what made you think Noah came to Austin?"

"It's logical. He likes music. It's on the circuit."

"The circuit?"

"Yeah. Travelers go from Seattle all the way down to Miami, depending on the weather and stuff. Then they turn around and come back the other way. He's not here or I would have found him by now. I'm thinking he's already moved on to New Orleans. Austin's been great and all, but it's not like I can live with you forever."

Lorelei let things hang a moment, but Emily didn't take the bait.

"So anyway," the girl said. "Mardi Gras is coming up. Wanna go?"

"What?"

"Let's go to Mardi Gras."

"And do what?"

"And do whatever."

"I don't think so."

"Couldn't hack it on the streets?"

"I'd do just fine."

"Oh yeah, here." She handed Emily her empty coffee cup. "Go over there and ask that guy for a dollar."

"No way."

"Chicken."

"No. I'm not going to beg."

"See. You couldn't make it."

"I could too. I'm a bartender. I can get a job in any city."

"But don't you see that what you do isn't all that different from what I do? What do you think tips are? You're still living off a stranger's spare change. You spange. You just don't call it that."

"It's different. I work for it."

"You don't think I work to get money? Don't you think standing on a sidewalk all day trading your dignity for pocket change is work?" She picked up a bottle in the road and smashed it on a rock.

This startled Emily, but she decided to ignore it. "Why are we having this conversation?" she asked.

"Because you're being hypocritical."

"And you're being a little snot."

Emily liked her better when she didn't talk so much.

"Look," she said. "I know I can't stay with you forever. I appreciate the help, but it's time to vacate."

Emily nodded and said nothing. She felt guilty at how relieved she was, but not guilty enough to offer to let her stay longer.

Barbara

SHE TOOK a little Zoloft. Fifty milligrams every day just to take the edge off. All her friends took something. Everybody did, right?

Barbara popped the little white pill into her mouth and washed it down with a swirl of wine. Who could blame her for ignoring that pesky little alcohol warning on the prescription bottle? If she followed all the darned instructions she'd never get to have a glass of wine or a cocktail. And sometimes she needed a drink more than the pharmaceutical.

Her therapist called it self-medicating. Her daughter called it better living through chemistry. Barbara called it survival.

She wandered back into the office, where Gerald was paying bills.

"So what's the damage this month?" she asked.

Gerald removed the reading glasses from his nose and rubbed the red spots where they had pressed him.

"We'll survive another month."

She sipped her wine and nodded. No need to discuss their situation. Their life that had started as the typical American success story had ended up as the typical American financial disaster. In the beginning, they rode that big wave of money that washed over Austin during the tech boom. The city's nickname was Silicon Hills because of Dell, IBM, 3M, Motorola, Samsung, Texas Instruments and other companies that fed off the young energy of Austin. Gerald had been in software development in the middle of it all. Barbara had worked at a public relations firm.

They were flush. They bought a house. They bought stock. Emily arrived, so they bought a bigger house. For twenty years they had steadily increasing incomes, so they leveraged their future. A future they had never questioned would only get increasingly better.

Then the market soured, the tech bubble burst, and Gerald lost his job. They were left with a huge mortgage, three car payments and credit card debt that climbed each month.

Gerald was unemployed for nearly two years. A situation that devoured their meager savings and cut a gash in their marriage that Barbara was unsure would ever heal. They continued to wait for the real estate market to recover and prayed that their stock portfolio would rebound.

"So, we're okay? No need to tap the line of credit this month?" Barbara asked.

"No. No. We're good. Really."

The job Gerald eventually landed was a step down in stature and pay. They discussed moving if he got a good out-of-state offer. But their house was worth half of what they had paid for it, so they kept holding on, hoping for the real estate market to recover. Barbara used to drive around collecting the white sale sheets out of the plastic tubes on her neighbors' lawns. Asking prices kept declining. Barbara finally gave up and quit torturing herself.

Gerald said the recession hit Austin earlier than other parts of the country. Big boom. Big bust.

He pushed a button and the computer screen went black.

"I'm going to watch a movie. You game?" he asked.

"What movie?"

"*Wall Street.*"

"God, no. Thanks, but I'll pass. Why do you beat yourself up with that depressing stuff?"

"I don't know. Guess I like to think it will help me figure things out."

"Phfffff."

Sometimes Gerald puzzled her. They had both been downsized about the same time—a double whammy of bad luck. It seemed Gerald had taken the loss harder. Barbara immediately started freelancing and now had a dozen clients. No big accounts yet, but she was steadily increasing her customer base. It was a new phase for her, always on the scramble for the next job, the next injection of money to keep them afloat. She didn't like the stress, but somehow she seemed to thrive when there was more at stake.

But that wasn't Gerald. He was the slow and steady guy—the dependable, methodical worker who liked parameters and knowing what to expect. When he should have been fighting the hardest, he'd given up. Instead of looking for a job, he'd gone into a funk and started drinking. She'd made the mistake of forcing him out the door with his golf bag. He'd just gone to the country club (a contractual expense they couldn't easily shed) and spent money they didn't have at the club bar with equally miserable unemployed members. Even when he was home, he wasn't really present. He'd shut himself in the theater room until Barbara was sure he was going to develop a vitamin D deficiency. That was one habit he had yet to shake. He could shut himself up for hours in that dark room.

Emily had inherited some of Gerald's need for routine and solitude. Neither seemed to embrace change or challenge. Emily had been a mediocre student and her lackluster performance hadn't earned her any prizes in life.

Barbara heard the rumble of the surround sound and she felt sad and alone. It was hard being the one who worried and planned and pushed. No wonder she self-medicated.

She hauled herself up the stairs to Emily's room. She used the handrail to steady herself, but only once. Barbara flipped on the light in her daughter's room. The dresser glittered with costume jewelry and evaporated bottles of cheap perfume. The corkboard still held Emily's photography, strange things she thought deserved to be documented.

Barbara knew it was melancholy to comfort herself with her daughter's life, but she missed her. She missed all the little clues that meant her daughter was still a part of their home—headbands strewn around the house, long shiny hair in Barbara's brush. Her delicate wet footprints fading on the tile after a shower. Her laugh, like sunshine.

Sure, they'd had difficulties, but Barbara chose to dwell on the beautiful aspects of her daughter. Like labor, it was easy to forget the pain of having a disgruntled, rude teenager.

An ache gripped Barbara's chest like an invisible hand. All mothers know these hurting moments when your child burns so strong in your heart that you need them physically. She lay on the bed beside Emily's favorite stuffed animal. The toy had been dragged through the dirt in the park, thrown up on in the car, lost on the floor of the grocery and abandoned when Emily went to college.

"Hello, you old bear," Barbara said. "Are you lonely up here all by yourself?" Miranda Panda didn't respond, so Barbara tipped her wine glass toward the creature's stitched mouth. "There now, how's that? All better?"

She'd never admit it, but Barbara mourned the days she hadn't been the one to take Emily to the park. They'd splurged on the very best daycare, the one that promised an enriched experience, but Barbara envied the women who got to spend their days with her daughter. She had missed so much of Emily's young life, and now that she was grown and gone, Barbara felt an acute sense of loss. She'd bought her things to make up for not being there for her, things to ease her own guilt. And where were those things now?

Barbara had been torn. She had wanted to work, and she'd felt an obligation to help keep up their lifestyle. The Bryces had grown accustomed to nice things and it never occurred to them to cut back. They simply worked harder.

That's what people did in the eighties and nineties. They embraced the pursuit of wealth. It was exciting and stressful in a good way. Everybody was competitive. Business was fun.

Then it all crashed and burned.

Being an adult was complicated and often not much fun. Every day brought a fresh difficulty. So, while it was frustrating to watch, Barbara found it hard to fault her daughter for being a reluctant adult.

Life is hard.

That's why Zoloft remained Barbara's best friend.

Lorelei

IT SUCKED to leave Emily's house, but Lorelei knew when to move on. She didn't want to burn her chances of ever crashing there again. Emily had developed that impatient look adults get when you've become a drag.

She set off on foot toward downtown on a main road. The van guy who had rescued her had driven it and she knew that path was a straight shot back to Shoal Creek. She crossed a big bridge into the city and stopped to look over the edge. While the water had receded, the corridor below the bridge was still forbidding.

Gnarls of trees amassed against pilings. Odd bits of humanity, clothes and garbage and yard art were twisted into the mix. All the squatting spots by the creek would still be underwater. She reassessed and headed toward campus. She needed to find a place to crash before dark.

Along the way she often stopped to consider some strange result of the storm. People were out everywhere, washing steps and righting muddy lawn furniture.

As she neared campus, she stopped to follow the source of laughter from an alley. In the closing light, she could make out a girl watching two guys chase something. They seemed to snare the small animal. They whooped with victory and stuffed the poor thing into a cardboard box.

She hoped it wasn't a kitten.

"Lorelei." It was Fiona. "Oh, hey. You're still around."

"Yeah."

"You wanna come with us? We're going to hang out with some people at somebody's apartment."

"Cool."

"Come on."

They all headed toward a bumper sticker-strewn old van leaning on the far side of the street. At their approach, a girl turned from the passenger seat. She spilled some liquid into her mouth from a giant beer can.

"Who's that?" she asked, waving her beer at the newcomer.

"Her? Oh, that's Lorelei," Fiona said. "She's chill."

Lorelei threw her pack in the back and crawled into the dark depths of the vehicle. It was dirty, what her mother would have called filthy. Fast-food wrappers and paper cups with liquid inside rolled around on the floor. A mangy dog that smelled like death slept in a corner. The others tumbled inside and slid the door shut, cutting off sunlight. It was stuffy and Lorelei began to sweat.

"That's Tweak," Fiona said of one boy. He raised a beer can to her. "And this is Toby." This one looked fresh off the farm, but there was something girly about him too. "And that's Malcolm driving, and that's his girl, Ajaicia."

"How you doin, mon?" Malcolm said. Rasta. No dreads, but his grill was golden. His girlfriend ran her hands down his arm to show he was taken. She looked sort of like Elda, just not as pretty.

"Hey," Ajaicia said, more friendly this time. "Oh my God, your tat is badass."

"We're going to my place to hang," Malcolm said. "You're welcome. Everybody welcome." He was older. Lorelei gauged him to be in his thirties. What was he doing hanging out with street kids? He was either a social worker or a drug dealer. She bet drug dealer, but either way, a floor where she could sack out sounded fine for now. They would probably even scare up some food.

The animal scratched inside the box. She hoped they didn't intend to eat whatever was in there.

"Have you seen Mook or Elda or anybody from that group?" Lorelei asked Fiona as they bumped along on the hard van floor.

"No, man, they like, took off to Mook's mom's or something," she said. "That's where he runs off to."

"What about Freestyle and Minion?"

She scoffed. "What? Those losers. I mean Minion, he's okay. But Freestyle, he's a loser for sure. Crazy foster scare motherfucker."

Freestyle had never mentioned that part of his background. That explained a lot.

They pulled into a ratty apartment complex with a faded sign that read *Siesta Gardens*. The once adobe-colored walls were streaked with rust leaked from the roof, giving the whole complex the appearance of melting. Empty liquor bottles and cigarette butts littered their way. Tiny faces with round hopeful eyes peeked from behind windows smudged with grime. Malcolm led their group past scarred doors. One was kicked in. The doorframe was splintered where a deadbolt had been.

Lorelei got the feeling this was going to be a flophouse. One step inside the apartment and she knew she was right.

Unlike a community house where things were marginally safe, a flophouse was anything but. These were lousy places where you could get drugs, robbed, laid, arrested, raped or worse. Lorelei knew she wouldn't be staying the night, but she decided to hang around for a while just to see who might arrive. It was surprising the people who showed up at a flophouse.

Before her eyes even adjusted to the darkness, Lorelei was hit with the smell of nicotine and stale beer. Kids were scattered around on an old couch, an armchair, the floor, about a dozen in all now that their group had arrived. A coffee table held an armada of beer cans. A few were stacked into a pyramid among overflowing ashtrays and empty plastic pop bottles.

A grossly thin guy in a wheelchair smoked a cigarette, and Lorelei could feel his eyes on her. It didn't take her long to surmise that Malcolm shared the apartment with him. Or maybe it was this guy's apartment and Malcolm was a squatter. She avoided the thin man's vulpine stare.

A round of applause went up when Tweak arrived with the box. Malcolm emerged from a back room with a giant cage. People grabbed beer cans and cleared the table. He set the cage on the table.

Everyone turned to look at the guy in the wheelchair, and that's when Lorelei noticed the snake wrapped around his arm. He uncoiled the redtail boa. Her brother's snake had had the same pattern that reminded her of chromosomes she had studied in science class. She was creeped out by how the pattern repeated through the reptile's eyes. Glass over yellow scales that made it look as if it could read your every thought. Her brother's snake had made her feel naked, like it could see her in a way impossible to others. She had been glad when the morbid thing slithered into the wilderness behind their house. She knew it wouldn't survive the winter.

The boa slowly encircled Malcolm's arm and inched its way toward his neck. He seemed affectionate toward the animal and was careful when he lowered her into the cage. He turned the cardboard box upside down and a small rat fell out. It looked half-dead and Lorelei figured the boys had stomped it.

The snake didn't move. It seemed almost as if it didn't even realize prey was near. The rat smelled danger and made a feeble attempt to flee, making it to the corner of the cage where it collapsed in terror. The predator inched forward and froze again. The room was silent, everyone poised for the strike. The serpent was patient. It watched, flicking its tongue.

It struck and clamped down on the rat's head. The rodent squealed and struggled. The snake aggressively coiled her body around her prey until only one twitching rat claw flailed outside the spirals of sinew. The predator cinched tighter. There was one tiny squeak and the twitching claw wilted.

The room rumbled. Girls shrieked. Boy's high-fived each other.

"Duuuuude!"

"Oh, man, that was harsh."

"Wicked!"

Lorelei decided to find a bathroom instead of watching the slow, methodic swallowing process. As she made her way toward the hall, a thin hand with dirty nails reached out and snatched her arm.

"What's your name?" the guy in the wheelchair asked. His teeth were yellow, his eyes roadmaps.

"Lorelei."

"I can't remember that. I'll call you Phoenix. Do you got any cigarettes, Phoenix?" Cigarettes were a sure way to make friends, and she usually kept a pack in her bag for just such a situation. Unfortunately, she wasn't holding.

"I'm sorry. I don't smoke."

He let her arm go. "Pity," he said.

"Dude," Malcolm said. "I got your foul smokes, here." He pitched a pack to him. "You ought to give that shit up and just smoke more weed, mon."

Wheelchair guy became engrossed in opening the cigarette

pack, and Lorelei slipped away. Down the short hall she found the bathroom. It was extra large, with sturdy handholds and a shower that a wheelchair could roll into. It was dirty and smelled like men's toilets at gas stations. Cigarette butts floated in old shampoo bottles. The toilet paper roll was empty.

She opened her pack and pulled out her toilet paper stash. She hovered above the seat as she peed. A roach scratched as it climbed between the folds of the clear shower curtain next to her. She heard more people arrive outside. Music cranked—a tune by Everclear that Lorelei loved. People shouted to be heard. There was laughter. She finished and wiped. Before she left, she squished the bug inside the curtain, adding its oozy guts to the soap scum and mildew.

"Hey." Tweak was in her face as soon as she opened the bathroom door. "I wondered where you went. Here, have a beer." Lorelei didn't really like beer, but to be sociable she took the offering. She hadn't eaten, and if she drank, she would get woozy, so she sipped slowly while she planned what she intended to do for the night. She couldn't stay. There would be a lot of things going on here all night, but sleeping wasn't one of them. Besides, if she fell asleep in this crowd, she'd most likely wake up to find her backpack taken.

A couple began groping next to her in the hall, but there were so many people crammed into the small apartment that there was hardly anywhere else to go. Fiona pushed past her.

"Girlfriend, come on," Fiona said and grabbed Lorelei's hand, pulling her into a back bedroom. People squeezed against the walls as she passed, and she realized with a shot of dread that the guy in the wheelchair was behind her. Fiona pushed open a door and the group filed inside—Ajaicia, Tweak and Fiona dropped onto a bare, stained mattress. The bed had handrails, one pillow and a nasty blanket.

"I'm Lawrence," the guy in the wheelchair said to her. "This is my place."

Lorelei thought this wasn't something she'd be proud of, but all she did was nod and calculate how quickly she could make her exit. Fiona zipped open her pack and fanned out drugs on the splotchy mattress. The others gathered around. Lawrence pulled a wad of cash from his pocket. Lorelei had thought him needy when he'd asked for a cigarette, but he had a huge roll of bills. He began to count money.

"You know what I want," Lawrence said. He pitched a worn

leather pouch on the bed, and Fiona pulled out his works. Lorelei felt the walls start a slow inward creep. Lawrence lit a cigarette, and she wanted to gag. Her ears buzzed. Tweak had probably put something in her drink. This had happened to her before, and she had awoken to a guy pawing her clothes off, his hot breath in her face. She had tried to push him away, but her arms were heavy. Somebody, Lorelei could never remember if it was a guy or a girl, but some kind stranger had come into the room and stopped him.

She needed to get out, but Lawrence's wheelchair blocked the door. They were on the first floor, so Lorelei looked to the window. It was open, an old screen hung on at the edges, but the middle was busted where somebody had pushed through from outside. Everybody was focused on the drugs arrayed on the bed. Nobody paid any attention to her as she slipped through the shredded spines of metal that frayed the hole in the screen.

She managed to get half of her body through the screen when she got stuck. Thinking her pack was hung on the scratchy screen, she lunged forward to rip herself free. Suddenly, she was jerked back inside the room.

"Hey!" she yelled, grabbing at the screen where ragged edges punctured her hands. One of her legs still dangled outside the window. The weight of the pack held her off-kilter.

"Where you think you're going, girl?" Tweak hissed in her ear.

"Let go!" Lorelei tried to shove him away, but he held tight to the shoulder straps of her pack. "Let go!" Her head felt like it was shrinking, squeezing rational thought out, filling her with fear and anger. She couldn't breathe.

"That's not very nice. I give you a beer and you try and run out on me?"

"Dude, let her go!" she heard Fiona say.

"Please, *please*, stop!" Lorelei cried.

"You got to stay and party with us. You're being rude," Tweak said.

"I said let her go, motherfucker. You're such a douche." Fiona again.

Lorelei was being dragged down, backward, onto the floor. She squeezed her arms behind her back and slid out of the pack. She was suddenly light. She heard Tweak hit the floor and curse. The room exploded with laughter.

She had to get out. She couldn't breathe. Lorelei shoved through the screen, scratching her face, lacerating her sweatshirt. She hit the sidewalk on one shoulder, but she felt no pain.

There was yelling inside the room, but Lorelei didn't wait to see the outcome of the fight. She stumbled around the corner and ran past the open front door of the apartment, where the party had spilled outside. She dodged people. Some of them called out to her, but she didn't hear them. She ran to the street outside the complex.

A city bus arrived. She stumbled on. Luckily, she had her zippered money pouch in her pocket. She couldn't count. Her hands felt numb. She held the leather bag open. The bus driver frowned at her and clicked his tongue, but he picked the correct change out and sent the silver tinkling down into the coin slot.

"Don't throw up on my bus," he said. "Pull the cord if you need to stop."

Her legs felt like jelly, but her mind was weird and agitated. There was no telling what Tweak had had put in that beer.

Maybe the bus would drive by something she recognized. She needed campus. She'd find that church and sleep in the cemetery like she had her first night in town.

At least that was her plan. She rode for what seemed like hours, fighting to stay awake. She didn't want to wake up to a cop in her face. She felt sick and she panicked and pulled the bell cord. The bus dumped her out in front of a metal-sided restaurant. She barely made it off the sidewalk before she collapsed into a bank of scrubby, sticky bushes. She crawled into the interior of the landscaping, balled herself into a fetal position and passed out.

Emily

"SAY CHEESEBURGER!" the mother said.

No reaction.

"Actually, it's okay if he doesn't smile. They don't want us to force the children to smile if they don't want to," Emily explained, but she could tell the boy was on the edge of breaking out a grin, so she said, "Okay, say boogers!"

The boy suddenly showed pink gummy gaps where baby teeth used to live.

"Boogers!" he yelled. "Boogers! Boogers!"

Emily released the shutter and checked her screen. It was a cute shot.

"That's enough," his mother said to him. "I'm sorry. He's a little hyper today."

"No worries. He's awesome." Emily lined his photo up on the identification software and sent it to print. When the printer spit out the creamy card with his smiling face, she handed it to the mother. "Here, take this to fingerprinting next."

She thanked Emily, took her son's hand and led him away to the table where volunteers would roll his fat little fingers in ink and press them inside ten rectangular boxes on the card for safekeeping. At another table, someone would swab the child's mouth and secure his DNA sample inside two plastic bags.

Unlike the volunteers here, Emily was being paid for her time.

Barbara had called in a panic. She had organized this Print-A-Thon as a community goodwill event for a banking client. They were set up under a white tent in the bank's parking lot where for four hours, Emily manned the photo station. Barbara's original photographer had dumped on her and she'd decided Emily was the perfect person to step in to help. It had turned out to be a lot of fun.

Little ones skipped to their parents' cars with balloons tied to their wrists, white candy sticks poking out of their plump lips. Less enthusiastic parents trailed behind, identification bags in hand. They were trying to push away thoughts of the solemn need for the service—precautions in case their child is ever kidnapped or runs away.

Emily had photographed more than two hundred kids. Even she had tried to avoid morbid thoughts of dreadful things ever happening to any of them. In a perfect world, none of this would be necessary.

By the time the event wrapped that afternoon, her stomach was growling. Barbara offered to buy lunch.

"You go on. I'll meet you in a few minutes. I've got to finish up here and shut things down. Order me a margarita—rocks, no salt," she said.

Emily stowed her camera equipment in the MINI, then dashed across traffic toward Chuy's, thinking about their thin crunchy chips and amazing green chili salsa. The sun was blinding, and if it hadn't been for her polarized lenses she might not have seen the Doc Martens in the shrubs along the side of Chuy's parking lot. The black boots were ubiquitous to the young homeless.

Emily stood in a dusty parking space wondering what to do. If somebody else discovered this person they might call the police. She decided to go inside, order a sandwich and drink to go, and see if she could get this kid up and moving before the cops arrived.

It was after the lunch rush, so she got the sandwich and drink quickly. She walked back out to the parking lot half hoping the person would be gone, but they hadn't stirred.

"Hey," Emily said.

Nothing.

"Hey, wake up."

It suddenly occurred to her that they might be dead. Great. And here she stood, like a dummy, trying to pawn food off on a corpse.

"Hey, wake up," she said louder this time. She gave the boot a nudge.

There was a groan. Then, "Huh?"

"I've got you some food."

"Go away."

Emily recognized the tangle of hair. "Lorelei?"

The girl slowly righted herself. Her head came up out of the brush last. Her hair was matted with scaly strands of cedar spines. One side of her face was scratched and imprinted with the saw-toothed pattern of the brush.

"Emily?"

"Lorelei? Holy crap. What are you doing here?"

"I don't know. I guess I passed out."

"Here? In Chuy's parking lot?"

"I don't know."

"Get up."

"I'm fine. Leave me alone."

"You're not fine. You're sleeping in a parking lot."

"No, I'm not."

She seemed weak, as if her mind were detached from her current situation.

"Don't you have somewhere to sleep?"

"Sure I do."

"Then how'd you end up here?" Emily leaned forward into the brush and handed her the drink. Lorelei took it with shaky hands and gulped it down.

"What happened to your hands and your face? You're all scratched up."

Lorelei tried to stand, but tumbled back to her butt. "I'm fine. Don't worry about me."

Emily suddenly remembered Barbara was on her way. She couldn't let her see Lorelei like this.

"Stay here," she told her. "My car's across the street. I'll take you anywhere you want to go."

Without waiting for an answer, Emily sprinted back across the road to the tent. She found her mother shoving the last few boxes into the back of her SUV.

"Hey, Barbara," she said. "Look, change of plans. I ran into a friend and I need to give her a ride somewhere. Can I take a rain check on lunch?"

"Of course. Stand your old mother up."

"Next time, it's my treat."

"Sure. Well, thanks for your help. I couldn't have done it without you."

"Love you. Gotta go."

Emily prayed that Lorelei hadn't bolted. The girl was unsteady as she got into the car, but Emily knew enough not to offer help. Lorelei got in, turned toward the window and curled up into herself.

"So, where do you want to go?"

"The Drag."

"Okay." Emily pulled out, and Lorelei began to cry. Tears turned into full sobs and sobs turned into simply out of control. Emily found a tree-lined edge of a parking lot and pulled over into shade. They sat in the idling car. Lorelei wiped her nose on a sleeve. Emily searched around for a tissue, but found nothing.

"Did something happen to you?" Emily finally asked. "Did somebody hurt you?"

Tears plopped into the girl's lap.

"No."

"Are you homesick?"

"No."

"Then what's wrong?"

She didn't reply for a moment. "I lost my pack."

"Shit. Did it have all your stuff?"

She nodded. "Everything. I'll never get it back now."

"You forgot and left it somewhere?"

"No. Some jerk boy took it."

She was breathing fast, snot dripping. She opened the passenger door and blew her nose onto the ground. She ran her sweatshirt sleeve across her face.

"Sorry," she managed to croak out.

"Calm down. It's not the end of the world."

"You . . . don't . . . under . . . stand." Who was this girl falling apart in her car? What happened to the tough Lorelei who didn't need anybody?

"There's no reason to get so upset over a backpack."

"It had my clothes . . . and stuff . . . stuff I need."

"Yeah, so? We'll get more."

"And a library book."

"That sucks. I guess you have to return that. So," Emily sighed, "where'd you leave it? I'll drive you wherever."

This calmed her some. Still she said, "I'll never get it back.

Never."

"You don't know that. Let's see if we can find it."

"It's somewhere . . . somewhere you won't want to go."

"You'd be surprised where I'm willing to go. Where is this place?"

"Some crummy apartments, like Fiesta Gardens or Siesta Gardens or something."

"I know it. I knew some people there once, but that was a long time ago." Siesta Gardens had indeed fallen down since the days when her old acquaintances lived there. It was a place she would never go, on an entire street where she would never go.

"Is this it?" Emily asked, hoping the girl would say it wasn't, but Lorelei nodded yes.

They got out at the same time, and Lorelei turned to her and said, "You don't have to go in."

"I don't mind." In truth, Emily didn't want to be left waiting and wondering if Lorelei was going to come back out.

Lorelei led the way to an apartment that lived at the end of a long row of sorrow. The door was open and people were talking inside. The smell of weed wafted out the door. Lorelei stopped at the threshold.

"Ah, Fiona's friend. You decided to come back," some guy said. "And you brought somebody new. Come on in, Phoenix. Pretty women are always welcome."

The apartment was dark. UT stadium blankets blocked the windows, and nobody had bothered to turn on a lamp. Everybody was focused on a cage in the middle of the room. It took a few moments before Emily made out what was in the cage—a five-foot snake with a lump in its middle the size of a softball.

"They fed it last night," Lorelei whispered. "Street rat."

"She never goes hungry," a guy in a wheelchair said, "although I can't say as much for the rest of these folks." He waved a bony hand around the room at the skeletal people, their bodies as wasted as their minds. Drugs were one way to take your thoughts off a grumbling stomach.

"I came to get my backpack," Lorelei said to him. "Have you seen it?"

"Sure, Phoenix. Fiona kept it for you. Wrestled it away from Tweak. Smacked the shit out of him for harassing you. I thought you might come back for it. It's in my bedroom. Under the bed. Fiona's still asleep back there."

"Passed out you mean," somebody said.

Emily didn't bother to follow Lorelei into the back. A joint was lit, and it traveled around the room. When it came her way, Emily took it, hit it and passed it on, although she tried to keep from actually touching her lips.

"I'm Lawrence," the guy said. He started introducing people. They all sounded like cartoon characters. "That's Star, Skittles, Monkey, Tweak and Ajaicia."

"Yeah, man. We know each other," Star said.

"We do?" Emily had thought she remembered a couple of the kids from somewhere, but they all tended to have that same unwashed, scraggly appearance. Then reality hit her. These were the kids she and Travis had rescued from the flood. They looked much different dry. The girl in particular had taken on an air of authority that was surprising in contrast to the shivering girl Emily had helped to save.

"Look what I swiped." Star opened her messenger bag and pulled out a blue plastic piercing gun like the ones used at kiosks and cheap jewelry stores in malls. "I stole some earrings too. Who wants something pierced? How about you, Emily?"

"No thanks."

"She's not street," Monkey said. He had festering snakebites on his bottom lip. Emily remembered him now, the metal vibrating with the chattering of his teeth. Emily had kissed a few guys with lip jewelry, but never labrets.

Lorelei finally reappeared carrying her pack.

Star clicked the piercing gun and everybody oohed.

"How about you, Lorelei? You want a nose ring or another hole in your ear? This thing'll do cartilage like butter."

"I don't care. I'll do it," Lorelei said. Monkey gave her his chair. She sifted through the earrings and selected a silver hoop.

"Where you want it?" Star asked.

Lorelei pointed to her right nostril. "Okay, but it's easier to do your lip." Lorelei shrugged as if she couldn't have cared less. She pinched her bottom lip between two fingers and pulled it forward, exposing the thin vein-threaded flesh inside. Star positioned the device on either side of her lip and held the gun like she was ready to put a bullet in Lorelei's head.

"Stop!" Emily blurted. "Don't do that. I mean . . . I mean, I know you guys are bored and all, but shit, that's not sanitary. I mean, those piercing guns aren't even sanitary in the mall. How many people has that thing been used on?"

She was met with blank stares, as if the message didn't register.

"You know?" she continued. "Hep C? HIV? AIDS?"

"Look, Miss Buzzkill. Mind your own business," Star snapped.

So much for gratitude, Emily thought.

"You guys have to think about this. Shit, throw that thing away."

"She's got a point," Lawrence said. "I wouldn't do it." An unexpected voice of reason.

"Shut up, Lawrence," Star said. "I've seen you share dirty rigs, so just shut up."

Lorelei let go of her lip and leaned back, clearly having second thoughts.

"We're leaving now," Emily said. "You guys do whatever you want. Nice to meet you Lawrence. Thanks for keeping Lorelei's backpack for her. That was real nice."

Emily walked toward the door, fully expecting Lorelei to follow. It never occurred to Emily that she would want to stay, but when she looked back, the girl was still in the chair.

"Lorelei," she prodded. "Come on, let's go get something to eat."

"Yeah, Lorelei, your mommy's calling you. You better go now," Star said.

"I'm about sick of you, Star," Lawrence said. "Why don't you get the fuck out of here?"

Star turned her rage on Lawrence.

"Why? 'Cause I don't bring you ice like your druggie girlfriend?"

Trash talk flew.

Lorelei silently slipped out the door behind Emily.

They drove toward downtown. Emily tried to talk, but Lorelei was somber. She balled up into herself again and leaned against the passenger door, pressing her forehead to the window, staring out, focused on nothing.

"Lorelei, I've never seen you like this. What's wrong?"

No response. She seemed hollowed-out, flat, emotionless.

"If you're mad at me about the piercing gun, too bad. I can't say I'm sorry. Who knows what sick person she's been poking with that thing?"

"That's not it," she said as if she were so tired she could hardly form words. "You can't possibly understand."

"So try me."

She turned soulful eyes to Emily, and a single tear ran down her cheek. It made an optical illusion, as if the bird on her skin were weeping.

"Oh, more tears. Look. We got your pack back. Buck up."

"Whatever," Lorelei muttered.

This girl was so confusing, so hard to reach. Was this what parents had to deal with, unexplainable mood swings, bad judgment and derision?

"Look, maybe I don't understand. But I'd like to. Explain things to me."

Lorelei sighed and rubbed her eyes so hard that Emily was afraid she would hurt herself.

"It's just that sometimes you don't really care what happens to you," Lorelei said. "You don't care about anything."

"So you go looking for danger? For some way to hurt yourself?"

"I guess. It's like nothing matters," she said. "Sometimes you just don't care anymore. Sometimes you just want to die."

They drove a few blocks in silence.

Suddenly, Lorelei said, "Let me out." Her eyes were dark and wild. "Let me out," she said, getting louder each time. "Let me out. Let me out! Let me out right now!"

"Okay, Jesus. Calm down." Emily pulled close to the rumpled sidewalk.

Lorelei jumped out, dragging her pack behind her.

"Hey," Emily called, but the girl slammed the door on the rest of her words and walked away in the direction of Siesta Gardens.

David

WEDNESDAY WAS triage day. Amelia and Steve led the staff in reviewing active cases. This was the time they all came together—the counselors, mental health specialists, the sexual assault counselor and the education specialist—to work on an action plan for each youth.

Everybody looked tired, but despite the long hours and difficulties caused by the flood, there had been recent successes. Everybody was in a good mood, joking and laughing.

"Okay. Let's get on with business," David said. "Who's up first? Amelia, you want to go?"

"Sure. Pretty good week. I got to send four kids back to their parents, and I felt like they were all positive returns."

Everybody applauded.

"I've got some others, though," she whistled and shook her head. "These are some tough cases here. I've got a boy right now. His name is Jeremy Flynn. Street name, Cargo. He's been on bipolar and depression meds in the past." Amelia kept the paper work flowing for food stamps, birth certificates, identification and Social Security cards, but this kid seemed to need much more than the basics.

"He won't talk to me until he gets a sleeping bag. David, I saw some stuff in black garbage bags on the loading dock this morning."

"Yeah, big donation," Steve said.

"Think we've got any sleeping bags in there?"

"I'll be happy to go check. Carry on. I'll be right back."

David picked through the dozens of possibilities on his giant key ring as he walked to the back to see what had arrived.

He was surprised to find the pantry open. Fiona was leaning against the jamb talking to somebody inside. The bare bulb in the pantry threw harsh light on Fiona, accentuating her thin frame and the mascara bruises under her eyes.

"Fiona, how are you?" he asked.

"Great, man." She had the liquid body movements of someone impaired.

"You hungry or did you just come to see me because of my sparkling personality?"

It took a second too long for her to laugh.

"Ha. Yeah, man. Right. That's funny."

"Hey, Fiona. Look at me."

She raised her dreamy eyes to his.

Now was not a good time to talk to her about her mother, but he had no choice. She could disappear on him again.

"Fiona, I had a conversation with your mother the other day."

No response.

"Your mom, she wants you to come home."

Fiona wrinkled her nose, an indication that some part of the message had gotten through.

"No fucking way, man. I'm never going back there."

"She says she's getting divorced, that she believes you. She wants you to come home."

"That's a lie. She lies, lies, lies about . . . about everything."

"Why don't you call her? You can use the phone in my office."

"She's a bitch. I'm never . . . ever . . . ever . . . going to talk to her again." She jabbed her finger at David for emphasis. "Never. Never. Never." Jab. Jab. Jab.

"She may come to Austin looking for you."

Her eyes snapped clear for a second. "Don't you let her come here."

"I can't stop her. Free country."

"No man. No. No." She ran her hands over her face as if she were rubbing the mere thought of her mother out of her head.

He decided to change the subject.

"Forget it. Look, you seen Lorelei lately?"

"Uh, yeah," she said, drifting away again. "Yeah, man. She's around."

"Hey, look at me. Have you seen her since the flood? Is everybody back down at Shoal Creek?"

"Huh? No. Mook got busted for public uri . . . uri . . . for pissing in public."

"He get a ticket?"

"Yeah, like seventy-five bucks or something. Ain't that some shit?"

"So you haven't seen Lorelei?"

"She's hanging with . . . that bartender girl."

"Who is that?"

"Emily . . . Emily . . . ah . . . somebody."

"Oh, yeah. I remember her saying something about having a friend. What's the name of that bar her friend works at?"

"I don't know."

"Group Therapy. Isn't that the one? Group Therapy?"

"Ding, ding, ding, ding! That's right!" She snapped her fingers slowly, but no sound came. "That's right. You win!" She cupped her hands to the sides of her mouth and made a sound like the cheer of a distant crowd. "Whhaaaaaaaa!"

David didn't want Fiona wandering around in her condition.

"Fiona, go over and sit on the couch. Drink some water," he instructed.

"Whatever." She stumbled away and crumpled onto the couch. She was burning bright and then came the sudden fade. He recognized the heroin oblivion slide. Drugs were the usual aftermath of hitting the streets, not the cause as so many people thought. Drugs temporarily washed away the anxiety and constant struggle of homelessness. Everybody needed to check out at times.

He covered her with a blanket. When she woke up she was going to feel like shit.

David pulled his bike to the curb and continued his ten-hour workday with a stop at the bar to see if he could track down Lorelei. His job could be 24/7 if he let it. He often thought it was good that he wasn't married with kids.

He recognized Group Therapy as somewhere he'd been a couple of times when he was in college. Inside it looked like a bar and it smelled like a bar. When he saw the bartender, he felt another tug of recognition. He never forgot a face, and this one had walked into the drop-in right after the flood with that pushy reporter. So, this was Emily. She had a wide smile and a wispy sort of grace. Her skin was smooth and sun-kissed. David was suddenly glad he wasn't married with kids for a different reason.

She finished ringing up her customer and laughed off the guy's attempt to flirt. She hit a button on the sound system, then came David's way.

"Hi, what can I get you?" she called over the first few chords of Tom Petty's *Mary Jane's Last Dance.*

"I'm looking for Emily."

"I'm Emily. Oh, hey. Do I know you?"

"I'm David Simpson. We met one day at the drop-in, right after the flood."

She said, "Ooooh, yeah. Sorry about that. Travis can be a little aggressive at times."

"Not a problem. I'm used to aggressive. Do you know a young lady named Lorelei?"

Her expression changed. "Yeah, I know her. What's up?"

"Have you seen her since the flood?"

"Sure, she stayed with me for like five days right after."

"You two friends?"

"Not really. I mean, I don't know if she considers me a friend or not."

"Can we talk?"

"Sure. Let me get somebody to cover for me. Sit over there, okay?" She pointed to a round booth in the corner next to the bar.

A burly Mexican guy in an apron came out of the back to take over the bar. Emily brought a couple of beers and set a frosty mug in front of him.

"Lone Star, okay?"

"Absolutely. Man, I needed this."

"Long day?"

"Long month."

"So what's up? I haven't seen Lorelei in a while."

"I'm just glad she made it through the flood. Is she doing okay?"

"I wouldn't say she's okay. She was hanging out in some crap hole apartment with a bunch of filthy kids the last time I saw her. I think they were shooting up. She seems like a wreck. Really depressed. Not thinking straight."

"The younger kids usually have a harder time. They just can't navigate the streets like the older kids. Where was this apartment?"

"In that old Siesta Gardens over on the east side of town."

"Yeah. I know the place. You think she's still hanging around there?"

"I wouldn't know. I took her there so she could retrieve a backpack she'd left behind. She freaked on me, jumped out of my car and ran away. I had hoped she'd go to the drop-in. She never showed up?"

"We haven't seen her since the flood."

"Well, maybe she moved on to look for her brother."

"I don't know anything about her having a brother."

"Noah. Apparently he's homeless too. Schizophrenic. Older. Parents didn't want to take care of him anymore. She's looking for him."

David took a long drink of beer. "Well, that makes sense. Probably half my kids have some form of mental illness—depression, bipolar, schizophrenia. If she's used to mental illness then she can handle being around unpredictable people. Probably one reason why she's surviving."

Emily scanned the bar, an unconscious habit he could tell. Her eyes darted to different people, to the bar, back to David.

"So," she said, "is it normal for you to search for these kids at night like this?"

"This is unusual, you know, with the flood and all. Plus, she seems so young. I try to keep an eye on the really young ones."

"That's got to be hard."

David couldn't tell if she meant hard for the kids or hard for him.

"You know anything about her? Anything that would help me find her?"

"Nope. That kid, she's a mystery. She doesn't talk much and when she does, I get the feeling you should only believe about half of what comes out of her mouth."

David studied a bead of condensation creeping down the side of his beer to keep himself from looking at Emily's lips.

"Tell me about it," he said. "They're all guarded, but she seems to be particularly difficult to read."

Emily

EMILY SAT cross-legged on the counter next to her bathroom
sink. She leaned close to the vanity mirror and applied a perfect
swish of black eyeliner. Her gaze fell on the faded club stamps on
her hand. The things hung around for days, like afterthoughts on
her skin.

She licked her hand. One by one she rubbed away the stains.
She liked the statement they made but also their temporary nature.

Her phone rang out *For the Love of Money* by the O'Jays.

She considered not answering, but she flipped it open and said,
"Hola, Barbara."

"Hello sweetheart. Are you getting ready for bed?"

"It's Friday night. You know I'm getting ready to go out."

There was a pause. "At eleven?"

"Did you need something?"

"Oh, yes. I'll be brief. Just . . ."

Emily waited. This happened sometimes. Her mother would
call wanting to talk about something, but then she'd have second
thoughts after her finger had already dialed.

"Barbara, is something wrong?"

"Let me ask you. Why do you always call me Barbara? Why don't
you ever call me Mom?"

"You called me to ask why I don't call you Mom?"

"No. It just occurred to me. Why do you call your father and me by our first names?"

"I don't know. I just always have."

"I know. Don't you think that's strange?"

"I know some other kids who use their parents' first names."

"Well, whatever. I really called to ask if you think your father is acting strange."

"What do you mean?"

"I mean, different. Do you think he's been acting different lately? You know, more depressed, like a couple of years ago."

"I haven't noticed."

"He's so moody. He just comes home from work and shuts himself up in that theater room."

"Maybe he likes movies."

"Emily, don't be so flip."

"If you think something is wrong why don't you just ask him?"

"You know how he is—the strong silent type. He'd never admit anything was wrong. I thought we could all go to dinner. See if you think he's in a funk."

"I think you're creating a problem where there isn't one."

"I'm just worried about him. He's in a mood."

"Just relax. He'll come out of it."

"Maybe. Maybe." Emily could tell she was fishing for something else to talk about. This happened too. Sometimes her mother would call without a reason, just to check up on her. "So, it's been a while since we spoke. How's that little street urchin you've become friends with?"

"Lorelei? Oh, she's okay I guess. I haven't seen her in a while."

"Really?"

"Yeah, why?"

"Well, I just couldn't help but notice that when you ditched me at Chuy's the other day you drove off with her in your car. I didn't realize you were still friends."

Emily bit her lip and climbed down off of the counter. She walked to her bedroom closet and began snapping hangers to the side, looking for something to wear.

"Look, I just gave her a ride somewhere."

"So, she's not living with you?"

"No. She's not living with me."

"So you just happened to run into her in Chuy's parking lot. You're not hiding her from me?"

"My God, what is with the third degree?"

"I'm just concerned."

Emily sighed. "Did you call for any reason other than to complain about Dad and give me the third degree?"

"Well, excuse me for my concern." There was silence, then Barbara said more brightly, "So, do you have a date tonight?"

"No."

"Any nice young men on the horizon?"

"Maybe."

"Oh, tell me. Tell me." Emily knew that was her mother's way of trying to connect, but if they went down that avenue, the discussion always ended up on Emily's lack of appropriate suitors.

"It's just somebody I've got my eye on." She wasn't going to tell her it was Travis Roberts. Her mother had called him an asshole, but she didn't really know him. Emily had no idea why her mother had formed such a low opinion of Travis. Sure, he could be pushy and he had a little ego thing going on, but he'd only grown more appealing to Emily as they worked together. The day they shot the flood story, she felt something click. He wasn't like most of the guys she dated. He was older. Serious. Mysterious. Employed.

The only problem was he didn't show much interest in her, a reaction she didn't often experience.

Maybe it was good to move slowly. She'd been thinking about her life since that day she ran into Beth at Whole Foods. Maybe Travis was more than a one-night stand. Maybe she needed to take a long-term approach with him.

"It's nobody," she said to her mother.

"Did I ever tell you how your father and I met?"

"You were working as a waitress."

"That's right, but did I ever tell you what he did?"

Emily didn't want to hear some long ago love story of her parents, but she decided to giver her mother five more minutes. She put her on speaker and began to wiggle into jeans and a T-shirt.

"One of the other waitresses came up to me and said, 'That guy over there paid for a drink, but he wanted you to bring it to him.' He was so shy. I didn't think I'd like him because he seemed so, oh, I don't know, normal, with his wire-framed glasses and his wool sweater. He'd been coming in for weeks before he finally got up enough nerve to ask me out."

Emily could hear a little affection creeping into her mother's voice, and she sat down on the end of her bed to listen.

"So, what happened?"

"Well, I took the drink over and set it on the table. He was so nervous. It was really cute. He asked if I'd go out with him, and I told him that I didn't date customers, so he said he'd never come back in my restaurant again if I'd go out with him."

That made Emily smile.

"Anyway, I didn't really want to go out with him, but he said he'd take me to any restaurant I wanted to go to in Austin. I was pretty poor back then, so that sounded like a good offer. I figured if I didn't like him at least I'd get a good meal out of the deal."

"So, what happened?"

"Well, he turned out to be charming. And I never went out with anybody else again. And the rest, as they say, is history."

"That's a nice story."

"I suppose the moral of the story is that sometimes the less glamorous man can be the right man."

So there it was, the life lesson. Nothing could ever be just a good story.

"Look, Barbara," Emily said, "I gotta go."

On her way out, Emily stopped to close her laptop. Before she powered down, she scrolled through the tiny photos of men she had tagged as possibilities on a dating website. She had told herself that it had been only curiosity that made her sign up, that it had nothing to do with her looming twenty-seventh birthday or her ten-year reunion.

She'd taken the chemistry test to help with matches. There were questions she'd never really asked herself. How much money did she need a guy to make? What religion did she prefer? Smoking or non? Did she have a political preference? Should he be athletic? Well-read? Artistic? Should he like music? What about traveling? Should he love animals? Would she date someone divorced? A man with children? Should he want to get married? To have children with her? It had taken Emily three attempts to finish the quiz and submit her preferences.

Then there was the other side of the equation. The part that required considerably more introspection than Emily liked. What did she have to offer a man? She wasn't financially solid. She didn't have an interesting career or even much education. She wasn't particularly cultured, unless you counted current music. She liked to eat but didn't really cook. Sure she was fun and spontaneous, but what man wants his wife bartending until two in the morning? On paper, she didn't have much to offer, and she'd had to resist the urge to fudge her profile.

Her matches were intriguing, although Emily suspected that a number of them had stretched the truth. The ones with flat abs drew her attention, but she made herself delete those immediately. No more ego trips. She clicked through the profiles, deleting any that said they had a four-wheeler or guns. She deleted any that seemed religious. She made a point of staying away from musicians since they tended to eat your food, sleep over, then vanish. She didn't particularly like bald guys, but a lot of them seemed to make up for their lack of hair with a whole lot of money. It would be great to go on a date with a guy who didn't look to her when it came time to buy a second round of drinks.

Maybe her mother had a point. Maybe sometimes the less glamorous man could be the right man. Perhaps it was time that she took a hard look at herself. What did she have to keep a man interested outside of the bedroom? What would make her a good mate? So far, she hadn't been able to commit to hardly anything. Why would a serious guy take a chance on her?

Emily was cowed by the prospect of connecting through such an artificial, screened arrangement, so she had read a few blogs with tips for successful online dating. One woman wrote that she always took a camera photo of a new date and texted the picture and the guy's info to a couple of friends. That way he knew he was identified, and she could relax and enjoy herself without being paranoid.

That one gave Emily pause. She had spent years dragging random men through her bed. Never once had she considered that what she was doing was dangerous. Never once had anything untoward happened to her. Was she just lucky?

She hadn't contacted any of her matches yet. She just couldn't bring herself to take that step. She'd received an invitation to the Austin Singles Roundup! Apparently, it was a meet-and-greet where people mingled and sized each other up. She envisioned this as a refined method of barhopping, where you swam in a concentrated pool of prospects. There seemed to be plenty of fish in the ocean, but after taking her chemistry test, Emily felt like a minnow.

Travis

AS USUAL, Emo's had a slamming band playing. During a break, the massive speakers blared Devo and everybody piled out on the dance floor cracking an imaginary whip. Travis doubted if any of the bar crowd was old enough to remember the early 80s.

He was nursing his third beer when he spotted Emily in the pulsing crowd. She was with a group flinging themselves around like high school kids. Maybe some of them were.

Her friends laughed and tumbled toward the bar, knocking into each other. They ordered and the bartender handed them clear plastic cups of iced yellowish liquid, probably vodka and Red Bull.

Like magnetism, Emily's eyes fell on his. She waved, and he lifted a few fingers her direction. The music cranked up again. She came toward him. Bass vibrated the bar under his fingertips.

"Hi!" she shouted as she shoved through people lined up at the bar.

"Hi."

"Are you following me?" She leaned into him. He could feel the heat coming off of her.

"Maybe."

She bit her bottom lip and something stirred in him.

"You like the band? Aren't they totally awesome?" Her T-shirt hugged her curves. Jeans rode low on her hips.

"Yeah, awesome."

He swirled beer around in his bottle and wished for a cigarette, anything to take his mind off the sections of sweaty hair stuck along her neck.

"Oh my God, you've got to come over to my house and see some of my photographs."

She was persistent. He had to give her that.

"Okay. When?"

"How about now? We're all just getting ready to go hang at my place. I'll show you my shots."

"A party at your house?"

"Sure. Come on over. I'll give you the address."

He handed her a pen. Emily shoved up his sleeve and wrote her address on the inside of his arm.

"You could have just written that on a napkin."

"What fun would that be?" She flung her hair over her shoulder and bounced away into the crowd.

Emily's friends were basically the same people Travis had hung out with in his twenties. The longhaired musicians went straight for the CDs and started fighting over what to play. The pale, thin vegan girl and her overly stoned boyfriend sat in the swing on the porch all night. There was the obligatory loud guy trying to impress two fashion victim girls with his shirt. The front pictured George Bush Sr. with the thought bubble, "I should have pulled out."

People came and went, the party swelling, getting loud and hot enough inside to push people out to the porch. At other times, the gathering would ebb until only a few people were scattered around listening to music. A debate raged on possible bands for future Austin City Limits and South by Southwest festivals.

Travis sauntered into the kitchen to grab a beer from a cooler. Outside the back door, two girls were perched on the top step, their outlines grainy through the screen door. One was crying while the other comforted her. The only thing missing was someone puking in the bushes in the side yard.

Twenty-something gatherings could be so weird when you passed thirty. His conversations at parties were typically more elevated than which beer had the most foam. Of course, if he drank enough beer he might regress.

But the thing that really marked you as an older dude was low-party endurance. About two he started to fade. He sat in the swing with Emily, trying to hang in. He suppressed a yawn.

"So, are you ever going to show me your photos or not?" he chided.

"Oh, I forgot. Stay right here." She was back in a moment with her MacBook. When she opened her photography file, Travis was suddenly awake. She'd captured gutter punks crawling out of dumpsters, some of them piled together sleeping in an alley. She had a series of action shots from a Hacky Sack game in the park. A couple of girls panhandled with a mangy mutt in front of a pet store. They had scored a bag of dog food far too large for them to carry.

"Impressive."

She smiled. "Thank you. Now, I'm going to show you something that I promised I wouldn't show anybody." She giggled, clearly more than a beer past her limit.

"Okay."

She clicked around on her laptop until she found the right image. The girl in the picture was hollow-eyed and haunting, a tattoo raking her face, her stomach nearly concave. She looked young and vulnerable and sexy and strange. Emily had shot her slightly overexposed, as if the girl were caught unawares, startled by the flash.

He turned the screen for a full-on study.

"This is an incredible shot. We have to use this one."

"Oh, sorry. No can do. I can't use any of this, girl. I promised her." She twisted her mouth in a contemplative way. "She's a strange little thing."

"We have to use this image. Get her permission."

"She'd never give it. She doesn't like to be photographed."

Suddenly, ZZ Top blared from the house.

"That's it, I'm pissed," she said. "Here, hold this." She passed the laptop to him and stomped over to her open front door.

"Guys," she yelled inside. His eyes followed the curve of her back under her tight shirt. "Guys!"

The music stopped.

"I hate to tell you this, but you know the drill," she said. "You don't have to go home . . ." They joined her in finishing the old bartender adage, *"But you can't stay here!"*

"That's right! Closing time. Vamoose. Chop. Chop. Get the hell out!" she said.

A few minutes later, the last of the late night partiers spilled out onto the front porch.

"Hey, man. Have a good one," one said as he walked off into the night.

"Yeah, see ya, man," Travis said. Emily crossed her arms and watched them disappear.

"That go for me too?" Travis asked her.

She smiled that crooked smile. "What? Am I running you off too?"

"Yeah."

She leaned against the doorframe. "Um, well. That depends."

"On what?"

"On you."

It was his turn to make a move. Travis ambled over to her, his eyes wandering down her neck, over her breasts and then lower to where skin peeked from the crevice between her shirt and jeans. She wasn't shy. She just stood there and let him look. He liked her confidence. Lust surged through him.

"Take off your bra."

She reached up under her shirt, unhooked her bra and pulled it out a sleeve. Her breasts fell heavy and full against the thin fabric.

"Anything else you'd like?"

"I'll see what I can think of," he said. He leaned in for the kiss, his hands cupping her, her nipples alert to his touch.

She tasted like honey beer. He walked her backward into the house. He pressed her into the sofa and kissed her, feeling her sharp little teeth, her warm willing tongue. Travis wedged himself between her legs and pressed. She ground against him until the metal buttons on their jeans caught. It caused them to laugh and broke their momentum.

"Come on," she said and took his hand.

He let himself be led to a back room where a queen-sized bed was still unmade from the previous night.

"Didn't your mother ever teach you to make up your bed?"

She laughed again. "What? And waste time on that when I could be doing this?"

She stripped off her jeans in one quick motion. She slid her tongue into his mouth and pulled him into cool, rumpled sheets. She ran her fingernails through his hair, and chills tingled his shoulders.

He pushed her away, shed his jeans and kicked them to the floor.

He flung his shirt on a chair.

When their flesh met it was like smooth fire.

Her breasts were soft as clouds, her nipples like velvet. He ran his tongue over her, in her mouth, along her salty neck, over the silky skin of her stomach, down in the heat between her legs. She swam in the sheets, breathless, quivering under him.

She pulled him up, and when he pushed inside her, he was rushed with pleasure so intense he had to concentrate to hold back. He pulled out and focused on her. He wasn't going to disappoint. They fucked for half an hour, hard and physical, like a competition.

Afterward, spent and proud of himself, Travis gathered his things and left Emily drowsy and content, her cheeks flushed, her hair sinuous across a pillow.

Emily

THE LAST time she had been with Lorelei was the day they went to that nasty apartment to retrieve her backpack. Lorelei had been sick and weird, had yelled at Emily in the car, then jumped out and stomped away. Emily hadn't heard from her in weeks, and then suddenly, out of the nowhere, Lorelei was on the phone, in crazy good spirits, asking if Emily would like to meet some of her friends. She promised to give her a feel for real street life, to show Emily things to photograph.

Emily found her talking with an older girl on the front steps of University Baptist. They were laughing, watching three guys kicking around a Hacky Sack. Lorelei wore a ratty plaid schoolgirl skirt with ripped black tights and a flouncy blouse Emily hadn't seen before.

"I like your new look," Emily said to ease into things.

Lorelei looked down at herself, and Emily could see she'd decided to be casual about the compliment.

"It's amazing what you can get from the library lost and found," the girl replied.

Emily just nodded. Did she really dress from lost and found boxes?

"This is Fiona," Lorelei said. "This is Emily."

"Hey," Emily said. "You're the friend who rescued Lorelei's backpack. That was cool."

"Right on," the girl said. "So a bunch of us are going over to this guy's house. He's got an old PlayStation 2. Wanna come?"

Emily hated dating gamers, so watching a bunch of juvenile guys yelling at a television had no appeal. But if she didn't go along she could forget about an afternoon with Lorelei and friends.

"This isn't going to be another skanky drug den like that Lawrence dude's place is it? Because I really don't feel like getting pierced or watching some snake digest a rat," Emily said.

"Ha," Fiona laughed. "That's funny. No. It's Mook's mom's place. She's cool. There's nothing going on there."

"Mook has a home?"

She shrugged. "A lot of us have homes, just not like, good ones with a warm bed where good ol' mom and pop are waiting up for us with milk and cookies."

Emily had never envisioned Drag kids as having any sort of home life. But it was reasonable that a few of them had families simply unable to care for them or parents who were plain ol' disinterested.

Within a couple of blocks they met with a familiar group of guys—Mook, Minion and Freestyle. Mook recognized Emily.

"What's she doing here?"

"She's with me," Lorelei said. "She's chill."

"I don't think so," he said.

Fiona interceded. "Oh, come on, Mook. You're bringing those idiots, so why can't my friends come? Betsy won't care."

He thought about it, then said, "No pictures, photo girl."

"No pictures," Emily promised.

"Well, let's go then," he said impatiently, as if his time were a most valuable commodity. He took off down the street. Freestyle let his skateboard clatter to the sidewalk. He stepped on and pushed off, his wheels making a zipper sound. Minion carried a guitar.

The girls followed. Fiona stopped to gaze in store windows, but the boys plowed ahead.

"Don't we need to keep up with them?" Emily asked.

"No biggie," Fiona said. "They'll be playing all afternoon."

Oddly, Lorelei and Fiona were drawn to pretty dresses, unlike their rough, ripped street style. Perhaps there was a time in their lives when they had party dresses, a time when they had been prized children. Emily imagined them without their rough edges, in pastels instead of black. Clean and rested and fed girls. Girls who went to high school and proms and took dance lessons and learned to play the piano. How were they before they hit the streets? How long had they lived this way?

The apartment complex had seen better days. The pool had
been dry so long that people had filled the bottom with flowerpots
and plastic patio chairs. Summer's plants were wilted. A couple had
only stalks left, which made Emily think something must have been
harvested from them.

Fiona led the way upstairs and let herself into a unit by the street.
Inside, the boys surrounded an old thirty-inch television, their faces
scrunched in concentration. Emily recognized the rapid-fire blasts
and thundering detonations of *Call of Duty*. They groaned in unison.
A frail woman smoked a cigarette in the kitchen. Fiona went forward
and kissed her on the cheek.

"Hi, sweetie," the woman said, and pushed back the dreads
around Fiona's face.

"Hey, Betsy. How you feeling?"

"Some days are better than others."

"These are my friends, Lorelei and Emily."

They both said, "Hey." You could tell that Betsy had once been
attractive, but her face had the furrowed look of a smoker and her
voice was gravely and deep. Her winged 70s hairstyle was flecked
with gray.

"I'd offer you girls something to eat, but I just don't have a thing
in the house," Betsy said.

"That's okay. We just ate," Fiona said, although that was unlikely.

The den erupted in hysteria, but in ten seconds there came
another massive groan.

Betsy grinned thinly. "They sure do like those games."

Minion was perched on an arm of the sofa, his guitar balanced
on one thigh.

"Can you play that thing or is it just for effect?" Emily asked him.

He began to pick out chords, and she immediately recognized
a Radiohead song. He had a nice voice. His music drew the girls to
him. Within a few bars the game was paused and all the kids had
joined in. They sang about being a creep, about being a weirdo.
About wishing they were special.

Betsy put the cigarette to her lips and inhaled.

"I hate that song," she said to Emily. "These songs these kids
like, they're so sad and negative."

"Sometimes it's hard to stay positive."

"You got that right," Betsy said. "I've got this fibromyalgia, and I can't work no more. Disability barely gets me by, and my son can't live with me or I lose my apartment, but you don't see me moaning about it. Singing songs about how bad I got it."

"They're kids."

"I love 'em all. They're good, you know. They're all good kids. They got their whole lives ahead of them. I try to get my son to go back to school, but he thinks it's romantic to live on the street. Well, he won't think that when he's my age. I've never been homeless, but I've been damn close. That shit ain't funny."

They finished their song, and Betsy broke in.

"You girls come outside with me so I don't smoke everybody out," she said.

They followed her tiny frame out onto the second-story walkway that looked down on the forlorn pool below. From the back, Betsy appeared young in her worn jeans and baggy T-shirt. You could feel the girl inside, but hard life had nearly extinguished her. She had smoked her cigarette down to the filter, so she lighted another from the butt.

"You girls being careful?" she asked. "There's lots of crazy people out there, crazy men. You stay around my Johnny. He'll take care of you. Johnny's a good boy."

"Johnny?" Emily asked.

Fiona laughed. "Mook. Johnny. Whatever."

"Where's Elda?" Betsy asked.

"She's taking the GED today," Fiona said.

"Well, good for her," Betsy said. "Good for her. I like that Elda." She reached up and touched Fiona's cheek. "But you'll always be my favorite."

Fiona saw Emily's curiosity, so she said, "I used to be Mook's girlfriend. We broke up. Elda's cool with it, but I don't get to see Betsy as much as I'd like to. Betsy's like my mom. Betsy's like everybody's mom."

Lorelei

BETSY'S BATHROOM was so clean it made Lorelei long to take a bath. It had been months since she'd soaked in a tub, but she didn't dare take advantage. Betsy had seemed pleased she had something to share, but Mook felt differently.

"Just don't stay in there too long," he'd warned Fiona. "Mom has to pay the water bill."

"Chill out, Johnny boy," Fiona said.

Lorelei stepped into the spray of water and turned it hot against her back. She ran conditioner through her hair, separating knots with her fingers. She lost track of time as the sensation caressed her body. One of the boys banged on the door, snapping her back to reality. Lorelei ignored his knock, but she reluctantly got out of the shower.

After she had dried off, Lorelei looked inside the medicine cabinet for nail clippers and found dozens of prescription bottles. She wondered how sick Betsy must be. She checked the labels. Some were pain meds, others she had never heard of. She knew Mook's friends would steal the pain pills.

"Get out of the way," Fiona said on the other side of the door. There was a knock. "Lorelei, let me in. I've got something for you."

She unlocked the door and Fiona slipped inside.

"Here," she said. "Look what I got." Tags dangled from the

clothing she pulled from her bag. "Pick out something. Last week me and some friends did a commando on the steampunk store."

Lorelei picked out a frilly top and skirt with a jagged hem. She pulled them on and stretched to look at herself in the tiny mirror on the medicine cabinet.

"Cute," Fiona said. "Take these tights. I got, like, five pairs of those things."

The tights were as soft as clouds on her legs.

"These feel great."

"I know, right?"

Fiona had introduced Lorelei to steampunk—fingerless gloves, layered skirts, ruffled shirts, top hats, old trousers and leather jewelry with clock gears. Some of the kids even wore goggles, which reminded Lorelei of the old movie *Chitty Chitty Bang Bang*. Steampunk was more like costuming than dressing. The style reminded her of the artwork in her mangas and graphic novels.

"Try this," Fiona said, handing Lorelei a tube of fuchsia lip gloss. A few minutes later, the two emerged from the bathroom with black-rimmed eyes and bright lips. Lorelei even wore a fake nose ring held in place by a magnet.

Freestyle, immune to the girls' transformation, pushed past them.

"It's about damn time," he grumbled, and slammed the bathroom door. Fiona went to the wall phone in Betsy's kitchen and made a call. Lorelei looked around for Emily, but didn't see her.

"Where'd Emily go?" she asked Mook.

"She split," he said without taking his eyes from his game. "Said she had to go to work."

Fiona hung up the phone and came into the front room.

"Gotta fly. Wanna come?"

Lorelei shrugged. "I got nowhere else to go."

The girls said their goodbyes to Betsy and walked down to the road, where they sat on a low wall. A few minutes passed and a shiny black BMW pulled up to the curb. Fiona walked over.

"Don't stand there like some stupid hooker, bitch," the driver said.

Fiona opened the back door and slid in. Lorelei followed. The car pulled into traffic. The driver was a gangsta-wannabe, a white guy with grills, chains and probably other, more dangerous, hardware tucked away somewhere. The front seat passenger was a casually dressed black guy who seemed to be in charge.

The black guy turned around and said, "What you got for me, Fi?"

Fiona pulled out a wad of cash and handed it to him.

"Now that's what I'm talking 'bout," he said. He reached into the console between the front seats and handed Fiona a small brown paper bag. "Same deal. We cool?"

"Yeah, sure," Fiona said. "Cool."

The guy smiled. "Excellent. And what about your friend here? How about it sweetheart? You wanna do a little business?"

"What about it Lorelei, you want to earn some cash?" Fiona asked. "It's really easy."

Panic tightened Lorelei's stomach. She'd been around drugs enough to know that dealers were never friends. She'd seen what they did to people who pissed them off. She rubbed her hands up and down her arms to ease the flare of tingle from her tattoos. She had to get away.

"No thanks," Lorelei said. "I'm good."

"Fi, your friend a little junkie?" the dealer said. "Look like something got a hold on her."

"Nah," Fiona said. "I think she's clean."

Lorelei began to rock. She needed to get out of the car.

"Riiiight." He dragged the word out. He held money toward her. "How about I spot you a twenty and we'll call it an advance in case you change your mind?"

Lorelei just stared at the money.

"Take it," Fiona said, but Lorelei couldn't bring her hand up to grasp the offered bills.

"Go on," the guy said. "Never mind about the deal. Just take it and get something to eat. You too damn skinny, girl."

She took the money, then stuffed it into a pocket.

"We finished," he said to the driver.

They pulled up to the curb along the Colorado River near a section of the Town Lake river walk.

"Shit," Fiona said. "Can't you take me back downtown?"

"Naw, baby. We ain't headed that way. You getting out here."

Fiona didn't argue. She opened the door and stepped out onto the wide sidewalk. Lorelei scooted across to get out behind her when the dealer reached around and grabbed her arm. A flash of terror ripped through her.

"I'll be looking for you," he said. "Pretty bird girl."

Lorelei shook off his hold and got out. The car accelerated before the back door even closed.

"Well, that's just fucking great. Dump us out here. Shit," Fiona said.

"It's not that far back."

"Couple of miles. Let's go down to the walkway and then cut up the Shoal Creek Greenway. Maybe Mook will be back at camp."

"Don't you think he's staying the night at Betsy's?"

"Who knows? Come on. I don't like to walk up on the street when I'm carrying this much."

Lorelei followed Fiona down to the river. It was dark and few people lingered. A couple of guys were kissing on a park bench. In the distance, an old homeless man pulled a metal shopping caddy behind him, his dirty possessions trailing along the crushed gravel path. He turned off onto a trail Lorelei knew led along Shoal Creek. It wasn't a polished park path like the one around Town Lake. The Shoal Creek trail was rough, natural terrain that connected a few public spaces along the way. It was an artery the homeless used to move around below street level.

Lorelei's tats tingled again, and she said, "I got this twenty. Let's get a cab back."

"Keep your money. I'll let you buy me a breakfast burrito."

They walked toward the spot where the old guy disappeared toward the creek. Then they heard voices.

"Here comes some customers," Fiona said, and stopped.

"Don't do that now," Lorelei said. "Can't you wait until we get back?"

"Look, I need some cash. Chillax."

Three guys sauntered toward them, shadows moving over them as they walked in and out of the path's lighting. They were dressed in jeans and fleece jackets. They all had hats pulled low.

"Hey," Fiona said as they neared.

"Hey fellows. Look what we got here," one of them said. Lorelei smelled alcohol and cigarettes, but there was something else about them that made her skin crawl.

"You looking to score?" Fiona asked.

"That depends. What you got?" one guy said.

Fiona motioned for them to step into the shadows of the trailhead. Two of them followed her. Lorelei lagged behind, and that was when she noticed that the third guy had a tiny video camera.

The guy brought the camera up to his eye and started filming.

"Hey, put that thing away," Fiona said.

"Man, you're bossy," one of them said. "You holding or not?"

"Put away the camera or no deal," Fiona said.

"Come on, man," another one said. "I don't want to mess with these skanks."

"That's so uncool, man," Fiona said. "You wanna do business or not?"

"Maybe we'll just take what you got, junkie."

"Fuck off," Fiona said.

Their laughter crawled through Lorelei. She saw the baseball bat that one held down by his side, and a sick wave of adrenaline surged to her legs. She checked for escape routes. Woods surrounded them. She couldn't outrun the boys in her heavy boots.

"Ooooooh. She's a tough girl. That right? You a tough girl, skank?"

"You're the skank."

"Stop," Lorelei said. "Stop it. She didn't mean anything by it."

All three guys turned toward Lorelei.

"You got something to say, Miss Ink Stain? What's with all those tattoos? You think you're some tough shit too?"

"No," Lorelei said.

That was when she felt the stings on her leg, blinding pain that made her fall to the ground. Two bright splashes of yellow spread across her black tights. They'd shot her with a paintball gun.

"Shoot her again," the one with the bat said.

"No. Please. Just leave us alone," Lorelei said. "Please."

"We don't want your kind in our parks, brushing your teeth in our water fountains, making everything smell like piss." The guy with the gun shot her again, this time in the ankle. He turned his bravado on the camera. "People pick up after their dogs, but you bums just leave your shit where you drop it, like wild animals."

"Yeah," the one with the bat said. "Like animals. That's what you are." He raised the bat at Fiona. She scrambled backward and fell against tree roots.

He began his swing. She braced for the blow. He balked. She cowered. They laughed, a drunken, hateful chorus.

"Hey," the one with the bat said. He pointed farther down the path. "There's an old one."

Leaving the terrified girls, the first two took off. The cameraman
hesitated, then he turned and hissed, "Get out of here."

The stalkers moved quickly, silently, melting into the shadows
of the path.

"Bum hunters," Fiona said. "They're going to beat down that old
guy."

The girls stood paralyzed. They heard distant voices, then a cry
for help.

"We should find a cop," Lorelei said.

"No time," Fiona said. "They're going to kill him."

Without warning, the homeless man tumbled out of the darkness.
The tattered old guy made a noble escape attempt, but the boys were
on him like wolves. One held him down while another kicked him
in the stomach. The cameraman moved smoothly, careful to get all
angles of the scuffle. One kick snapped the man's head back and he
vomited violently.

"Stop it!" Fiona screamed. "Stop it!"

The kicker lunged for Fiona and caught her by her hair. Fiona
kicked at him and caught him in the shin with a heavy boot.

"Fuck that hurt!" he yelled. "Big mistake, skank."

The one with the bat came toward Lorelei, and a flock of birds
took flight in her chest. She couldn't outrun him or fight him off
empty-handed.

Her assailant closed in with the bat. His eyes were black and
soulless. Hate floated on his breath. She was hit from the side and
sent sprawling onto the walkway, air knocked from her lungs. She
lay crunched up on her side, hoping they would turn their fury back
to the old man. Her line of vision was askew, fuzzy at the edges,
but she could make out Fiona's thrashing boots as her friend was
dragged into the darkness of the trees.

Barbara

"WHAT'S THE matter with you?"

"What?" Gerald mumbled. They were watching one of the last games of UT's season play. They used to go to every home game of their alma mater, but like other things they'd enjoyed in the past, season football tickets were now too expensive.

"I asked you if you wanted some popcorn. You've been so distracted lately. What's going on with you?"

"Huh?"

"Never mind. Lord." She went into the kitchen and got out the popcorn maker. The crowd erupted, and Barbara looked up to see an ocean of orange and white fluttering on the plasma screen. It's true that a widescreen is always the best seat in the house, but Barbara missed tailgating and the electricity of the stadium.

Normally, Gerald would have yelled, "Touchdown!" Today, he just sat plastered to his chair, only grunting if something went wrong with a play.

Barbara wondered if he was slipping back into depression. It was something she fought off herself. The thrum of financial struggle was always in the background, a constant gnaw on their psyches.

Recently, they'd had to dip into Emily's unused college fund. Gerald had insisted that her money was not to be touched, but Barbara's attitude was, use it or lose it. She certainly wasn't going to give her daughter the money for anything other than college.

Gerald had put on a little weight. He ate when he wasn't happy. He still hadn't made peace with the customer service position he'd landed a couple of years ago selling computers for Dell. He had complained a lot at first—he deserved to be in development, it wasn't enough money, there were no opportunities for advancement, his talents were being overlooked. After a while he stopped complaining and just trudged off to work each morning with his head hung. It was hard on him, going from senior staff to peon, but at least being a peon brought home a paycheck. They still had friends who had been unemployed for years because they wouldn't take a job they felt was beneath them.

Or maybe there was something else going on. Things had been cool in the bedroom for years. Was it possible he had found a new love interest and guilt was pulling him down? Barbara doubted it was somebody at the office. She couldn't imagine that her husband would ever have enough gumption to rustle up a little ass on the side, but then she'd come to realize that anything is possible.

Over the past few years, they'd watched their friends' marriages dissolve as quickly as their bank accounts. When there was plenty of money, everybody could stay together. Even couples that were apparently unhappy continued to vacation together and show up for cocktail parties, less to keep up appearances than just to avoid the drama of divorce. Why upset the kids? Even infidelities could be overlooked when nobody was willing to change their lifestyle.

But when money problems forced a lifestyle change anyway, couples split up. Love didn't seem to count for much of the equation in modern marriage. Today, marriage was more a partnership, a business venture void of romance, so when things went sour there was very little affection to keep couples together.

Luckily, she and Gerald had somehow managed to stay glued. They had true affection for each other. At least she still did for him, at least most of the time she did. But he was so stoic that she couldn't always read him. Still, she didn't think he would take a chance on infidelity. Divorce would certainly bankrupt them both, so it seemed that common sense, just basic practicality, would keep him from straying. So perhaps they weren't so different than other couples that stayed together out of convenience.

Or maybe it wasn't some big secret. Maybe he was just going through a midlife crisis. She'd read a magazine article about male menopause caused by a gradual decline in testosterone. It said the symptoms could be fatigue, weakness, depression and sexual problems.

Just great, Barbara thought, recalling the article. *Something else to look forward to.*

The popcorn maker whined and spun the kernels in its heated centrifuge. She loved the slightly burned smell that always came out first. As the popcorn began its tiny staccato explosions there was a television timeout. A local news brief came on. Barbara couldn't hear it over the popcorn noise, but she could see police sedans and people standing around at night looking concerned and confused.

The screen cut to people strolling through a mall, shopping bags dangling from their hands, little kids trailing behind. Holiday decorations littered the scene behind them.

The popcorn maker whirred and spit out fat white puffs. Barbara stared at her husband's bald spot above his chair in the other room. Emily had said she didn't detect anything amiss with her father, but how could she? Gerald had never shown their daughter his weak side, never let her in on problems. He insisted that they always hide troubles from her, never fight in front of her. Always avoid conflict. Act as if nothing is ever wrong. He wanted her life to be easy, but really, had he done her any favors?

Barbara dumped popcorn into separate bowls and shook organic cheddar salt on top. She had long ago nixed the real salt and butter Gerald liked so much.

"What was on the news?" she asked when she handed him his bowl. She slid back onto the couch and tucked her feet up under her.

"Ah, something down around Town Lake. Somebody got mugged or something."

"That all? There sure was a lot of response for just a mugging. What was the other story about?"

"Some big Thanksgiving sale. I don't know what. Apparently, retail sales are projected to be up this year."

"Well, that's a relief. I can't wait for this economy to turn around."

Emily

SHE ADJUSTED the flight on one of her darts, aimed and nailed the bull's eye. Her opponent grumbled under his breath. Emily was hot even though she was distracted by thoughts of her lusty night with Travis. She was remembering the scratch of his beard on her skin, their smell lingering in the room when she awoke in the morning.

Emily was angry with herself for being so quick to jump into bed with him, but old habits died hard. It had been a while since their hookup and not a word from him. She hadn't expected a call the next morning, but by now she expected he would have at least sent her a courtesy text.

Maybe she'd take another look at that dating site. Figure out how to go on a proper date with a fellow who might actually turn out to have a little moral character or at least some sort of future.

"Hey Emily, did you hear about the dead girl?" someone behind her asked.

She stopped mid-throw, "What dead girl?"

It was one of her regulars. A cop. "Right down there around Town Lake. Street kid, I think."

"When did this happen?"

"I saw the lights coming over here. Just other side of the bridge. Stopped to see if they needed an assist."

She handed her darts over to a friend.

"Here, finish my game," she said.

Behind the bar, she opened the drawer where she stashed all the business cards guys left for her. On top was Lorelei's social worker. She stuffed the card into a pocket and punched Travis's number on speed dial on her way out. It certainly wouldn't hurt her position with him if she gave him a lead on a story.

She rolled her bike into the alley and pressed Travis's number. It rang only once and went to voice mail.

"Travis, it's Emily. It's about one a.m. and I'm headed down to Town Lake. One of my cop customers said they just found the body of a street kid on the walk. A girl. Call me."

It took only five minutes for her to ride down to the lake. The spot wasn't hard to find. She just followed the blue lights raking the dark tree line.

Emily prayed that the dead girl wasn't Lorelei. The few times Lorelei had opened up she had talked about begging drunks for money. Maybe one of her early morning spanging marks had turned on her. Or she was prostituting. That never turned out good.

Or maybe she'd overdosed. She'd told of sitting in fast-food joints all night, nursing a cup of coffee so they wouldn't run her off, but nobody could go night after night without sleeping. That meant some sort of stimulant. Meth users didn't sleep. Coke users didn't sleep either, but that was an expensive drug. She could be huffing. *Chroming* the kids called it now. Maybe she had a run-in with her drug dealer. Finding her passed out in Chuy's landscaping had pretty much solidified her as a user in Emily's mind.

A group of uniforms and lights collected in a wooded part of the park. The body wasn't yet covered, and Emily caught her breath. The girl was face down in a tangle of autumn leaves, her head covered by a dirty sweatshirt. Her pleated skirt and hole-riddled tights seemed untouched. She looked flung down, discarded, heavy boots at odd angles, arms loose in their sockets. Tears rushed to Emily's eyes.

She saw Travis was already there, busy talking to people, taking notes. He probably hadn't even listened to her message yet.

Crime scene took photos. EMS put the body in a black glossy bag and hauled it up out of the park. They walked not ten feet from Emily. A city cop labored up the hill behind them as if he carried the world in the girl's worn out backpack. A weird watch face and a couple of cogs dangled from a zipper. Emily had seen that pack before.

She suddenly wished for her camera and then felt guilty for the impulse. She heard someone say, "Homicide."

David appeared, hands shoved deep into his pockets, his head down as he came up the hill toward her.

"It's not her," he said.

"I thought as much," Emily said. "That's not Lorelei's backpack. Do you know the girl?"

"She calls herself Fiona," he said.

"Oh, I know her." Emily couldn't stop herself from raising a hand to her mouth in horror. She now knew a dead person, a murdered person. Someone younger than she was. It seemed impossible.

"She's a good kid." He struggled for what to say next. "Was a good kid. A little messed up, but . . ."

"I'm so sorry."

"What? No. This happens."

"Not in my world."

He sighed and hung his head again. "Now I have to make a phone call."

She waited for him to go on. Blue lights flashed across his weary eyes.

"Her mother called a while back looking for her. I'd been trying to get Fiona to respond. Maybe go home. But she wouldn't even talk to me about it. I have to call her mother back. Better coming from me than from the morgue."

She looked down the hill at Travis. He was talking to the cops, scribbling on his long notepad, unshaken by any of it.

"You going to tell the police?" Emily asked.

"Not yet," David said. "I mean, I'm pretty sure Fiona is this woman's daughter, but she'll have to provide some positive ID. That is if she even wants to come get the body."

Lorelei

She had accompanied Mook and Elda to the plasma center, a ritual of the homeless who could fake a permanent address. Every week, sometimes multiple times, they sold their plasma for twenty dollars a pop by claiming they lived with his mother.

Lorelei, who couldn't prove she was of age and didn't have an address, wasn't allowed to join her friends in the donation area with lounge chairs. Instead, she waited in the lobby in hard-molded plastic while her friends had their blood filtered.

She hadn't told them anything about what had happened in the park the night before. She was afraid they would turn on her for not defending Fiona. After all, Fiona was one of them. They might force her out, or worse, Mook might make her talk to some of the cops he knew. So she had told them that she and Fiona had gone their separate ways after Betsy's.

Everybody in town already knew about Fiona's death. It was all over the news. Lorelei had watched it twice on the small television mounted to the waiting room wall. Speculation was a drug related crime, an implication that her dealer had killed her. Another theory was tension between street tribes. Then there was the person who saw an old hobo with bloody hands come from the same area of the park. He was a prime suspect. They'd found his shopping caddy near the body.

Would anyone ever know the truth? The old man made a

comeback, ramming her assailant from behind. She was suddenly
clawing her way from underneath the fight. She ran and didn't look
back. She saw a blue emergency call box. She tore away the shield
and flipped the handle. She ran again, staggering up a ramp to
street level. She made it down an alley where she crouched behind
a dumpster and listened for footfalls. She waited, wild with terror.
She watched, hoping her friend would emerge from the park, fearing
their attackers would appear instead.

For many minutes, she waited, blood pounding in her ears, fear
like metal in her mouth. She didn't know how long she waited, but
her legs began to ache, and she touched the spots where she had
been shot and winced. She was about ready to give up and move
on when she saw movement on the ramp. Her heart leaped, then
fell. Painfully, slowly, the beaten and bloody old man rose from the
depths of the park. He walked several feet, then stopped to brace
himself against a handrail.

Lorelei wanted to rush to him and ask what had happened to
her friend. She stood and cautiously moved his direction, but sirens
suddenly blared, and she stepped back into the alley. Two cop cars
converged on the spot. Officers poured out of the vehicles and rushed
down the ramps.

When Lorelei checked again, the old man had disappeared. Only
a bloody handprint on a railing remained.

The old hobo had saved her, but he hadn't been able to save
Fiona. Maybe he hadn't intended to save either one of them.
Self-preservation was most likely his only ambition. Wasn't that
everybody's main goal, including her own? Lorelei figured that as
soon as the thugs realized they had killed Fiona they had forgotten
all about the old man and fled. He hadn't fought them off, they'd just
decided to save themselves too.

Through the plasma center's grimy windows Lorelei spotted
a familiar face across the street. Angel was standing outside a
nondescript building with a cluster of smokers. Lorelei knew an AA
meeting when she saw one. She could pick them out in every city,
no matter the time of day or how clandestine the location. She had
a sudden urge to cross the street and throw her arms around the
stocky Mexican cook. He'd been kind, but she couldn't risk that he
would be sympathetic again.

Mook and Elda came out with tan bandages around their
elbows. Down the street, Mook sprang for a bag of tacos from a

corner vendor, then they took a city bus to the Ramp Ranch, the new free skate park. Mook planned to be scarce so cops wouldn't question them about Fiona. Lorelei normally loved skate parks, had practically lived in them in L.A., but today the rasp of boards against concrete wasn't satisfying.

The skate park was organized chaos. Boys were lined up five deep on each end of the bowl to drop in. Freestyle had scrawled Fiona's name on his board, then pushed off toward a section of stairs where other guys were grinding a rail.

"She doesn't want to spend eternity with that pedophile stepdad standing over her grave," Mook said. Elda insisted that he had to clue the police into Fiona's personal life. If he didn't, she would be buried in a pauper's grave. Lorelei kept tight lipped on the subject.

A boy in skinny jeans zoomed by like a superhero, his shirt flapping behind. His board made a monster zip when he ripped tile at the lip of the bowl below them.

"If I ever find out who killed her I'm going to kill that fucker myself. I was hoping she just OD'ed. Went out high. That would be the way to go."

"It happens," Elda said to Lorelei. "A bunch of people decide they don't like gutter punks, and they start picking us off one by one."

Another bare chested boy sailed by, and Lorelei checked out the winged wheels on his shoulder. Suddenly, he jacked his board onto a rail with a loud ping and scraped down the metal edge. He fell and quickly recovered, but the knees of his pants were mangled.

A couple of boys on BMX bikes laughed at his wipeout. "Epic fail!" they called. They gave him the hook 'em horns hand signal every Texas fan knew.

"Fuck. There's Travis," Mook said. At the far end of the park was a guy Lorelei recognized. She'd seen him around, talking to other kids.

"Who's he?" Lorelei asked.

"Reporter for *Be Here Now*," Elda said. "Travis Roberts."

A couple of the gay skaters whooshed by, scarves around their heads, the ends flying behind them. A skinhead waited his turn, a cigarette dangling from his snarl. The reporter walked up to the skinhead and started talking. He lit the skater's smoke, then one of his own.

They watched as the reporter made his way along the edges of the park, talking to clusters of people. Lorelei expected Mook to wander away, but he just sat on the wall waiting.

"Mook, man. Zup?" the reporter said.

"I just can't get away from you, can I?" Mook smirked.

"Now you hurt my feelings. Why don't you introduce me to your friend?"

Mook gestured. "This here is Lorelei. This is Travis. He's our local do-good reporter of all things political. He's a liberal at heart, but don't cross him or he'll write some shit about you."

"I'm flattered. Hey, what do you guys think about the improvements to the park?"

"That what your story is about? I thought you were probably here to ask around about Fiona. That's why we got the hell out of Dodge. We don't want to talk about her."

"So you came out here to avoid the po-po? It's not very far out."

"Good enough to lose them. Not good enough to lose you, I guess."

"I know she was your woman once. I'm sorry, man." Travis frowned and kicked at the pavement. He looked into the distance, pulled on his cigarette. "It's got to be hard."

Mook stomped one end of his board and popped it into his hand. "Look, I came here to skate." He shoved off and glided away.

"What about you? You know anything about Fiona?" Travis asked the girls. Elda just walked away, but Lorelei stayed.

"You're not really writing about the park. Are you?"

He shrugged. "Looking for a story."

She shrugged back, mimicking him. "Well, I don't talk to reporters. You guys always get it wrong."

"I've seen you around. How long have you been in Austin?"

"A while."

"Where you from?"

"Everywhere. Nowhere."

"Yeah, right. So what do you think happened to Fiona? I understand she had a bad habit."

"So? Who doesn't? You should find out what happened to her. That would make you a good reporter. Us kids, we don't know nothing."

"Somebody knows something," he said. He smoked for a while, leaving the line of conversation open.

Elda returned. "Hey, let's go grab a wash at Mickey D's."

"I'm down." Lorelei grabbed her pack and roll. "Later."

They hiked across a field, briars picking at their legs. They dodged traffic to cross a busy road to a McDonald's. A honey-haired mother saw them coming and hurriedly crammed her child into a car seat. She climbed into the SUV and slammed her own door before the girls drew near. As they walked by, the young mother's caution registered in oval reflective surfaces. The car's locks engaged.

They slipped in a side entrance and went directly to the bathroom, hoping for a single with a lock on the door, but there was no such luck. At least the bathroom had two sinks. Elda filled one with warm soapy water. She took a handful of the brown paper towels and used them to bathe.

Lorelei brushed her teeth, then flossed. She was pulling the slick thread through her molars when the door opened and in walked a rotund woman with a child dangling from either hand.

"Oh," the woman said. "Oh, excuse me." She tugged the children out the door. One cried out, "But I gotta pee pee!"

"Better hurry," Elda said.

A minute later, the door flung wide, and a manager was standing there, all polyester and greasy face.

"You have to leave. This restroom is for paying customers only."

"We are paying customers," Elda said bluntly. "If you'll just give us a chance."

"Yeah," Lorelei said. "Can't wait for the Big Mac and fries. Yum. I'm lovin' it."

"We're not serving you," the manager said. "Leave now and don't come back. I'm sick of you trashy kids thinking you can come in here and wash your hair in a restaurant's bathroom. That's unsanitary. Don't they have places for your kind?"

"Our kind?" Lorelei took a halfhearted swipe at the woman, who jumped back out the door. It swished closed.

Elda sighed. "Shit. Now you've done it. Let's go."

Back across the road, they ran through the brushy field to the skate park. Mook was waiting for them.

"We gotta split," Elda said. "Lorelei scared the manager over at Mickey D's. Five-oh are probably already on their way."

"Oh my God, did you see her face?" Lorelei said. "She was, like, totally freaking."

"'That's unsanitary,'" Elda said in a mocking high-pitched voice. "'Don't they have places for *your kind*?'"

"But we scared her I think," Lorelei said. "We scared her good."

"Of course you scared her," Mook said. "Somebody with nothing to lose is the scariest person of all."

Emily

EMILY PERUSED the short article "Body Found at Town Lake" online in the city's main newspaper. Authorities had released a thorough description, including details of the tattoos on Fiona's body, but no one had come forward to identify her. The reporter wrote about obvious signs of trauma on the body of the girl, "known simply as Fiona." It was noted that she had not been shot. Police asked anyone who had seen the girl in recent days to contact them.

She hoped Travis would do a more thorough job covering the story when *Be Here Now* came out later in the week. Fiona deserved more.

Her doorbell chimed and a soft knock followed.

The last person Emily expected to see on her doorstep was her father. He looked sheepish and a little sweaty.

"Hey, what are you doing here?"

"Hey, honey. I just wanted to come by and see you. Is that okay?"

"Well, sure. Come on in."

He followed her inside.

"You want some coffee or tea? A Coke maybe?"

"Coffee would be nice."

"Fine. Come on in the kitchen and talk to me while I make it."

"Okay."

He sat at her table and watched her measure out coffee and pour water.

"So," Emily said as she got cups out of the cabinet. "What's up?"

In all her days of living here, her father had never paid a spontaneous social call. He was always with her mother or he came with a specific purpose like delivering something.

He cleared his throat and ran a nervous hand through his remaining hair. This last gesture made her heart flutter, and she settled into the chair across from him.

"Something's wrong," she said flatly.

"Well, no reason to beat around the bush anymore. I think I'm going to lose my job."

"Oh, Dad. No. Are you sure?"

He nodded. "Pretty sure. Yes. I'm positive."

She had a flash of memory of the day after the flood at home. He'd been making pancakes, and he'd told her he needed to speak with her about something, but she'd gotten distracted, and then she'd never followed up.

"Is this what you wanted to talk to me about?"

He nodded again. "I . . . I've been thinking it was going to happen. Now, I'm sure."

"You'll just have to find another job. I know you can do it."

He let go a small breathy chuckle. "Right. Right."

"Dad, you're a great guy. You're super smart. I know you'll find another job."

He shook his head and she saw what she thought was a tear. "I'm afraid your mother will leave me this time."

"Oh, no. Don't think that. She'd never leave you."

"No. She would. I know she would. Our lives, our marriage. None of it has lived up to her expectations. I made promises to her before we were married. Promises that I haven't kept."

"Like what?"

"I told her I'd always take care of her, but look how things have turned out. It's the other way around. Now, she's taking care of me."

"You guys are taking care of each other. You're a team. So what? When one of you is down the other one holds things together. There's no shame in that. Has she *said* she's going to leave you?"

"No, but I can feel it. Maybe I don't blame her. Maybe I'd leave me too if I were her."

"That's crazy talk. She's not going to leave you." But then Emily thought about it and reconsidered. There was, actually, the very real possibility that her mother would walk away. Say what you will about Barbara Bryce, but she was always a survivor.

"They're only giving four weeks severance. Four weeks. One month. That's nothing."

"Are you guys pressed, financially I mean?"

He nodded again, a pitiful thing. "I'm not going to lie to you. We're stretched pretty thin."

Emily thought things were bad, but she hadn't known just how bad. They had scaled back, tried to get things under control. But apparently the loss of her father's job could be catastrophic for them.

"I didn't want her to know until I was sure." He shook his head. "Oh, I'm so sorry. I shouldn't have come here and burdened you with this."

"No. No. I'm glad to help. I'll keep my ears open. If I hear of any jobs I'll let you know, but I don't usually run with the software crowd."

He just nodded.

"Maybe it's time to reinvent yourself. Do something different. Go into business for yourself."

"You need start-up capital to do that. Besides, I don't know what I would do. I can't think of any retail business that would be good to start in this economy, and I wouldn't know how to run something like a restaurant. I'm too old to go work somewhere that's manual labor. I'm out of luck."

"Geez, come on. You're not obsolete just yet."

He looked around her little kitchen and fidgeted. The coffee maker spurted and groaned, indicating it had completed its job. Emily got up to fill their mugs and then it hit her.

"What about my college money? You guys still have that, right?"

"Sure. But I don't want to even think about your money. It needs to be there for you. You know, when you decide you want it."

"Why don't you use that for start-up money? You can pay the account back when you start making a profit. Be your own man, that way you don't ever have to worry about getting fired ever again."

"I won't use your money."

She handed him his coffee, black.

"That's stupid. Of course you'll use it. You saved it. It's technically your money."

"No. I don't see that as an option."

"Okay. But just think about it."

Her cell phone rang. She hated that it happened once again at a crucial time with her father.

David's name appeared.

"I hate to do this," she said. "Is it okay if I take this?"

"Of course, don't let me interrupt," her father said.

She took the call in her bedroom. "Hey David. What's up?"

"How'd you like to go for a ride?"

"Where?"

"I'm going to check a few locations kids like to hang out, away from downtown. The skate park. Barton Springs. Something bad happens like the Fiona thing and they make themselves scarce."

"Looking for Lorelei?"

"Among others."

When she came out of the bedroom, her father was standing by the front door.

"No. Wait. Don't leave."

"I've bothered you enough for one day. Please don't say anything to your mother until I have a chance to talk to her."

"I won't. Look, I know how you feel. Mom has super-high expectations. I've spent my entire life trying to please her. I finally grew up and gave up. You can only do what you can do. You don't owe her anything."

His smile was weak. "That's not exactly true, honey. When you're married you'll understand."

"Maybe. If I ever get married."

"Well," he hedged a moment before he leaned forward and kissed her on the cheek. "You'll find somebody. You're just being picky, and that's a good thing."

Her heart ached at his sad smile.

He reached up and touched her cheek.

"You're a beautiful person, Emily. I've always been proud of you."

She flung her arms around him. "I love you, Daddy."

"I love you too."

Her heart felt too big for her chest as she watched him walk toward his car at the curb. He'd adopted a hunched posture that she didn't recognize. Was it age or was he truly in trouble this time? Her mother had been right. He did have a big secret.

Fifteen minutes later, David rumbled up in the front yard, sun flashing off chrome. The day was pleasant. The bike purred beneath them. He drove fast, gliding smoothly through traffic. Wind lashed her hair against her cheeks in stinging streaks. She could feel David's stomach tighten as he leaned into curves. She hadn't thought about what he looked like under his shirt, but he suddenly seemed much more appealing. She had the desire to lay her head against his back and hug him close, but that would have been much too familiar.

David

BARTON SPRINGS was still green and overhung with shade. As always, the aquifer pool was clear and calm. Below the expansive concrete reservoir, in the rock tumbled streambed, people sat along the banks and threw sticks into the water for their dogs.

"I'll be damned. There she is." David couldn't believe they'd found her so quickly. Lorelei was perched on a giant rock about ten feet into the water. She sat up straight, her arms wrapped around her knees as she gazed off into the woods.

David parked and walked to the bank next to her spot.

"Hey," he called.

She slowly turned his way. "Oh, hi."

He jumped from rock to rock until he reached her and sat down. The stone was sun-warmed and comforting.

A shirt she had washed was plastered across another rock.

"Come here often?" he said, trying to make light.

"I get around."

"You been okay?"

"I'm fine."

"Haven't seen you in a while."

"Decided to move zones. You know, with people getting killed and all."

"That's so wrong about Fiona. I know you guys were friends."

"Yeah. Whatever."

The Zilker Park kiddy train made a high-pitched whistle in the distance, and Lorelei paused to listen. Her eyes darted with her thoughts. Emily had crouched on a nearby boulder. She picked up a few pebbles and tossed them into the water one by one.

"Do you know something about what happened to her?"

"Look, I don't want to get involved," Lorelei said.

"I won't rat you out. If you know something you should tell me before somebody else gets hurt. Somebody beat her pretty bad. Anybody we know?"

He waited.

"There's some guys."

"Yeah?"

"Bum hunters. They were picking on some old dude, and then Fiona yelled at them to stop and they started pounding her. That's when I split."

"Okay."

"I don't know if they meant to kill anybody, but they had a bat and a paintball gun. Check it." She pulled up her pant leg. Two angry bruises bloomed on her thigh.

"They shot you."

"Hurt like crazy."

"Looks like it. Did they see you?"

"Sure they saw me."

"So they'd recognize you?"

"Most likely. That's why I'm hanging out around here. Look, none of the other kids know about this, okay?"

"You didn't tell anybody?"

"No. They'd hate me if they knew I took off and let Fiona get killed."

"That was in no way your fault. Fiona was murdered. If you'd hung around you might have ended up dead too."

"You've got to do something. Make them find those guys. You're right. They could hurt somebody else."

"Are you scared?"

"Just cautious."

"You camp around here?"

She suddenly grew irritated. "Look, I don't need you to worry about me. I only told you because I didn't want that old homeless dude to go to jail for killing Fiona. They jumped him too. He was all bloody and stuff."

"Okay."

"That just wouldn't be right, you know?"

"Sure. I totally understand."

"One of them had a camera. A video camera. He taped the whole thing."

This sort of thing went on. David had watched it on YouTube.

They listened to the water's trickle for a while. A golden retriever splashed after a branch.

"You got any money?" Lorelei said.

"How about something to eat?" David asked. "You gals hungry? I'm starving. How about it, Lorelei? Want a sandwich?"

"I could eat."

"Great. Come on, Emily. I need you to hold the food. We'll be right back."

In the parking lot, Emily said, "You think she'll be there when we get back?"

"Probably. If she thinks she'll get a free feed. I just needed to know she was okay."

They drove across the road to a health food restaurant carved into the rocky side of a hill. David ordered sandwiches and smoothies to go. Emily had a shot of wheatgrass while they waited outside on the deck.

"If she needs somewhere to stay she can crash with me again for a few days," she said.

"That's not a good idea."

"Why not?"

"Look, you can do what you want, but it's important to have boundaries."

"That why you invited me to come along today? Because you thought I needed better boundaries?"

That stung. She was right. How could he explain why he invited her?

"Okay. You have a point. What I mean is, you have to know where your line is. I don't give kids money. I don't let them live with me. I usually don't give them rides."

"Then what do you do to help?"

"I help them help themselves. Street kids are unpredictable. It's important that you don't become emotionally involved. It rarely ends up the way you'd like."

"I can't believe I'm hearing this from you. I'd think that any kind of help would be good."

"Not always. Look, you have to set healthy boundaries or else she'll have you on edge all the time. Just like this disappearing act. She knows when she's gone that people think about her. I'd imagine that's her hope anyway."

"No cash money?"

"That's up to you. I'm not sure she'd use it for drugs. She doesn't seem to have much of a drug habit, but you never know. She seems a little unstable. Quick-tempered. She hangs around with kids who use."

"Siesta Gardens."

"Right."

"Was Fiona using?"

"On a daily basis."

"Think it was a drug deal gone bad?"

"Could be. This assault Lorelei's talking about sounds very much like a bad drug deal. We may never know."

"Like anybody is going to put a big effort into finding out who killed some homeless kid."

"Right. So I'm just saying be aware of her behavior and try not to react to it personally."

"You're right. I know you're right. I don't even know why I care."

"Because you do. Some of us just do."

They weren't gone ten minutes, but when they got back with the food, Lorelei was nowhere to be found.

"Great," Emily said. "Just great."

"Like I said, these kids are unpredictable. If they don't want to talk they can be ghosts."

"But you let her get away."

His was a smile of surrender. "It has to be her choice."

Barbara

GERALD CUT off another bite of chicken fried steak and dragged it through a mound of mashed potatoes smothered in milk gravy.

They had just left Barbara's parents and had stopped on the way home for some comfort food. She looked out the window of the restaurant where she worked as a teenager and envisioned waves of bluebonnets. Spring would bring its familiar rolling blanket of purple blossoms to these hills.

She took another sip of tea. The waitress arrived with the plastic refill pitcher, but Barbara waved her hand over the lip of her glass.

"Oh, that's right, darlin'. You want *unsweet*," the waitress said as if Barbara were a lunatic.

"Yes. Thank you."

"With no Splenda or nothing?"

"No. Thank you though." Barbara pulled a tight smile for the benefit of the waitress. She was proud of her self-control, but at times it was difficult. Like right now. Right now she wanted to reach over and slap Gerald.

How long had he known he was losing his job?

As soon as the waitress left, tears tickled Barbara's eyes. She touched them with a napkin.

"I can't believe we have to go through this again," she said.

"I'm sorry," Gerald said. He stuffed another forkful of steak into his mouth and glanced out the window. He had been looking anywhere expect directly at her.

"Why did you wait until now to tell me? Now that you have your walking papers there's nothing we can do."

He swallowed. Adjusted his glasses. Took a sip of tea. Then he said in an even tone, "Barbara, sweetheart. I assure you I did everything I could. There is nothing more that could be done. The company is downsizing. Last hired. First fired."

"So . . . so . . . well, I'm speechless."

"I didn't want to worry you earlier than necessary. I thought it might blow over."

"No wonder you've been acting weird the past few weeks."

His expression changed. "I wasn't aware that it showed."

"Right. I can read you like a book. I knew something was up." She struggled to tamp down her emotions. She thought he was a coward for dropping this bomb on her in public where he knew she wouldn't make a scene.

"How can you sit there and eat like that?" she snapped. "This conversation has made me lose my appetite."

"Stop being so dramatic. We've been through worse. We'll be fine."

"You have to promise me something."

"What?"

"You have to promise me that you'll go see a doctor this time and get some antidepressants. Something that will keep you out of the theater room and looking for a job."

"I'll think about it."

"And no boozing either."

"I promise, but I want you to promise *me* something."

"What's that?"

"That you will have some faith in me."

"I have faith in you, Gerald."

"No you don't. You don't trust me, and I can understand why. When we entered into this marriage I vowed that I'd take care of you and I intend to do that."

"Lord, Gerald. This isn't 1910. I think I can pull my weight."

"That's not the point. The point is that a man prides himself on being able to take care of his family. Now, I don't know how I'm going to do it. I haven't got that part figured out. But I can tell you that working for somebody else doesn't work for me. I'm thinking about other options."

"Like what?"

"Well, I'm not sure yet, but we can discuss it. I value your input."

Barbara wiped another tear. "Everybody is lying to me."

"What do you mean?"

"You lied to me through omission. Emily lies to my face. Are you aware that she is still involved with that street girl she brought to our house?"

"No, but I fail to see how that affects us. Emily's a grown woman."

"Hardly. Do grown women have their daddies buy them a set of new tires?"

He raised an eyebrow in surprise.

"Don't think I don't know what you did," she said. "I saw the new tires before you gave her back the MINI. And they were the nice ones too, not the cheap kind. See, lying by omission."

Barbara knew he hadn't thought of his actions in quite that way, but she couldn't resist the jab.

"You're right," he said, "But that's my way of going into her room and crying over her old clothes and teddy bears."

It was Barbara's turn to feel stung. How had he known about her days in Emily's room? He grinned that he'd gotten the better of her, then returned to his detached expression.

"She needed them," he said. "A dad's got to be good for some things."

The waitress finally brought the unsweetened tea and slipped the bill onto the checkered tablecloth. She didn't offer up her idle chatter, so Barbara knew she sensed something was up at table nine.

"That homeless girl that got killed at Town Lake, Emily knew her," Barbara said. "She said that she'd met her the day before. She said somebody is beating street kids to death with ball bats."

"That sounds a little melodramatic."

"How in the world could Emily know a girl who got murdered? Emily needs better friends. You know she has absolutely no people filter."

"Uh-huh. I've heard that a few times."

"She let that street urchin move in with her right after the flood."

"How do you know this?"

"A mother knows things."

"You spied on her?"

"I sensed something was up, so I drove by, and the girl was there while Emily was at work. I let her borrow the Acadia under the stipulation that she *would not* let that girl move in with her. Emily assured me she wouldn't, and then she went straight home and did exactly that."

"The girl's just down on her luck."

"She's a runaway."

"Of course she's a runaway. The question is why."

"She probably didn't like rules. Or she didn't like school. Thought she'd have a life of adventure. I bet I could find her parents."

"Where would you even start looking?"

"I don't know. Maybe those people who send that card in the circulars once a week with that little picture—*Have you seen this child?* Maybe I could get the Print-A-Thon folks to help."

"Do you remember what she looks like well enough to pick her out of a lineup?"

"I wonder what she looked like before she ruined her face. I mean, really, that child is going to cost somebody a fortune in laser removal."

"Have you thought about how you can help the girl? That's all Emily is trying to do, just help."

"Gerald, be realistic. That girl doesn't want help. She just wants to take what she can get from any willing victim, then she moves on."

"We all make mistakes," he said. "Emily has a right to make her own mistakes. She may not have turned out like you planned, but she's got a good head on her shoulders. If she doesn't come to us for help then we need to stay out of her business."

Emily

"OH MY God. What am I supposed to do about this?"

She held a copy of *Be Here Now*. Lorelei's face stared at her, an accusation in black-and-white.

"Nothing. It's done," Barbara said.

"Can I sue them?"

"You can. Good luck. The press club has excellent lawyers. They win a lot. Make them give you a job instead."

"I don't want to work for people who will steal your creativity."

"I understand. I wouldn't either."

"I'm going to call him and cuss him out."

"Make sure he doesn't put you on speaker phone or worse, record you."

"Great. I hadn't thought about that."

"How's Lorelei going to react?"

"She's going to freak."

"Is she dangerous? Do you need to come home so you can avoid her?"

Her mother devolved to that tone that set Emily's nerves on edge. She regretted calling her.

After they hung up, Emily was washed in a wave of gloom. Her high over her photography being published was sullied. A guy she had trusted, a guy she had liked, had turned out to be a total jerk. Her friendship with Lorelei was ruined. Emily had actually put the girl's life in jeopardy. The situation couldn't get much worse.

She had Travis on speed dial.

He answered on the fourth ring.

"At least you've got enough balls to answer the phone."

"Let me explain."

"Yes. Please do explain exactly how you got that photograph. Did you download it before or after you fucked me?"

"Before."

"Well, so glad you stuck around."

"Look, this will eventually work out to be a good thing. I promise you."

"I could sue the shit out of you."

"You wouldn't win."

There was a tense lull.

"You idiot, that girl has a very legitimate reason for not wanting her photograph on the front of your magazine. There's some creepy stalker looking for her."

"What do you mean?"

"Some older guy she shacked up with in Arizona. She's scared to death of him. You'd better hope he doesn't show up and kill her."

A long pause.

"Do you think that's really possible?" he asked.

Emily wouldn't tell him anything about Fiona's murder. He was a newshound, not a friend. His actions had made that clear. If he printed anything about Lorelei in connection with Fiona's murder, even a description of her, it would put Lorelei in even more danger.

So she said, "Look at that girl who was beaten to death in the park." Another extended pause. "Things are scary. The least you can do is find Lorelei's parents."

"What?"

"Throw down your investigative thing and find out who she is."

"Do you know anything about her?"

"Not really. She's been all up and down the West Coast. Says she's got a brother, Noah, she's looking for. He's apparently been vagrant for a number of years."

"Is Noah even a real name?"

"Who knows?"

"Where's she from?"

"I'm thinking Midwest somewhere."

"Wow. That's extremely helpful."

"I don't care if you have to look through ten thousand photos of missing children. You need to find her. It's the right thing to do."

"You're asking a lot."

"You owe me a lot. You'll be lucky if I don't sue you and the paper."

"We both know that's not going to happen."

Travis

EMILY CALLED him some colorful nouns and adjectives before they finally hung up. Sure, Travis knew it was a rotten thing to do, but the photo had turned out perfect. Guaranteed to be a picked up cover.

But if Bob found out how Travis got the shot, things would turn ugly.

And what about some goon stalking this girl? Was it true or was Emily spinning a tale to make him feel bad?

Travis had desk duty, his turn to watch the wires for breaking news. A number of writers were working late—last minute layouts, headlines and deadlines. Things were slow, so Travis started digging. He had a photo of Lorelei, but no name, no state.

He needed to redeem himself with Emily before she called Bob and went off. He was supposed to always have signed releases to publish photos, but nobody ever asked if he did. Bob had just assumed that because the paper had worked with Emily on the flood story that they were cleared to use her shots again.

Travis had abused Bob's trust, just like he'd abused Emily's.

He was a scoundrel. But he was a scoundrel who got the story.

The telephone was still a journalist's most powerful tool. If the first person you contacted couldn't help they were usually happy to refer you to somebody who could. Travis would play dumb, ask for their assistance and make them the expert. People loved to feel like the expert.

Problem was, he had nobody to call, nowhere to start, not even one lead. He could spend hours culling through the thousands of runaway photos on various national databases. For once, he lacked resources. He was at a dead end before he even started.

He thought to call one of his connections at the Austin PD to get some direction on how to start a search. He could also call David at the Tumbleweed Center, but Travis wondered if he had burned that connection. David was a reasonable guy. Maybe if he explained the gravity of the situation, David would forgive his aggressive rainy day photo op.

His desk phone rang.

"Travis Roberts."

"Are you the guy that wrote that article about the homeless in Austin?"

"That would be me."

"That girl on the cover. Do you know her?"

"Sort of. Why?"

"Because I think that's my sister."

Emily

NOT LONG after she finished cursing out Travis, he called back. Group had been slow all afternoon, and even though it was Happy Hour she had only two customers nursing beers.

"This better be good news," she said.

"Is Lorelei looking for a long-lost brother?"

"How'd you know that?"

"He's on the other line. Can I give him your number?"

Sixty seconds later, Emily was talking with the mystery man.

"Do you know the girl on the cover?"

"Lorelei."

"Yes. Do you know where I can find her?"

"You told Travis you're her brother."

"Right. Noah. Do you know where she is?"

"Can we meet?" she asked.

"Where?"

"I'm at work. Group Therapy, it's a bar."

"I can find it."

When they hung up, she dialed David.

He said, "I'll be there in fifteen."

They sat in the staff booth waiting for Noah. Angel hovered around the bar, keeping an eye on things. The last bit of daylight blazed through the open door, and Emily held her breath.

He was larger than she had expected, but then again, Lorelei was a tall girl.

He hesitated, scanned the room. When his eyes fell on David, they nodded to each other. He walked in their direction. Emily had pictured Noah as a slight person, with pale straight hair and effeminate ways. She supposed she thought of him as vulnerable. But this was a dark-haired gym rat with enough tattoos woven between his fingers to make her think he had a full body suit under his long sleeves and jeans.

"You're not Noah," she said. She made eye contact with Angel. He walked to her end of the bar.

"Name's Leo."

"You're the tattoo artist."

"It's that apparent?"

Emily scowled at him.

"Can I sit?"

David waved to a seat next to him.

"So," David said, "why did you lie about being Noah?"

He shrugged. "I thought it would be the easiest way to get her to talk to me."

"Do you know Noah?"

"No."

"You came all the way from Phoenix?" Emily asked.

"L.A."

"I thought your studio was in Phoenix."

"No. It's in L.A." He reached into his pocket and removed a business card. Japanese designs swirled in red and black across the back of the card. "Leo's L.A. That's my studio."

"So why'd she tell me you were in Phoenix?"

"First of all, let me ask, if you don't mind, who are *you*?"

That seemed like a reasonable enough question, so she said, "I'm Emily. I'm just a friend. This is David. He's her . . . what are you to her, David?"

"I'm a friend too. I work with the homeless kids around here. So, how did you find out she was in Austin?"

"That newspaper," Leo answered. "I got buddies work at studios here in Austin. They recognized my work. Called me up. I looked it up online. Pretty easy."

"Didn't you have some sort of relationship with her?" Emily

asked.

"I did."

"Don't you think you're a little old for her?"

"She needed somebody to take care of her, and I'm not immune to her feminine charms." He raised an eyebrow to David as if he would understand, but got no response. "What's a guy to do? She lived with me. Ran away once, but I can't stand to see her on the streets. I found her, but that lasted about another month, then she left again."

"So you what?" she asked. "You want her back? This sixteen-year-old girl."

"Fuck. No way. Is that how old she is?"

"I don't know," David said. "She could be."

"Did you tattoo her face?"

"I *fixed* her face," he said defensively.

"She said you did it to her while she was drunk."

"What? No way. She had this crap stick and poke tat under her eye. I fixed it. Covered it up. Now it looks great."

"That's totally fucked up, tattooing a child's face," Emily said.

David gave her a look that said pull back.

"I'd never do anything to hurt her. She had a bunch of tats when I met her—train tracks and owls and all kinds of work. Look, why am I on trial here? I'm just trying to help her. Keep her off the streets. Keep her from doing drugs and other shit that'll fuck her up."

"What drugs does she do?" David asked.

"All kinds I think. She's up one minute and down the next. Crazy stuff. Look, you going to help me find her or not?"

"We don't know where she is," Emily said. "Haven't seen her in a while."

He nodded. "She does have a way of just vanishing."

"You're too old for her."

"I agree, but I love her. I worry about her."

"Uh-huh."

David said, "Do you know anything about her that could help reconnect her with her family? Her real name, where she's from?"

"She's from Utah."

"Where in Utah?"

"I don't know. Like Mormon central or something."

"Salt Lake?"

"That would be my guess."

"Do you know her real name?"

"Wish I could help you out, man. All she ever told me was Lorelei. Here, take a couple more of my cards. Please, have her call me."

"I don't think so," Emily said. "You'd better leave or I'll tell the cops you're a stalker pedophile."

"I'll be in town awhile." He looked directly at David as he said this. "Call me if anybody on your end changes their mind."

Travis

Emily was hacked off. His mobile crackled with her anger, cutting out as she yelled.

"You total ass . . . that guy wasn't . . . brother . . . tattooed jerk that's after her." Then loud and clear, *"What the hell is wrong with you?"*

Unsure how to respond, he said, "Wait. Back off. How was I supposed to know that?" He came off as too defensive and silently cursed himself.

"You're not supposed to make things worse. I mean, geez," she said.

"I was just the messenger."

"Oh, no. You're not responsible for any of this are you?"

"What do you want from me?"

"Find her parents."

"I'm trying, but I don't have a lot to go on."

"Try Utah."

"Utah? All of Utah?"

"Start with Salt Lake."

"Okay."

"Call me as soon as you get anything."

"Okay."

"I mean it. You'd better call me."

When they hung up Travis could still hear Emily's words stinging his ear. So she had been telling the truth about Lorelei's stalker. That bit of information did change the gravity of the situation. Maybe Emily was right. Maybe he was somewhat responsible for the girl.

Travis checked the National Runaway Switchboard but got nowhere. Next, he tried the National Center for Missing & Exploited

Children's website. If she was from Utah, and if her parents cared enough to file a missing persons report, he might have luck.

On the first page he found a search engine. He checked Female, Utah. How long missing? He guessed and entered two years.

Four photos appeared. First one was a black girl, but the next three were all possibilities. He looked closely. One girl had promise, but this girl was healthy, her cheeks round with youth, her hair shiny and long. She was smiling. Travis held the cover image of Lorelei up next to the monitor and compared the girls.

The stats read:

Name: Rose Kimball
Case Type: Endangered Runaway
DOB: Sept. 1, 1996
Missing Date: Sept. 6, 2010
Missing State: Utah
Sex: Female
Race: White
Height: 5'10"
Weight 135 lbs.
Hair Color: Brown
Eye Color: Green/Blue

This girl was much heavier than Lorelei. He could see the perfectly aligned teeth of the happy child in the photo, but there were no teeth showing in Emily's photo. Still, it could be the same girl.

He found the contact number for the Salt Lake City Police Department online and got in touch with a Lieutenant Smith in missing persons. He confirmed for Travis that he still had three missing teenage girls. One had come home.

"Can you shoot me over that picture? I got some face identification software that'll tell me if it's a match or not," Smith said.

Travis e-mailed Lorelei's image. He waited on the line while the officer opened the file and ran the analysis.

"Wow," the lieutenant said. "If she was trying to change her appearance she sure accomplished that."

"So we got a match?" Travis asked.

"It's a match," the officer said. "No doubt about it."

Barbara

IT WAS another clear day. The capitol's golden dome shimmered in the afternoon sun as Barbara approached downtown. She had just picked up her Acadia from being detailed for a second time. The first job hadn't touched the stagnant water funk emanating from the carpet after Emily borrowed it. This time around her vehicle smelled almost like a new car again.

Barbara switched radio channels on the way into the city, making mental notes about which talk shows were in which time slots. Radio talent moved frequently. She used her drive time to keep up.

She switched to conservative talk radio. Emily called it hate radio. She said the talk always focused on what was wrong with the other guy, never on personal responsibility. Barbara had to admit conservative radio loved to lay blame.

Still, Barbara could usually find a grain of truth in conservative talk. After all, somebody has to be responsible for the economic mess the country was in, and she didn't think that somebody was her or Gerald. It was validating to have her frustrations expressed, even if the announcers and guests did tend to be a little on the angry side. She could always use a good dose of vitriol about illegal immigrants or taxes.

Her usual exit was blocked by a semi. She was stuck five cars back, perfect pickings for the homeless guy who'd been working this territory for the past ten years. Today his sign read *Homeless*

Hungry VET. Sometimes he waited for drivers to beckon him over. Other times, he walked along the traffic jam like a fireman collecting money for burned children.

Barbara reached into the center console between her seats and pulled out a granola bar. She always had a moment of panic when anyone of his sort approached. She rolled the window open a few inches and passed the food through the slit.

"Thank you, ma'am," he said. "God bless you." He didn't seem drunk, but you never knew.

The intersection cleared, traffic moved, and she gladly left the bedraggled man behind.

Talk shows warned listeners against giving money to the homeless. The general thinking was any money given would go directly to alcohol or drugs. Then the vagrants ended up in the emergency room, and taxpayers got stuck with the outrageous unpaid ER bills. Barbara supported clinics to help poor people as a better, less expensive way to provide indigent care.

She had been thinking a lot about the homeless since Emily dragged that strange, hungry, tattooed girl into her house. That poor child was beyond help. There is no way to clean her up and make her presentable. Nobody would hire her except maybe as a clerk in a comic book shop or an adult toy store.

Contrary to what Emily and Gerald might think, Barbara was not unsympathetic to this little Lorelei's plight. Although she'd never told anyone, Barbara had seen hunger. She'd gone to college on scholarship, but her parents hadn't been able to help with other expenses. She had been on her own when it came to room and board, so Barbara got a restaurant job and scrounged food. Restaurants expected the college kids who worked for them to pinch a little food here and there.

And she had dated for dinner too. Although she had never been reduced to having sex for food, she had known girls who did. After all, birth control on campus was free. Food was not.

Barbara had seen need and the desperation that comes with it. She sensed the trouble that followed Lorelei, and although Emily wasn't forthcoming with information, Barbara knew the girl was still hanging around. If she didn't take action, Lorelei was bound to bring bad luck into Emily's life.

Gerald would say she was overstepping her boundaries, but Barbara didn't care. A mother had to do what a mother had to do.

Barbara turned onto Guadalupe and followed it downtown. She found a parking space on the street and retrieved the cardboard box from the backseat. She reached into the center console again and dumped the rest of the granola bars into the box. She crossed the street and stood in a barren plaza, looking around for the entrance.

"You looking for the drop-in?" a boy asked.

"Yes. I am."

"It's down there," he said, pointing to concrete steps that ended at a gray metal door.

"Thank you."

Inside, the place was empty of ragtag teenagers. She walked around, calling out for anyone. A plump, middle-aged woman stuck her head out of a small office.

"Can I help you?" she asked.

"I'm looking for David. We met a while back."

"He's not here right now. I'm Amelia. Is there anything I can do for you? Do you have something you'd like to donate?" she said, motioning to the box.

"Well, no. Actually, I'm looking for a young girl named Lorelei."

The woman shook her head. "We haven't seen Lorelei around here for a while."

"Do you have any suggestions for where I might look? I really need to find her."

"Sorry. I couldn't say." She was getting nowhere with this woman, so Barbara thanked her and wandered back out to the plaza. The same boy was talking with friends.

"Excuse me," she said as she approached them. "I'm looking for a girl named Lorelei."

"Yeah, I know her," he said, offering no other help. He had two metal studs on the outsides of his lower lips, the kind of thing that you can't stop looking at. The punctures were angry red, obviously infected. She tried to pull her eyes away.

Barbara was relieved when a girl said, "She's the one with the bird on her face."

"Yes, that's her. Do you know where she is?"

"She hangs with Mook's clan, doesn't she?" the girl said. "Down at Pease."

"Pease Park?"

"Yeah, but like, she's been AWOL for days."

The boy said, "Yeah. Last time I saw her she was hanging with

Fiona."

"Fiona? That name sounds familiar," Barbara said.

"She's the dead girl they found at Town Lake."

"Oh, yes. That's so sad. Did they ever find out what happened to her?"

"She was a slinger. I bet the East Austin mafia got her," the boy said.

"I don't understand."

"A slinger, a broker, a scrub?" the girl said. "She sold drugs to UT students for a dealer. Sort of a go-between so she could pay for her own habit."

"She was a burnout," the boy said. "She probably ripped them off or something. Piss them off and they'll f . . . uh, mess you up."

The girl said, "Oh yeah. For sure."

"So Lorelei hung around with this girl?"

"Yeah. I saw them together. They were friends. They were at Lawrence's, right?"

The boy nodded his agreement.

"Who is Lawrence?"

"Just some strung-out old paralyzed dude. She's probably not there," the girl said.

"She could be, if she took Fiona's business," the boy said. "Or maybe she got spooked and went stealth."

"Is this place in East Austin?" Barbara asked.

"You don't want to go there," the girl said. "It's drugland. No place for a lady like you in a nice ride like that."

All three turned to look at her SUV.

"We got a ride in one of those once," Star said. Something passed between the two friends. Barbara couldn't read their expressions, and she had a sudden fear that they would rob her.

"Yes, well." Barbara was unsure what to say next. Then she realized how to manage things. "I have clothes in this box. They're about your size. Would you like a jacket?"

"Depends."

Barbara opened the box and held out one of Emily's old velour sweatshirts. It was black with *Juicy* in cursive on the back. Barbara had always hated the expensive, tacky thing and was relieved when Emily wore it only once and pushed it to the back of her closet.

"It's cute. I'll take it," the girl said.

"A trade," Barbara said. "You tell me the address of drugland."

"Sure lady. It's your funeral," she said.

The boy gave her an address. She thanked them.

"You might find her just walking around somewhere," he said and motioned down the street. "We're not allowed to stay in one spot very long or we violate camping rules. Just drive around. You might get lucky and run up on her."

"Thank you."

"If you go to East Austin, don't get out of your fancy ride," the girl said.

"I won't."

"And if you find Lorelei, tell her Star and Monkey said hey." They looked at each other with an odd grin, as if they knew an inside joke.

She drove up the hill into the Penbrooke neighborhood, behind Pease Park and across the Winsor Street Bridge, without any sign of Lorelei. In a parking lot, she asked a few teens if they had seen her. Barbara drove to all the spots in the city that made sense, but she had no luck. Desperate, she decided to give East Austin a try.

The last time she'd spent any time in East Austin was back in the eighties when Gerald brought her to the Victory Grill to see Stevie Ray Vaughan. Before they had a child, Gerald used to drag her to jazz clubs and blues clubs. But that seemed like a lifetime ago as she rolled slowly along the streets wondering exactly what she was looking for.

She passed through parts of town where things were looking up. New construction. New restaurants. Retail.

Then suddenly, there was the expected decline.

Barbara was used to illegals waiting for offers of work on Cesar Chavez. They wanted to be inconspicuous except to those who would offer a job for the day. But she immediately felt a different street presence driving into this part of town. All eyes were on her.

In squalid apartment complexes, men in sunglasses peered from dark doorways, televisions flickering behind them. A few dominated the sidewalk, making direct eye contact as she drove by. It was a life she'd only seen on cable and in the movies.

A pitiful man in a wheelchair gazed longingly out his door. Children played with beer bottles in parking lots. How could a child ever survive this? Why would any girl voluntarily come here? Even one who warned the world away with tough tattoos?

On her second pass through the neighborhood, a man wearing a wife beater and enough hardware in his face to attract lightning approached her. Barbara stepped on the gas and crushed his curses with the growl of the engine, although there was no mistaking his sign language in the rearview mirror.

Lorelei

SHE HAD serious cramps. In the bathroom at a fast-food joint, she'd neatly folded toilet paper into a thick square and positioned it in her panties, but that wouldn't hold her flow for long.

Elda went into the drugstore with her. Mook went in separately with the intention of creating a diversion so they could rack a box of tampons and some Midol. Lorelei hated to steal, but tampons were expensive.

The feminine hygiene aisle was directly in front of the cash register, but the pimply teen checking out a loud woman didn't seem to be paying attention to them. At the other end of the aisle was a door with a one-way window. Lorelei decided it was too risky and leaned into Elda to whisper this when they heard the crash.

Cans rolled toward the front door, something metal pinged across the hard floor and Mook called out, "Oh, man, I'm so sorry! Oh, man, I'll clean it up. Here, let me clean it up."

The door on the office flew open and a rotund man with wire-framed glasses and a bad comb-over was on the job.

"Get out of here!" He flapped his arms at Mook. "You kids are nothing but trouble! Get out!"

The girls shoved boxes of tampons and drugs into their packs. When Lorelei turned, the cashier was looking past his customer directly at her.

"Please," she mouthed.

He nodded only slightly toward the door. Elda pushed her and they ran. Mook was right behind them. They sprinted a couple of blocks and ducked into an alley.

When they were sure nobody was following, they walked on. They passed a few cafés with tables on the sidewalk. At one empty table, Mook snatched an abandoned sandwich off a plate without missing a step. He walked along casually, chewing and talking. Foot traffic parted for them. Parents pulled their children aside to let them pass.

The first person to see it was Mook.

"Shit. Look at that." He opened the glass door of a newspaper stand and pulled out a copy of *Be Here Now.*

"That's Lorelei," Elda said. "Look, Lorelei. It's you."

All three stared at the cover.

"I can't believe it. She told me nobody would ever see those pictures. She promised. Open it up. See if there are more."

Elda took the paper and stood between them. She found the spread on being young and homeless in Austin. There were three color photos on the double truck spread. One was a shot of Mook playing video games.

"She did it to me too," he said. "That bitch."

Elda said, "She took pictures of Betsy that day too. I thought you knew."

"That's *so* fucked up," he said.

"You're a rock star, Lorelei. Really," Elda said. "You look amazing."

"I can't believe she did this to me. She promised," Lorelei said. "Anybody got any minutes I can use to call her?"

"No, nobody's got any minutes," Mook said.

"I gotta go," Lorelei said, but she didn't move.

Then they all realized they were standing by a bus stop.

"I got a bus card with a few bucks left on it," Elda said. "You're welcome to it."

Thirty minutes on a swaying city bus siphoned her fury. Lorelei walked from SoCo to Emily's in a stupor. The house was dark when she arrived. She sat on the porch swing, trying to stoke her outrage and sense of betrayal, but part of her softened with the memory that she had been welcome here.

She noticed an open bedroom window, and she thought about climbing inside. She'd done it before, but only at abandoned houses. That's when she saw the box by the door. On the top, in bold letters, was written, *For Lorelei.*

Freaky. Had Emily known she was coming?

Inside the lock folded top of the cardboard box, Lorelei found a handful of granola bars, three pairs of jeans, four shirts, a hat, gloves and an awesomely cute jacket. The note read:

These are all for Lorelei. I didn't think you'd mind. Please make sure she gets them. Mom

The jacket was a little tight, but it would do. Lorelei unfurled a wad of dirty clothes from her backpack and filled it with the new things. There were even socks and pretty underwear. Lorelei put a sock to her nose and inhaled the perfume of fabric softener, a luxury that made her mother flash to mind.

She stuffed her old, dirty clothes into the box and carried it around back to the trash. She heard Emily's car approaching and sneaked back to the porch where she hid. There was no way Emily could have seen her. She waited, arms slack at her sides, peering through the front window from the shadows of the porch.

The kitchen light came on. Emily moved into the den and switched on a couple of lamps. She came toward the front door and Lorelei's heart fluttered, but Emily just leaned down and gathered mail from the floor inside the door. The lurking girl's anger simmered as she followed the sounds of movement from room to room through the open window. She waited, contemplating what she would say when she finally had the guts to knock on the door.

Emily came back into the den. Lorelei raised her hand to rap, hesitated, then knocked.

The porch light came on. The front door shuddered as Emily pulled it open.

"Lorelei, thank God," Emily said as she stepped outside. "I'm so happy to see you."

"Shut up! I've got something to say."

"Okay. I'm listening."

Lorelei hadn't expected that reaction. Emily waited while Lorelei searched for words, but when she saw the girl was unsure what to say, Emily blurted out her story.

"Travis stole your photos off my laptop."

"How'd he even know they were there? You showed him. I know

you did."

"He saw them when we were looking at other shots for his article. When Fiona's body was found, it kicked his entire story into high gear. It was wrong to let him see your photos. I can't tell you how sorry I am."

"I said don't talk."

"Okay."

"You took photos of Mook too."

"I did give Travis those shots, but I swear to you, I didn't give him your pictures."

"I said shut up! I never hurt you. I never did nothing to you. Look what you did to me."

Emily cast her eyes down.

"I trusted you, and you screwed me. I can't stay in Austin now. There's no way. Did you know that every single person that walks down the street in this town is going to know me now? Those guys, those bum hunters. They have a picture of me now."

"I know."

"Yes. Thanks to you I'm now the most recognizable person in Austin."

Emily's expression changed to puzzled. "Hey, I used to have a jacket just like that."

"Really. What a coincidence."

"Where'd you get that?"

"Shut up. You make me sick. You know what you are? You're a poser! You act like you care about somebody, like you want to be somebody's friend, but you don't. You wanted something from me, and when you got it you were like, so screw her."

"That's not true."

"It *is* true! You're two-faced. You're all like down on your parents and stuff, and then the first thing that goes wrong you go running right back to Mommy and Daddy. You'll never grow up because you'll always have them. And your buddies down at the bar. They've always got your back. Well, nobody's got my back. Nobody. Especially not you."

"I'm a good person."

"You don't even know who you are. You're a poser, even to yourself."

A different look came over Emily then, a sad resignation, and Lorelei knew that she had hit a nerve. They were at an impasse.

Lorelei said, "I said what I came to say."

She turned to go when Emily said, "Leo."

She faced her again. "What about Leo?"

"Leo's in town."

Lorelei held her breath.

"What?" she whispered. Then louder, "I can't believe you called Leo."

"No. He found you. You were right. His tattoo buddies here in Austin recognized his work. They contacted him. David and I met him. He's a perv."

"I told you that. I told you he's a perv. You drew him right to me. What am I supposed to do now that psycho stalker is in Austin looking for me too?"

"You should go to the police. They'll protect you and see that you get home to your family." She paused, then said, "Rose."

Nobody had called her Rose in so long that the name shot a burn of dread through Lorelei.

"That's you, isn't it? Rose Kimball?"

"How do you know my name?"

"National Missing Children's Database."

Lorelei picked up a cacti pot, and without hesitation, she heaved it through the double windows. The pot thudded against an inside wall and smashed to the floor amid tinkling glass.

Then she screamed. No words. Just a guttural explosion of rage.

"Shit," Emily said when Lorelei caught her breath. "Feel better?"

"No! I do not feel better!"

"I'm just trying to help. Please, just let me help you."

"Help me? You've done nothing but hurt me since I met you. I don't need your fake concern."

"You're not as tough as you act."

"You don't know anything about me."

"People care about you. *I* care about you."

Lorelei considered Emily's words. She really wanted to believe Emily was her friend. But Emily had betrayed her. In the end, all adults betrayed her, manipulated her, stifled her.

"Liar," Lorelei hissed. She slung her heavy pack over a shoulder and stomped down the steps. She snapped around at the sound of Emily's tears.

"Go on! Cry!" she shouted at Emily. "It'll be your fault if those thugs from the park get me or if Leo finds me before I can get out of town. I thought Austin might be the place I could stay for a while, but no. Now I have to move on again. All because of you and your stupid camera. I hate you for this. I really do. I hate your guts."

Emily

AS SHE waited in line for her latte, Emily texted Travis.

LL definitely Rose K. Any luck with parents? She's freaking about tattoo guy.

She grabbed her drink and cursed Travis under her breath. *Coward.* She was sure he would ignore her text when her phone bleeped.

Is she okay?

She thought to leave him hanging. He deserved it. But then she needed him.

For now.

Pause. Bleep.

Pretty sure I found her parents.

He was supposed to tell her things immediately.

She texted: *???????????????*

His reply: *Sorry. Double checking. Didn't want to be wrong again.*

She found a table and waited. It was nearly midnight when David walked in, his hair plastered to his head from the motorcycle helmet, his eyes red and bleary. Sleep was in his voice when she had called, but he had insisted that he was just watching television.

As usual, David was relaxed, in listening mode. He sipped his black coffee and searched the street outside, always on the lookout for someone in need. How difficult it would be to never turn that off.

She could barely handle the drama bomb of one girl. How could he deal with so many desperate young souls?

But something about his calm demeanor rankled her nerves. She wanted him to yell, to call her a bad person for betraying Lorelei, for bringing on such danger.

She should have protected the child. She should have tried to persuade her to go to David for help. But Emily had stood mute on her steps, frozen as Lorelei's words singed her ears. She had watched as the shadows of the yard swallowed the girl and had done nothing. Ineffectual. Once again, Emily had let opportunity pass.

"I hate you," Lorelei had said. "I hate your guts."

"So," Emily said to David. Her legs bounced nervously under the table as she stirred and stirred her drink. "So, how weird is it that I start out trying to help Lorelei, and she ends up being stalked by some muscle-bound, love-sick pedophile and a pack of bum hunters?"

"It's not your fault," David said.

"But it is. If I hadn't taken those shots of her when she didn't want me to... If I hadn't shown them to Travis."

"You trusted him."

"I'm a great judge of character, huh?" Suddenly, Emily disintegrated into tears. People in the coffee shop stole glances her way, then averted their eyes.

David handed her a napkin. She wiped her nose and blew. She tried to stop, but emotion kept seeping out of her.

"You're tired," David said. "You look exhausted."

"I'm so worried about Lorelei. What if we never find her?"

"Look. I'll take over now. I'm obligated to contact the authorities if I think anyone is in danger. This definitely qualifies. I'll need that photo of her."

"I thought you might." She touched her phone." I'm sending it to you now. Lord knows, everybody else in the world has seen it by now."

A couple of scruffy teenagers came in. They raised a hand to David and he nodded recognition. His phone chimed. He checked it.

"Got it." Then, "What about her parents? Any luck there?"

"Travis found them. At least he thinks it's them. Man, she is going to be so mad." Emily hated the fevered press of tears flavored with frustration and guilt.

"Hey," he said. He touched her hand, but she jerked away. The last thing she wanted was for David to think of her as another lost girl in need of his counseling services.

"I'm just concerned about her," she said. "Is that so wrong?"

"It's not wrong. It's just not productive." He sighed. "Look, don't underestimate her. She's smart. This will all work out."

"What if her parents turn out to be total assholes?"

"We'll cross that bridge when we come to it. Parents are always the first option, but you never know what situations these kids come from. They run away for a reason."

"Way to make me feel better."

"Emily, quit beating yourself up over this. You screwed up. So what? In the grand scheme of things that have happened to Lorelei in her short life, you're just a minor blip on her radar."

"Wow. Again, thanks."

"Look. At least now we know she's still in town. That's a start. I've got some friends in the Austin police force who'll be on the lookout for her."

"Will they put out an APB like on cop shows?"

"Something like that."

"Between you, me, Leo, those bum hunter guys, the cops and her parents, there's no way she can escape."

"Don't be so sure. These kids can be resourceful. They always surprise you." David hit a button on his phone. "Hello. Sgt. Jackson, please."

She was impressed. David had the police on speed dial.

Lorelei

LEO WOULD know where to look. Of this she was sure. He had found her in L.A. and he would find her in Austin. He'd hang around the shelters. He'd learn where all the soup kitchens were and which churches were open to street culture. He'd ask people about her. He'd hand out money to anybody who would give him information.

So even if she had felt safe from the bum hunters at the drop-in, she couldn't go anywhere near there now.

She had no choice. She had to get out of Austin. She needed transportation, but she wasn't likely to find a ride this late. Everybody was already bedded down. She needed some place safe to sleep, a location Leo wouldn't consider. It only took her a moment to decide.

She headed out of Emily's neighborhood toward Group Therapy. She could wait outside until the bar closed and then slip over the back fence again. She walked slowly. There was no need to rush since Group didn't close down until two. She had some granola bars, so she wouldn't have to dumpster dive. The thought of what she had eaten her last time there made her nauseated.

At the mouth of the alley, she assessed her situation. She could go hang out across the street as she had done before and watch for Angel and Tino to leave, or she could wait in the alley and hope they would come out and offer her another warm sandwich and glass of juice. She could scale the fence later.

The alley was sour with garbage stench. She moved past the reek into the depths of darkness. When she was sure she was out of site from the street, she crouched against a wall. She reached into her pack and took out the new knit cap and a thick pair of gloves. She took off her boots and pulled on clean wool socks. She put her boots back on. Using her backpack as a seat to buffer the cold ground, she leaned against the wall and waited.

A few people stumbled by the alley's entrance. They stopped and laughed, then moved on, happy silhouettes against the bright streetlights, their breath fogging the night around them.

She closed her eyes. Her adrenaline rush had faded, and now she felt drained, sad, exhausted and lonely. If only she could sleep, maybe she would feel better. She pulled her jacket around her, thankful for the newfound warmth.

As she began to doze, she told herself it would only be a few hours until she could climb the fence and make a fire. Then she could really sleep. And in the morning she would try the train yards. She could always find fellow travelers at train yards.

She heard the crunch of gravel under boot heels, but it didn't alarm her. She thought she was dreaming. She often dreamed of her father's footsteps, how he would pause outside their door to scrape snow from his boots, the solid thud as they thunked to the floor in the mudroom. As she floated in the twilight of her dreams, he spoke her name.

"Lorelei."

Panic shot through her like a flame, and she was on her feet.

"I told you I'd find you."

"Leo." His name was bitter on her tongue.

"Baby. Why'd you run away from me?"

"How . . . how'd you find me?"

"It doesn't matter." He stepped toward her, but she cowered into a corner. "All that matters is that I've come to take you home."

"Leave me alone, you obsessive freak."

"Now baby. Is that any way to talk to your old man?"

"You are not my old man. Get away from me." She lunged for her pack, but he was on her and had her in his arms. She fought him, kicked and clawed, but he held her tight.

"Go on. Get it out." His breath was sickening in her ear. "I'm here. I understand."

"Get off!" she screamed. "Get off me!"

"I love you, Lorelei. You're my girl."

"No!"

"Don't you miss me?" He forced his tongue into her mouth and she screamed.

"Stop!" A deep masculine voice bounced down the alley.

Leo tensed. Lorelei stopped struggling. Angel stood in a shaft of light streaming from the open kitchen door.

"Let her go," Angel growled. "She's just a kid."

"This is no business of yours, hombre," Leo said.

"I make it my business." He untied the apron at his waist and tossed it to the side.

"I've got no fight with you," Leo said. "We were just leaving."

"You'll have to come through me."

Leo let her go, turned and held his hands in the air. Lorelei snatched her backpack and moved toward Angel, but Leo grabbed her arm and jerked her back. He was strong, and her arm throbbed in his grip.

"Owww," she whined. "Stop it."

"I'm going to kick your ass," Angel said as he advanced toward them. He pushed up the sleeves of his shirt and bent forward into a fighting stance.

"You don't know who you're messing with, man. Back off," Leo said. He reached into a pocket with his free hand. The blade of a knife appeared with a snap. Leo didn't hesitate, but began to slowly circle around Angel, dragging Lorelei with him toward the exit.

Angel drew his fist up and swung. Leo jumped back.

Lorelei laughed and he jerked her arm. "Shut up."

"He won't use it," Lorelei taunted. "Go on. Punch him, Angel."

"Let her go," Angel said.

"Fuck off."

"Last chance, amigo."

Leo shoved her behind him and she fell back into the alley. The men were suddenly shoving and swinging, arms and legs flying. There was the smack of flesh when a hit landed. They grunted and cursed. They fell, kicking each other, grabbing for a hold. Leo's bulk was not an advantage in a brawl. He was bigger and stronger, but Angel was swift and knew how to fight.

Lorelei scrambled to her feet. She dodged the fray and took off for the mouth of the alley.

The men slammed into the dumpster with a hollow, resounding thud. She looked over her shoulder in time to see Angel jump to his feet. Leo stayed down. He wiped blood from his nose. They were frozen, panting, hurt. Each man's eyes darted her direction and then back to his foe.

"Run, chica, run!" Angel yelled. "Get away!"

Leo made a move toward her, but Angel swept a quick leg beneath him, and Leo went down again. They tumbled against the dumpster, and the fight raged. Leo banged Angel's head against the gray metal, and blood appeared over an eye.

Lorelei fled down South Congress toward the river. Angel had saved her, but for how long? He couldn't keep Leo occupied forever. She had to find an escape. The train station was her only option. She needed to find the train station.

Run, chica, run, she repeated to herself. *Get away.*

Emily

DAVID HAD warned her that the parents might not come. He said that often parents decided at the last minute that they just couldn't do it. But Lorelei's parents had been on a plane mere hours after David contacted them.

Emily and David waited at a four-top in the Driskill's opulent dark wooden bar. It was neutral ground, a popular location to meet in Austin. It was still early. Emily felt as if she hadn't slept in days and was grateful for the coffee their waitress brought.

She was admiring the bronze sculpture of cowboys and horses galloping through the bar when the Kimballs appeared, hesitant and out of place. Maggie Kimball's frumpy pastel sweater and pleated slacks channeled the 1980s. Her soft brown hair was held back in a pale blue bow more common to toddlers. Elias Kimball wore khakis and a frayed-collared sport shirt stretched over his paunch. He had a military-style haircut. "We should have met at a pancake house," Emily whispered before the couple approached them.

They shook hands, and introductions were made.

"Please, have a seat," David said.

Mrs. Kimball looked uncomfortable at the prospect of sitting on the hairy black-and-white cowhide chairs. The waitress returned, and Elias ordered water. Maggie said, "Nothing for me." Emily wondered if the woman had ever been in a bar.

"So," David said. "Thank you for coming, Mr. Kimball."

"Call me Elias," he said. "And my wife's Maggie. Where's Rose?"

"We're not sure," David said. "She's disappeared again."

"If you don't know where she is then why are we here?" Elias asked.

"We lost her since we spoke."

Emily wondered if David had misrepresented their knowledge of Lorelei's whereabouts on purpose. They had looked for her everywhere, but she had eluded them.

"This isn't just another run around is it? I don't have any more time for rigmarole and dead ends," the father said.

David reassured him. "We'll find her. I had friends in the Austin police force put a BOLO out on her."

"BOLO?"

"Sorry. It's short for 'be on the lookout.' If she's in town, they'll find her."

The older man said, "Let's just make sure we are talking about the right girl here before we go on."

Emily had printed out a clean copy of Lorelei's cover photo. David handed it to the mother. Maggie grabbed at her neck as if clutching imaginary pearls, and tears gushed out of her.

"Mercy," she wept. Elias put an arm around his wife.

Emily felt her own push of hot tears. She wished desperately to be less sensitive to other people's feelings, to have a more stoic side. David took her hand and squeezed softly. She managed to choke back her sympathy.

"The police told us they thought it was her, but we can't believe it. Could it be wrong? That police face identification thing?"

"It's possible I guess, but I doubt it."

He shook his head. "Put that away. Maggie doesn't want to ever see that again. That permanent, what she did to her face?"

"It can be removed with a laser," David said.

"What would that cost?

"I wouldn't know, sir."

"I don't know," he said. "I don't know. This thing she's done to herself. What else? There's no telling what else she's done."

Maggie took a tissue from her drab department store bag.

"Right now, we have to think about what we can do to help Rose," David said.

"We already done just about everything a parent could possibly do," he said, defeat underlying his words.

"Ask yourself why she would run away, get these tattoos," David said. "People do things for a reason. Something has to have pushed her to make these decisions."

Anger ignited in the father. "Are you saying this was our fault? 'Cause I can tell you right now that none of this is our fault. None of it!"

Emily was shocked by the man's sudden vitriol. His anger was such a stark contrast to her own father's gentle nature. Emily could see how Lorelei could feel threatened and controlled by this man.

"No, sir. Not at all," David said calmly. "I'm just asking what the reasons could be."

"Well, we've been asking ourselves the same thing for about three years now. And I can tell you . . ."

"She's sick," Maggie interjected.

Everyone waited.

"Mentally ill. That's what the doctors said."

"I understand," David said. "It's quite common for mental illness to run in families."

They both looked at David blankly.

"What do you mean?" Maggie asked in a tender voice.

"Your son, Noah. Rose tells us he's schizophrenic."

"You must be mistaken," Maggie said. "We don't have a son named Noah."

It was now David and Emily's turn to be confused.

"You do have other children?" David said.

"We have four boys," Elias said. "All married with children, living happy lives in Salt Lake. We don't have a schizophrenic son named Noah. Whatever gave you that idea?"

"Why would she say that?" Maggie asked her husband. "That's strange."

"She did, didn't she? Told you she had a brother named Noah. That's a new one."

David lowered his head in contemplation. The Kimballs looked at each other, at Emily, at David, then at each other again, waiting for somebody to make sense.

"Okay," Emily said. "She told us that she has been moving around the country looking for a long-lost brother, but you say there is no lost brother?"

"She lies," Elias said. "She lies all the time. You blame us. I know you do. Everybody always blames the parents. But she's very hard to control."

"There is no reason to place blame, Mr. Kimball," David said.

"Do you have any idea what it's like to watch your child change into a stranger? A kid making straight A's and then suddenly she's flunking? A kid who used to be all the teachers' favorite, and she starts getting in trouble for not paying attention and speaking out of turn in class? Don't act like you understand." His voice had continued to rise. His wife laid a hand on his leg. He got up and walked toward the lobby.

"Give him a minute, he'll come back," she said. "He's not a bad man. He just can't grasp why she won't just snap out of it and act like she's supposed to."

"You have to be her advocate," David said. "If your husband finds it difficult to be an effective parent, he could use some counseling of his own to help him deal with things."

She shook her head. "You can forget that."

"How old is Rose?"

"She'd be seventeen by now."

"She's seventeen?"

"She was fifteen when she left. Didn't even have her driver's license. I don't know how she's made it all over the country like she has."

"What was her diagnosis?" David asked. "Is it bipolar? We get a lot of kids who struggle with manic depression."

But before she could answer, Elias Kimball returned. He appeared much calmer.

Maggie took a big breath and whispered, "Yes. The doctors say it's bipolar."

When her husband spoke, Maggie demurred. "We just thought she was really moody, just acting out. Those tattoos. She really went overboard with those. They're hard to take. We're LDS. We believe tattoos defile the temple of your body. Why would she do that to herself? To us?"

"Many people with bipolar defy authority. It could be that. It could be that she enjoys the sensation of getting the tattoos. She could find it pleasurable. People with bipolar are high-level pleasure seekers. Anything that gives an adrenaline surge would be attractive to them. Addictive even."

"Like sex," the father said.

"Yes," David said quietly. "Sexual promiscuity is one of the most common symptoms of bipolar disorder."

"She did that. At home. We were afraid she was getting a reputation," the father hung his head as he spoke. "It all started about the same time, her school problems, her interest in boys. It's shameful. We raised Rose to be respectful of herself and others. But she turned out . . ." He couldn't continue.

"Mr. Kimball, Elias. Rose has a disease just like diabetes or cancer. She needs treatment and support. This is not a character flaw."

The mother twisted a tissue into corkscrews in her tiny hands. "We know you're right. She has crazy mood swings—one minute she'd be buzzing around the kitchen helping me. She'd cook a dozen dishes and bake pies and cookies and read. Lord, that girl could read two books a day. She never slept. Then, like somebody pulled a curtain over her, she'd take to bed, and I couldn't get her out, not to go to school or anything."

"Sounds like she's a rapid-cycler," David said.

"That's what the doctors called it," the mother said.

"At first we thought she was on drugs, so we sent her to counseling, but that didn't change a thing. It just seemed to make her mad," the father said. "The counselor said he couldn't tell if she was using or not. Big fat waste of money."

"So," the mother continued, "Elias decided to send her to one of those wilderness camps for troubled teens. He said it would straighten her out. When she came back, she seemed calmer, but that wore off too."

"So I had her committed," Elias said. "It was a last resort. She's old enough to drive, but I wasn't going to let her get her license until she calmed down. I couldn't have her out all wild, driving around, out of control. I have a responsibility to the community."

"Of course, that upset her," Maggie went on. "She was supposed to get her learner's permit, but Elias wouldn't let her until she shaped up. We thought for sure that would be something that would make her fly straight."

"But it was like she couldn't help herself. And lie, that girl would lie to your face and not blink. So I sent her to a mental hospital," he said, emotion tickling his voice.

"We did," Maggie said. "We sent her to a mental health facility for a month. That's when they told us her diagnosis. They started prescribing all these medications that caused all these side effects."

"But they calmed her butt down," Elias said defiantly.

"They did," the mother said, nodding agreement, looking at the twist of tissue in her lap. "But she hated them. She'd drag around like a zombie half the time. I don't know which was worse. As long as I controlled her pills it seemed like she came back into balance, but when we tried letting her do it herself, she'd always forget, or she'd say she felt fine and then she wouldn't take them, and in no time she'd be right back where she started."

"Then she ran away," Elias said. "She ran off after the hospital stay. This whole illness has been a financial disaster for us. We can't leave Rose alone. My wife lost her job because of absences. The older she gets, the worse it gets."

"It's the most desperate feeling in the world to watch your child destroy herself," Maggie said, her voice pleading for understanding. "Mood disorder. They called it that. A mood disorder."

"It sounds like you've done everything you could," David said. "Bipolar is difficult to recognize in kids. Sometimes, the depressive part of the disease shows up first, so people just think their children are depressed. When the manic part shows up later, it can seem like ADHD."

Mood disorder. It all made sense—Lorelei's abrupt arrivals and even quicker departures. Her fluctuating tides of energy. Her sexual advances. Quick anger. The tattoos.

And the brother story. There was logic to creating Noah to take the blame, a brother with all the same problems. Why not tell a story where Lorelei is the savior instead of the rejected one? She was convincing. Had she told the story so many times that she'd begun to believe it herself?

"Every time the phone rings," the mother said, "I never think it means my daughter is coming home. I always think someone is calling to tell me that they found Rose dead."

Lorelei

AFTER LORELEI fled the fight, she had come upon a church and slipped around back to the burial grounds. She bedded down in bushes, but there was no way she could sleep. She rocked, clutching her knees to her chest, her heart's rhythm matching her flurry of thoughts.

So Leo had found her. He had warned her that he would. The tail feathers on her phoenix had been tingling at the edge of her eye, making her think about him, so she should have known he would show up.

Lorelei had thought she could just leave him behind like she had so many other situations. She'd run away from her home, an unbearable life filled with her weeping mother and her angry father. Since then, her life had become a progression of a few months here a few months there. The community house, different friends. Her year with Leo had been a long stay in her otherwise transient existence. It had started out safe, romantic even, but ended up quite another way.

After her Haida boyfriend left in the middle of the night, Lorelei had taken up with a group of travelers. Along the way, she'd met Road Dogg. He was in his early twenties, tall and thin and sprinkled with tattoos. He had the traveler railroad tracks on his arm. Each letter of his name was inked across one of his knuckles. He talked about road literature like Jack Kerouac and Jack London. He liked Ray Bradbury's work and Stephen King.

He'd gotten her a job picking up nails on construction sites. Road Dogg had been all over the country and said that kids in the north worked while kids in the south begged. He said, "Never be a beggar." She'd earned enough that she didn't have to wear shelter clothes. She had a nice sleeping bag and a small tarp. Road Dogg kept her jumping, finding day jobs for them on Craigslist. They did drywall, framing and gardening.

The day he decided to leave for warmer climes, Lorelei had tagged along. They piled into an old minivan with a ragtag bunch of other kids. They left the massive green trees of Oregon for the steely cliffs of the Pacific Coast Highway. Lorelei had never seen the ocean and was so enthralled that she imagined flinging herself over the edge to see if she could fly off into the golden horizon.

The trip had taken weeks. New friends flowed in and out of their lives. They stopped at festivals where they found temporary work serving up vegan meals to patchouli-smelling crowds of groovy music lovers. They slept in fields and abandoned houses. But what started out as the best road trip ever took a turn for the worse when they rolled into Southern California.

Los Angeles was a tangle of highways. The first serious urban center she'd ever experienced, L.A. was all hard edges and concrete. She'd been surprised by the amount of barbed wire. To her, barbed wire was for keeping cattle in, but apparently in the city, it was for keeping people out. She liked the graffiti, but some of it was poorly rendered, and it gave her a creepy, depressed feeling. It reminded her of her latest tattoo, a lightning bolt she'd let someone scrape under her eye, an immediate regret.

They were disappointed to find that the community house where Road Dogg usually crashed had burned to the foundation. Somebody told them neighbors set the building afire because it had turned into a squat.

The rest of the pack decided to drive on to Vegas, but Road Dogg stayed to visit a friend with a tattoo studio. Road Dogg had become like a big brother to her, so Lorelei stayed too.

Inside Leo's L.A., mesmerizing music pinged softly underneath the razz of tattoo guns. It smelled sterile, like the entire studio had just been autoclaved. The walls were covered from floor to ceiling with colorful Japanese dragons and vivid lotus flowers, scarlet swelling hearts and 1940s hula girls. Snakes, skulls, crossbones and flames were tacked everywhere.

Road Dogg walked into the back, where the buzzing grew louder. Artists leaned over tables and massage chairs where clients exposed various body parts.

He stopped at an open doorway. Tracing paper with sketches lifted gently from the walls. There were pages cut from magazines and black-and-white photographs of arms and legs and backs.

It was magical.

"Hey, man. What up?" her friend said.

"Dogg! Come on in. Good to see you, man. Who's your chick?"

"This is Lorelei."

"Right on, man. Nice to meet you, Lorelei."

Leo wasn't like anyone she'd ever met. He had the exaggerated muscles of a body builder and the thick neck that Lorelei had always found repulsive on her school's football players. But somehow it all worked on Leo. The tattoos were plentiful, but not excessive. Somehow she felt an attraction to him even though he had to be in his thirties.

Road Dogg and Leo knuckle bumped like old friends.

"Still working I see," Road Dogg said.

"Yeah, man. You know me. I've got ink for blood."

"Got any new work?"

Leo pulled his shirt over his head to show an orange koi swimming from under his arm up over his left shoulder. Lorelei had never seen such an exquisite tattoo.

"That's freaking awesome, man," Road Dogg said.

Leo examined one of Road Dogg's arms. "You've got to do something about those rough tats. Stop with the stick and poke, dude."

"You know me, man. It's like a bad habit. Once you start, you can't stop. I don't have the money for somebody with your talents."

Leo turned to Lorelei. "What about you? This idiot here do that to your face?"

She touched the sad excuse for a lightning bolt.

"Hell, no. I didn't do that mess," Leo said. "You should fix her up, man. Can you make it look better?"

Leo nodded. "Sure, I can fix that."

"I don't have any money," Lorelei said.

"That's cool. Girl as pretty as you shouldn't be left with that mess on her face. You've got to think about it though. I'm not going to do a cover on you just to do a cover. It's got to be something you like."

"He's serious," Road Dogg said. "He won't do somebody who just walks in off the street and wants to pick one out of a book."

Leo gestured to one section of wall where recognizable designs dominated. "This is what you call flash stock art." He pointed to another section. "That's my original artwork. I prefer to do something that means something to a person."

She scanned the designs.

"Tattoos—longest shelf life of any product, highest buyer's remorse," Leo said.

Road Dogg and Lorelei found a camp of kids outside the city because he didn't like shelters. Road Dogg worked a lot and included Lorelei when she would come. They picked strawberries and broccoli in enormous fields where she met families of migrant workers who shared their beans and rice. They were illegals, the people her father talked about who took jobs in factories and slaughterhouses that rightfully belonged to Americans. Lorelei wasn't so sure that these people were hurting anybody.

One afternoon, while Road Dogg was out harvesting Brussels sprouts, she came into the city by herself. At the tattoo studio, a chesty brunette was in Leo's chair. He was detailing a flower on her hand while a drunken, sullen man looked on. The woman seemed so stoned that she might go to sleep even while needles punctured her skin.

It took Lorelei only a second to realize that the man was talking smack about his woman, and it was making Leo mad.

"Put my name on her ass," the guy said.

The woman nodded, "It's okay," she said.

Leo locked eyes with the man, but said to the woman, "I won't ink his name on you."

"You put what I tell you to put on her," the guy said.

"That's it," Leo said, stripping off his latex gloves—snap, snap. "We're done here. Take your business somewhere else."

"You got to finish her."

"You don't want me working on anybody as pissed off as I am right now."

"You haven't even done me yet. I want one of those hula girls there with her tits all hanging out. I want it here." He pointed to a vacant space among the lewd sleeve on his arm.

Something changed in Leo's eyes. He said, "Fine, have a seat."

The woman got up, and the man settled into Leo's chair. Lorelei watched from the doorway. Within minutes the idiot's forehead was sprinkled with beads of sweat. Lorelei could tell Leo held the needle in the same spot longer than necessary. She'd seen him work twice as fast. When the guy ended up with his head between his knees, his girlfriend moved in to console him.

As the idiot was leaving, he had turned to Leo and said, "You're the worst damn tattoo artist I've ever seen."

Leo just smiled.

"I can't believe you made him sick," Lorelei said.

"He deserved it. You don't treat a woman that way."

That was all it took.

She never went back to the migrant camp.

Leo lived in a modern apartment above the studio. Not the worst place she'd ever crashed. The first night was awkward. She'd assured him that she was eighteen. He looked dubious, but let the subject drop.

He was a considerate lover, but nothing like her Indian love. Just the thought of that lean, dark-skinned boy caused her owl tattoo to pulse. But Leo made her feel wanted and protected. And for a while, that was enough.

They looked through books and discussed the meanings of certain tattoos to fix her eye. She decided on a phoenix, the bird that self-destructs in flames, then rises from her own ashes, reborn beautiful and strong. After he'd drawn a dozen options, they finally arrived at a carefully considered bird that would mask her previously shoddy work.

Before she starting getting tattoos, the worst pain she had ever endured was the prick of a dentist. But being tattooed gave her a crystal clear burn that brought her clarity, a searing sensation, as if the world were made of glass. After a while, pain became a background to the hum of her thoughts, and she relaxed into a trance.

Once her face work was finished, Lorelei began to sneak into Leo's workspace and watermark the inside of her arm where the skin was thin and tender. It was worse than a bee sting, but the adrenaline jolt that seared her for that second left her alive and tingly. She'd be happy and calm for days afterward.

Leo had walked in and caught her blood lining—small strikes

she had cut into herself using water instead of ink.

"Stop it," he had said when he caught her. "What are you doing? Hurting yourself just to hurt yourself?"

"I like how it feels."

"Girl, you can't do that."

"Isn't that part of what you like about it? The rush?"

"Yeah, okay. That's part of it, but shit, you can't do it for recreation." After that, he secured his gun in a metal cabinet, and the other artists who rented space from him started locking their doors.

Leo fixed her other ratty tattoos. He took care of her and bought her clothes. He took her to Venice Beach, where nobody stared at her face. Leo bought her a pair of old roller skates, and she spent hours cruising Ocean Front Walk while he lifted weights at Muscle Beach. She sat in the sand and admired the bearded palm trees. She watched black neoprene clad surfers on waves in the distance. She danced to cheerful mariachis and watched fire-eaters and a magician with a monkey on his shoulder. Along the boardwalk, she ate shaved ice and shopped for cheap sunglasses. For the first time in her life, she grew tan. She streaked her hair blond. She was a California girl.

But one day, she noticed that she couldn't stand Leo's funky breath from the Asian food he favored. Soon came a feeling of dread at the end of the day when his cowboy boots clomped up the stairs.

In the beginning, she had felt better about herself when she was with Leo, but somehow things had soured like his breath. Without warning, her pleasant life with him was reduced to something disturbing. She quickly grew to dread his attention.

He'd take her out to eat and want sex when they got home. He'd buy her a pair of jeans and then expect a blowjob. His touch made her skin crawl. Twice, she threw up after they did it.

She hated who she became with him. And she hated him.

Leo noticed the change in her. As she'd pulled away, he'd grown controlling, desperate to hang on to her. She resented his condescending way of saying, "You'll understand when you're older."

She even hated the way his clothing, all metal buttons and studs, clanged around in the dryer in a foreboding rhythm—*You don't want this, you don't want this, you don't want this.*

So, she ran away.

Leo found her in Venice before she'd even had a chance to get out of town. She had put up scant resistance when he led her to his bike and drove her back to his apartment. He had given her a lecture on the dangers of the streets, as if she wasn't already aware. When he saw he wasn't getting anywhere with that line of reasoning, he professed his love and pleaded with her never to run away again. He started to cry, and she almost felt sorry for the sobbing hulk, but while she braced herself for his touch, her mind was calculating escape.

Soon after, Road Dogg showed up at the studio to say he was on his way to Phoenix.

"Please, take me with you," she begged when she finally got him alone. "I can't stay here another night."

"But what about Leo?" he asked.

"I have to get far away," she told him. "If I don't leave L.A., he'll keep finding me. He won't leave me alone. You have to let me come with you."

Road Dogg warned her that they would be hopping a train, a loud and dirty and dangerous proposition.

"Keep him talking," she said. "I'll meet you out back in ten minutes."

Road Dogg had burned his friendship with Leo to help her. She would never be able to repay him. But his was just another kindness that she'd never be able to repay.

She had a string of those—kind people, fun people. But of course there were also mean people and crazy people. And people who turned out to be problems.

Leo was just another one of those problem people she'd been trying to leave behind.

Morning approached, and she gathered her things and headed out. She stuck to second streets as she worked her way toward the train yard. Better safe than sorry.

She hated to leave Austin, but she was fresh out of options. Her steps were heavy. Blackness pushed at the edges of her mind, but she forced herself to put one foot in front of the other. She could take herself away from another bad situation. She'd just have to do it one step at a time.

David

SHOAL CREEK had returned to its good-natured ways, but the flood's aftermath was starkly apparent. The high water line was drawn in dried mud ten feet up all the tree trunks. Limbs were strewn with random urban oddities. The stench was earthy with a hint of sewer.

David led Emily down into the park along a well-worn path. It was nearly noon, around the time the urban campers began to stir. At shelters, the homeless were kicked out as early as seven, a big reason sleepy headed, homeless teenagers avoided them.

After David picked up Emily, they'd stopped by Bouldin Creek Coffee and bought a gallon carton of dark brew and a dozen bagels. They'd stuffed a bag with containers of cream cheese and plenty of sugar, cream, napkins, plastic knives and spoons.

It was a cool day. A slight breeze carried the welcome scent of a campfire. Burning restrictions had returned to normal. The city was on the mend.

They were all gathered around the fire—Mook, Elda, Freestyle, Minion and two new girls David hadn't seen before. Elda took over the job of food distribution. The new girls helped pour coffee. David and Emily took cups and perched on logs. They watched the ravenous kids chew and chew.

"So, David," Mook said, "I appreciate the feed and all, but I get the feeling you need something. What can I do for you, man?"

"It's Lorelei. We need to find her."

"None of us have seen her."

Elda said, "Last time we saw her was at the Ramp Ranch."

"The skate park?" David said.

"No, wait," Mook said. "Remember? After that we saw that article in *Be Here Now,* and she went off to bitch out Emily. By the way, what the fuck? I asked you not to take pictures of us."

"I know," Emily said. "That's one of the reasons I came today. I want to apologize. I was wrong. I just felt this pressure to prove myself and I didn't think how my actions would affect you. I'm sorry. Really sorry."

"That was messed up, but I'm not mad anymore. It was a good article, you know? I thought it was really real, like, dead-on how things are for us. That Travis dude's a jerk, but he sure can write."

"Thank you," Emily said. "I don't think I could stand it if you guys hated me."

"No worries." Mook hit his chest lightly with his fist. "No room for hate in my heart."

David could see something significant had happened.

"What's up, Mook?" he asked.

"Betsy died," Elda said softly.

"What? Oh, Mook. No," Emily said.

"Really, man," David said. "If there is anything I can do."

Mook hung his head, and his hair fell into a wall of tangled mats around his face. "It is what it is, man."

They all knew his reality. Mook was truly homeless now.

"I have a couple of photos of your mother. A great shot of your mother and Fiona. Would you like to have those?" Emily asked.

"Yeah, man. Thank you. I'd appreciate that."

"Okay. Sure. I'll print them out and leave them at the drop-in this week."

Their hungry, morose little group ate and sipped and stared at the fire.

Elda finally said, "So, did Lorelei ever make it to your house? She was super-freaked about the picture."

"Oh, she came to see me all right. She threw a clay pot through my front window."

"You didn't tell me that," David said.

Emily shrugged as if to say, *What difference would it make?*

"She probably just hopped a train," Elda said. "That's what I would do."

"To where?" David asked.

"I don't know. Sante Fe, Phoenix, New Orleans? Somewhere north. Take your pick."

"If she's still around town, any idea where she might hang out?"

"She's weird. She did a lot of library time."

"Okay, thanks," David said. "And Mook, I thought you'd want to know—Fiona's mother identified her body."

"How'd that happen?" he asked.

"Mother had her fingerprinted when she was about seven. Morgue matched the prints."

He nodded. "Did she come get her?"

David shook his head. "No. They buried her in the potter's field outside of town. I can show you where if you want to go see her."

Emily

THEY CHECKED the library, the Ramp Ranch, Zilker Park, Town Lake and Bouldin Creek. They tried University Baptist and other churches along The Drag. They searched the train depot at Lamar and Fifth, and with permission, walked the switching yard. David called his contact at the Austin PD, but the BOLO hadn't produced any results. They searched all day without a trace of Lorelei.

When David brought Emily home, they were exhausted.

"Come in," she said. "I'll feed you."

He quietly followed her inside and collapsed onto a kitchen chair.

She handed him a glass of Chianti.

"I guess we have to tell her parents we really have lost her," she said. "And then they'll go home and forget about her all over again."

He sighed. "But they won't forget about her."

"Seems to me they're not that interested in getting her back. Well, maybe the mother is, but the father, he's relieved to not have to deal with her anymore. I can see what would make Lorelei run. I mean I know she's sick, but that father of hers, he's not helping the situation any."

"They're conflicted. They've tried. Parents get worn down by a difficult child. I'm sure they're financially exhausted, mentally exhausted, emotionally exhausted."

They sipped wine while Emily booted up her laptop. David had never seen her gutter tribe shots. As she looked for the ones of Betsy and Fiona to give Mook, she clicked through all of them. David scooted his chair closer and leaned in to watch.

Each photo told a story. These kids were animated, dirty, laughing, passed out, dancing, crying, fighting, begging, eating, hugging, resting, running away. Those hollow eyes, the rotten teeth, the layers of dirt. Most people couldn't hide their disgust, their trepidation, but David looked at them with love. It made Emily ashamed to think how she used to pass by these kids and consider them just an unseemly part of Austin's landscape. Now, she wondered what brought each of these young people to such desperation.

Emily whispered, "My parents would go to the ends of the earth to find me. They'd sell the last thing they owned to see that I got treatment if I needed it."

David studied the photos.

"That may be true, but you have to understand the psychology that affects the Kimballs. They're still grieving their well child. They have to mourn the loss of their ideal, healthy child before they can accept one who is chronically ill. A bipolar diagnosis can devastate an entire family."

"You make it all sound so sterile, so . . . I don't know . . . unemotional."

"No. It's very emotional, but you can't help people if you get overly emotional too. You have to have healthy . . . "

"Boundaries. I know, healthy boundaries. I get it now."

She came across her series of black-and-whites of Lorelei against the rough kitchen walls. Her tattoos were bold while her eyes were so pale they seemed translucent.

"Wow," David said.

"The day I took these, she tried to put the moves on me. Right here in this kitchen. She kissed me. Only time I've ever been kissed by a girl."

"Don't take this the wrong way, but it was probably just survival sex. It's an easy barter for shelter or food. Their bodies are their only currency."

"It was like she thought she owed me something."

"Like Mook said, 'It is what it is.' Just get ready. A new batch of them arrives every spring just in time for the South by Southwest

Festival. I've always thought of them like the Congress bridge bats. They migrate here in the spring, stay all summer, then start moving on in the fall."

"Interesting observation."

"Hey, I've got a favor to ask you."

"What?"

"Our annual fundraiser is coming up. An art gallery in town has offered to host it this year. How great would it be if we used your photos? This is real. You can feel the emotions in your shots. We could use them for our publicity materials, maybe our brochure. That is, if you would let us. We don't have any money to pay you, but we can give you credit."

"I don't expect to get paid. Of course you can use them. We should get my mother to write the brochure for free. She cranks those things out all the time."

"Sure. Great."

Emily fished her mobile from a pocket and held down Barbara's speed dial number.

"Emily?" she said. "Is everything all right? Did you find the girl?" Emily had been keeping her mother abreast of the Lorelei situation, had told her about their meeting with the Kimballs.

"No. No luck."

"I'm sorry."

"I've got a favor to ask. Would you volunteer your time to write a brochure for Tumbleweed Young Adult Center's spring fundraiser?"

She paused only a moment. If she said no, Emily was going to remind her mother of all the times she had been dragged into her PR projects, but Barbara said, "Absolutely. I'd be happy to."

"They want to use my photographs to hang in an art gallery as the backdrop for the event."

"That's wonderful. Tell the gallery owner I want to write the media release for the show too."

"Okay, I will. Thanks, Mom."

"Happy to do it. And Emily."

"Yes?"

"I like it when you call me Mom."

Emily didn't know how to respond, so she simply said, "Okay. I'll remember that." Then she touched a button and her mother was gone.

"She's in," Emily said.

David smiled. Emily smoothed a curl away from his forehead and lightly kissed him on the lips.

"Why'd you do that?" he asked.

"Because you're a sweet person. Because you're a guy who really cares about somebody other than himself."

Emily moved to straddle his lap. He held his hands out to his sides, surprised by her boldness, but not protesting. She folded into him and laid her head on his shoulder. It felt natural, like on the bike, only now he could hug her back.

"Hold me," she whispered.

David ran his fingers through her hair and cradled her head against him. After a while their breathing synched, and their hearts fell into the same peaceful rhythm.

"Don't worry about Lorelei. She's street smart," he said. "She's a survivor. She'll be okay."

He raised her face to his. His kiss was a gift.

They stayed that way, slowly kissing. Their touch expressing things they had both felt, but had never dared speak.

David stood up and Emily clung to him, her legs around his waist. He carried her into the bedroom, still kissing her. There was no hurry. His movements were fluid as he gently lowered her to the bed. She watched from a pillow as he shed his shirt and loosened his jeans to reveal the taut stomach that she'd clung to on the bike.

He gently kissed her right arm up to her neck until he found that sensitive spot behind her ear. Emily's mind floated. He slid her shirt away and then her jeans.

David took his time. There was no urgency, no need to prove himself. As his mouth explored her body, she felt his heartbeat in every touch.

She needed him inside her, and she whispered, "Come here."

He held himself above her, and she watched the wave of his stomach muscles with each push. Her hands roamed his pulsing torso. He didn't look away or close his eyes to drift into fantasy. He focused on her. Their eyes locked as they moved together.

She pulled him down, and they shifted, scissoring their legs. He cupped her shoulders in his strong hands and buried his face in her hair. It was perfect. She let herself go. Her whole body vibrated with pleasure.

She felt his climax building, and she held him tight. His breath was halting in her ear, his body rigid with desire.

They fell apart, panting, smiling, staring at the ceiling.

"Oh my God," Emily said.

"Yeah, I know. Wow."

Emily felt satisfied in a way she didn't recognize.

"Water?" he asked her as he rose.

She watched him walk naked into her kitchen. As Emily's breathing slowed, her mind wandered, and suddenly, she was flooded with a reality. She had let many men into her bed, but she'd never opened her heart. The more men she was with, the less she had believed in love. But David was different. He was more real, more present.

She was used to the flush of desire. It was her overwhelming feelings for him that shocked her. She wanted him and not just for one night. David was not a man to play with and then discard. He was an adult, not the half-drawn men of extended adolescence that Emily was accustomed to. David was a man of substance, and if she let him in, he'd be around for a while. And she wanted that. For once, Emily was absolutely certain of what she wanted.

He returned with a cool glass of water. He crawled into bed and pulled the sheet up over them. He didn't fall asleep even though she knew he must be exhausted.

"You're an interesting guy, David."

"Why do you say that?"

"I guess I should say you interest me."

"Good." He rolled over and kissed her slowly. "Because you interest me."

They stayed in bed, talking until morning light fell in lacy patterns across the sheets.

"So why did you decide to do what you do? Help these kids?" she asked.

"Because people get better. I believe that."

"Really?"

He considered his words. "How can these kids endure life if nobody ever shows them love? How can they love themselves if they've not been told they were worth loving?"

"That's sad."

"I've led a fortunate life. Other people aren't so lucky. Helping people seemed the right thing to do, for me anyway."

His explanation made sense. She had always criticized her own home as bourgeois, but it had been a good, solid home with devoted parents. Perhaps, in some twisted way, it had been reassuring to have something solid to reject.

"I need to figure out what I'm going to do when I grow up," Emily said. "Maybe I'll do what you do."

"You're an artist."

"I'm a bartender. That makes me practically a psychologist. I listen, give advice, provide a shoulder to cry on. I think I'd be good at what you do."

"People choose it because their heart tells them they have to."

She rolled onto her stomach and propped herself up on her elbows. "In some strange way that I can't explain, I feel like I understand them."

"That's because you see them as people. They aren't just an annoyance or a burden or menace. They're real to you."

He reached up and gently touched her face. He pulled her to him and folded her into his warmth, a perfect fit. He stroked her hair, his breath tender against her cheek. His voice was a deep, soothing vibration.

"You do seem to have a way with the kids. They trust you. Think you'd like to volunteer? We could sure use your help. That way you can see what you're up against."

"I could do that, but that doesn't sound very hopeful."

He kissed her hair. "As long as people like you care, there is always hope."

Lorelei

IT HAD taken only moments for Austin to grow small and fade into the horizon line. At the train yard, a bunch of freight-hopping crusty punk kids on their way to New Orleans had told her it was an eighteen-hour ride.

The rhythm of the tracks lulled her travel companions into a stupor on the floor of the empty Union Pacific car, but Lorelei stayed awake, watching the flatlands of Texas slip away. She studied the limestone hills outside the city. Then came expansive empty plains, a prehistoric landscape with only the occasional footprint of man.

She recalled her last train ride. She'd tagged along with Road Dogg from L.A. toward Phoenix. They'd slept in the bottom of an empty coal hopper, bandanas over their faces to screen black dust. He had crawled up the sloped sides to peer out at the exact moment they were passing through a crossing. Stopped traffic saw his masked face peeking over the lip of the container. Homeland security hauled them off the train at the next stop.

Authorities hadn't been interested in Lorelei, but they had taken Road Dogg to the local jail. She had waited for him for three days. Finally, starving and lonely, Lorelei had moved on. She hitched the rest of the way to Phoenix and found the bus terminal.

So, she was extra careful. She didn't want to be found and questioned and held against her will. She didn't need counseling or therapy in some psych ward. She'd served her twenty-eight days of indignities, invasions of privacy and drugs that left her hollow and dull.

All these thoughts flowed like mercury through her mind, the past and future a seamless vision. She was thinking of the night before. How she had hidden from Leo behind a church. In the morning, she had gone to the Driskill to see if she could spange a quick twenty before she went on to the train yards. She'd been peering around a corner, on the lookout for the hotel's uniforms, when she'd spied her parents.

They were so out of place standing in front of the opulent hotel, considering the frilly arched entryway. Her mother smoothed down the front of her clothes as was her nervous habit. Her father touched the small of her mother's back reassuringly and propelled her inside. Lorelei sank to the sidewalk in a rush of disbelief.

She wanted to run to her mother, to fall into her arms and explain everything. To tell her she was sorry, so sorry. Lorelei blinked back tears. After everything she had destroyed for them, they were searching for her. For just a moment, Lorelei allowed herself to consider the possibility that they wanted her back.

But then she remembered her body art.

Lorelei fought to smother the dull pain of crushed hope. They would never accept her now. They hadn't liked the old her, so they certainly wouldn't like the new her.

She searched her heart for the right thing to do. She felt compelled to let them know she was still alive. She owed them that much. She'd write her mother a note and give it to the bellhop.

She shoved her hands into the pockets of Emily's old jacket, looking for a scrap of paper. Her search revealed an inside zippered pocket she hadn't noticed before. There she discovered the envelope and the note.

Lorelei,

Please allow me to help you. Here is enough money for a ticket back home. Please go home. Your parents must be worried sick about you. All parents want to know that their children are safe and not hungry or cold.

You're a smart girl. Do the right thing.

Safe travels,

Barbara

P.S. Please don't tell Emily. She wouldn't understand.

Inside the envelope she found five one hundred dollar bills—
Barbara Bryce's way of putting distance between her daughter and
the pathetic homeless girl. Emily had accused her mother of always
throwing money at a problem to make it go away. Emily had no idea
how right she was.

Lorelei fingered the money. Her immediate future suddenly
looked much more promising.

She scribbled her own short note on the back of the envelope.

I'm okay. Don't look for me. Love, Rose.

Lorelei waited until there was only one handsome young
bellhop outside of the hotel. She cautiously approached. He eyed her
suspiciously, waiting for her pitch, expecting her to ask for money.

"You want something?" he asked.

She held the envelope forward. She had folded it over so he
wouldn't see the note.

"Did you see that woman who just came through here with a bow
in her hair? The kind of country people?"

"Yeah."

"Okay. Can you give the woman this?"

"Why?"

"I'm her daughter. She's looking for me. I want her to know that
I'm okay."

He hesitated and then took the note.

"Can you give me a while to get out of here? I don't want them
to catch me."

He glanced around to see if he was being watched. "Okay."

"Think you can find her?"

"I'll try."

"Great. I appreciate it."

She turned to go when he said, "Hey, will they know who it's
from?"

This amused her, and she flung her arms wide as she walked
backwards down the sidewalk.

"Yeah, dude. They'll know who it's from. Believe me, there's only one me."

She would never know if the note had found its mark, but by the time the train's destination drew near, Lorelei had convinced herself that things were as they should be. She couldn't go home. She was out of options in Austin. That's the way things worked. There was no use in crying over it or wondering if things could be another way.

That wasn't to say that she didn't have regrets. Her illness had robbed people she loved of money and energy and time. Most of all, it had robbed them of peace of mind. Life's ordinary concerns got replaced with tension and worry over her. What would she do next? How could they control her?

After a while, everyone became exhausted, and that was when they tried to drug her into the right perspective with meds that smoothed out the rough edges of her baseless grief like cool water over river rock. The problem was that the meds also extinguished the times her mind ran like liquid fire. She needed that stimulation. How could she explain that music turned to beautiful colors in her head? That random words plastered themselves to the inside of her skull like graffiti she could read with her mind?

It was frustrating that others couldn't experience her reality. If they could live inside her head they would understand that there was poetry to her disorderly thoughts. There was a balance, a payoff for the bad times.

It was all in how you looked at things; hers just always seemed to be the wrong point of view.

She touched her traveler tracks. They had been stinging for days. They knew she was in trouble and it was time for another journey.

The train whistle slashed the night, announcing their arrival, confirming distance from the past.

She was filled with anticipation; her whole body buzzed. She couldn't wait to get to New Orleans—all those people, parades and parties, all that vivid happiness and weirdness. Nobody would pay attention to a girl with a few tattoos in a place like New Orleans. She was going to blend right in.

Epilogue

WHEN DAVID asked Emily to do an exhibition for the fundraiser, he had acted as if she would be doing him a favor. When she found out where the event was booked, Emily realized things were the other way around.

ArtHive curated their own exhibitions of emerging Texas artists. Their website billed the gallery as the center of activity for contemporary art in Austin. Emily's work would be merely a backdrop for a fundraiser for one night, not an exhibition selected by ArtHive, but she was still determined to make a statement.

Barbara rented one of ArtHive's studio spaces for her. Emily rearranged her Group work schedule so that she only bartended at night. Her days were spent in the studio. She grew accustomed to the thrum of the gallery's massive air system and the low echo of murmuring visitors. Her ears always recognized the clickety-click echo of the curator's spiked heels on the polished floors.

Lisa, ArtHive's head curator, often dropped by Emily's studio space to check on her progress. Lisa had been skeptical that a novice could pull off such an ambitious show as Emily had planned, but once she saw the photographs, Lisa quickly proclaimed Emily's work perfect for their experimental art venue.

Over the many months Emily had worked on the project, the gutter punks had let down their guard and allowed her into their culture. When she began culling images for the show, she had thousands of shots to consider. Lisa encouraged her to find what she called the through-line, the soul of the work that meshed all the images into a cohesive story. Lisa wasn't getting paid for doling out advice on a facility rental, but she seemed to have a connection with the Tumbleweed Center's event as so many people in Austin did.

Physically producing the show had been challenging. Her experience creating sets for her high school photography projects came in handy. She lifted images of dozens of kids from various photos and made life-sized reproductions. They were black-and-white, some were high-contrast, others grainy and pixilated. Emily left the back supporting structure of the standees exposed. She arranged them around the gallery in a series of vignettes. She hung background shots on walls.

She finished her installation just as the caterers arrived with their foil-covered trays and white tablecloths. The sound of rattling silverware ricocheted off the glassed atrium as Emily walked around for one last fine-tune. In the end, she touched nothing.

That night, ArtHive throbbed with energy. Emily was nervous, nearly sick with anticipation. She wanted other people to see what she saw in the kids—the moment laughter erupts, a much-needed hug, eyes filled with hunger, an intimate kiss. Some of the wooden gutter punks were crouched around the fire of a squat. She had captured a kid passed out beside a dumpster, and others in a park, their dog anticipating a Frisbee that Emily dangled yards away over the crowd. She created a queue of street kids in the food line outside the drop-in. These she hung individually from the ceiling by mobile cables, allowing them to move with the pulse of the party.

People asked questions that made Emily look at her work in a new way. They saw narratives she had never even considered. The range of reactions surprised and delighted her. The words most often used to describe the show were *compelling* and *strong*.

Emily was shocked to see Beth there. She was with her friend Kelly and they brought their husbands. They were sipping drinks and assessing the show. It seemed her mother had invited half of Juniper.

"Emily, I'm just so impressed," Beth cooed as she bounced her infant in her arms. "I had no idea you were so talented."

"I've got to say," Kelly said. "This will wreck your heart. I mean, those are somebody's children."

"It makes me want to do something," Beth said.

"I know," Kelly said. "We have to find a way to get involved."

Travis had extended an olive branch by making sure that the *Be Here Now* art reporter got in good images with the fundraising story. The reviewer was haughty and didn't ask a lot of questions, but she noted that, "Absorbing subjects, stark photography, metal cables and raw wood lent the show an industrial feel, hard, like the streets." She also wrote, "The unfinished backs of each standee gave an empty effect, as if the subjects were half-human." For all her snotty attitude, she got it.

Emily was astounded by the turnout, but David wasn't surprised. He said Austin always supported the homeless in its midst. There were people from every walk of life—the wealthy and the middle-class, the political and the bohemian, the artistic and the business-minded—a hundred passionate discussions pressing against the gallery walls, all concerned with her show.

Only the gutter punks were missing. She'd tried to sell them on coming, had given them tickets. She explained that they'd be the stars of the show, but they had been immune to her spiel. She'd spent the night checking the entrance, hoping they would come.

The only homeless person she had spotted was Leslie. He was dressed for the party in a leopard print dress, high heels and a glistening tiara. He was flamboyant as usual, although he seemed to realize the occasion called for modesty.

"Congratulations." Emily turned to see Travis's wickedly smooth smile aimed her direction. "Still sore at me?"

"I haven't thought a thing about you, you egomaniacal jerk."

"I deserve that." He smiled again. "Your show is terrific. Really on point."

"Thank you, but it's about the kids, and I'm disappointed that none of them came."

"Some of them did," Travis said. "I just passed Mook on my way in."

On the other side of the front glass windows, washed in ambient light from the gallery, Mook and Elda peered in. Elda wore a baggy dress cinched at the waist with a wide leather belt and ballet flats. She had flowers in her hair, no doubt stolen from someone's garden along the way. Mook had shaved, but his unruly hair still twisted out from his head in all directions. He wore a dress shirt and a pair of pants a size too small for his lanky body.

Emily walked out of the sliding glass doors to greet them.

"Hey guys. About time you showed up."

"See," Elda said to Mook. "It's cool."

"Is anybody else coming?"

"I doubt it," Elda said.

"I'm glad y'all came. I really want you to see the show. Come on."

Mook pushed his cracked black frames up on his nose. "We'll weird everybody out."

"You're wrong. Now come on or you're going to hurt my feelings." Elda took Emily's hand.

"I'm game," she said. "I'm ready to celebrate."

"What are we celebrating?" Emily somehow knew they weren't celebrating the Tumbleweed Center's event.

"She got her GED," Mook blurted.

"And the best part is," Elda said. "Me and Mook are going to move into transitional housing next week. After we get our apartment, I'm going to get a job."

"What about you, Mook? You going to work for the Man?"

"I haven't decided yet. I don't want her going off and leaving me, so . . . maybe."

Elda adjusted the collar of his shirt. She nodded her head toward the door. "Come on. Let's go in."

The doors swished apart, and the rumble of the gallery washed over them. Barbara was coming toward them. She suddenly stopped and relieved a surprised server of an entire tray of fluted glasses.

"Hello," her mother sang. "You must be friends of Emily's. I recognize you from her work. I'm so glad you could make it tonight. I'm Barbara. Would you like a glass of champagne?"

The evening was a success. The Tumbleweed Center made money. Mook and Elda had a good time. The most amazing part was that her exhibition was, as they say in the art world, well-received. As the party was shutting down, Lisa approached Emily about extending the exhibition.

"I think," Lisa said, "this show has had such an impact that we need to keep it up for a couple of weeks. More people need to see it."

Emily was elated, and even more so when Lisa said, "Next Saturday, admission to the gallery is free. You know, in case any of your street friends want to come see the show."

When Emily shared the good news with her parents, they offered to take her and David for drinks to celebrate. They walked across the street to a small restaurant for one last glass of wine while they waited for David to wrap up the event.

They found a banquette in a corner and slid in. Her mother ordered a bottle of sparkling wine and when their flutes were filled, her father held his up and said, "A toast."

Emily and Barbara raised their glasses.

He cleared his throat. "Okay. Here goes. First off, here's to our daughter, the lovely and most talented Miss Emily Bryce. Congratulations on a very successful show at the famous ArtHive. Way to go."

"Here, here," her mother said. They clinked and drank.

"And . . . " Gerald continued, "here's to our new venture. Your mother and I have decided that we are going to start our own public relations firm. Together."

"What?" Emily said. "Really?"

"Lord knows, he's been exposed to enough of it over the past thirty years that he should know what to do by now," Barbara said.

"Pray for me. Look who's my new boss," Gerald said, and winked.

"That's exciting. I'm so happy for you guys. What's the name of your company?"

"We're calling it City Public Relations," Barbara said. "You know, CPR. Breathing life into your business or something like that. We haven't fine-tuned the slogan just yet, but you get the idea."

"Your mother is going to be the front man and I'm going to run the office, do the finances, search out new clients and artists and writers."

"And photographers, like you. We want to buy you new photography equipment and get you on the payroll. I have all sorts of events coming up that need to be shot. It's almost time for Keep Austin Cleared again, and your pictures of the garbage dump last year were perfect."

Emily raised her glass. "I'm in. Just see if you can find me some projects more interesting than garbage. Okay?"

"Will do," her mother said, and they clinked again.

As she watched her parents slosh their fizzy drinks, Emily realized that they were a team. As imperfect and challenged as they were, they were stronger together than they were apart. She was lucky to be a part of their team, part of the family.

"I love you guys," Emily said. She scooted over in the booth and hugged her mother fiercely, holding on. At first, Barbara seemed hesitant, but she quickly melted into Emily's embrace. She caught her father's eyes and he nodded his silent approval. When they moved apart, her mother touched her eyes with a bar napkin.

"Thank you, Mom, for everything you've done for me," Emily said. "You really are the glue that's held me together all these years."

Emily parked in a slit of light that fell from the kitchen window into her backyard. As she fumbled for her keys, she remembered David's kiss after she had whispered the good news about her parents. He'd had to stay longer to clean up. He would let himself into her house later. Usually he slipped into her bed without waking her, but this night she intended to wait up.

As she was unlocking the door, her cat appeared. He rubbed around her legs, bumping her for attention.

"Hello, you handsome guy." She scratched his ears. Skinny Cat had been lost to her for months after the flood, but then, like an apparition, he had appeared again, hungry and without apology or explanation for his absence.

He followed Emily inside. While he crunched cat food, she put the teakettle on and wandered into the living room. She moved the mouse on her new desktop and the massive monitor jumped to life. She'd used some of her college funds for this new computer, Photoshop and a real desk and chair. No more working at the kitchen table.

She logged on to YouTube and watched the video again. The clip had gotten thousands of hits every hour since it had posted. They had thought they were so cool, so beyond the law, but they were stupid. Austin's bum hunters had posted one of their beat-downs on YouTube and in a matter of days, they had been identified and arrested. The videographer had turned on his friends and handed over the video of Fiona's death. All three were awaiting arraignment. Emily felt some satisfaction in knowing they were caught, but she wished Lorelei were around to testify.

Emily viewed the video again. It was grainy, shot at night. Fiona being beaten. An older man pushing into the fray. Lorelei at the edges of the screen, frightened, screaming.

"Stop, please, stop."

Then she ran. She left her friend to die. There had been no other choice.

Emily's eyes fell on her cover shot of Lorelei that she had framed and hung above the desk. She hadn't included any of Lorelei's images in the show. As much as she had wanted to use them, Emily couldn't. She had failed to keep her promise once. She wouldn't do it again.

Instead, she had chosen to hang this likeness of her young friend in the privacy of her home. It was a talisman, one simple shot that had changed her profoundly. Emily had learned that compassion was a dangerous but worthwhile emotion, and that good things can come from the most daunting of circumstances. The haunting image would always remind Emily how lucky she was to be loved and to have a life so filled with promise in a very complicated world.

Q&A with Janna McMahan

You've set novels all over the South. Why did you pick Austin
for Anonymity?

Austin has a young, hip vibe. It's an educated city with an
interesting mix of people. Austin touts itself as the live music capital
of the world with good reason. Every night is a party. On weekends,
a couple of main avenues are turned into pedestrian malls lined
with bars, comedy clubs and music venues. The thousands who
wander the streets are a people-watching smorgasbord for a writer.
The funny, the intriguing, the strange—I've seen it all on Sixth and
Congress. It's a predictably unpredictable place.

Austin is big on business too—Whole Foods and Dell computers
and dozens of other high-profile national and international companies
are headquartered there (including my brother's company, Gel Pro).
The University of Texas has one of the largest student populations
in the country. Austin is also the seat of government for Texas, yet
the city is super-liberal, making it rather out of place in the larger
culture of the state.

I often visit my brother and his family in Austin. I love the
vintage clothing stores and the odd shops. In *Anonymity*, I paid
homage to some of my favorite parts of Austin, like heavenly beef
brisket, Barton Springs and the city's most well-known resident,
a cross-dressing homeless man who habitually ran for mayor and
usually took a serious percentage of the vote.

There is always risk for a writer who sets a story in a real place
and time. I tried to be as accurate in my descriptions of Austin

and her people as I could while still serving the fictional aspect of my story. Most readers love this approach and enjoy mentions of familiar landmarks and personalities while fully accepting the slight inconsistencies that come with fiction.

What compelled you to write about the homeless?

I was intrigued by the scruffy teenagers hanging around an area people call The Drag. It's a commercial strip abutting UT's campus, made famous by that horrible clock tower shooting. These kids were queued up along an alley. When I asked why, I learned it was a food bank for homeless youth.

I had never given any thought to homeless young people. I grew up in a small town where nobody was homeless. If you were down on your luck you just moved in with a relative or you moved a trailer in your parents' backyard.

Then I moved to South Carolina where the most visible homeless population is primarily African-American men. That became my mental profile of the homeless, so when I saw the volume of young homeless in Austin, I was astounded.

There was one girl, who could not have been seventeen, whose face was a mask of tattoos, a decision that would impact her for life. I carried that girl's image in my mind for fifteen years before this story finally spun out. Sometimes a situation like that will make an impression on a writer, and we'll mull it over for years before coming up with a story to do it justice.

So you decided to write about that street urchin with the tattooed face?

Who was she before she became that girl? How did she come to be one of the ragged, hungry children in an Austin alley? She made me consider numerous story lines about how young people end up without anywhere to call home.

Before I did research for this book, I always thought of the young homeless population as runaways. There was a wave of runaway literature and movies back in the 70s that contributed to a widely held, yet wildly ill-informed view of why children are homeless. Like a lot of people, I thought teens ran away from home because they didn't like the rules mom and dad set. Or perhaps they did come from an abusive situation, but they decided a romantic version of life on the road would be better than staying with a relative and trying to finish high school.

What I found was that somewhere around half of all street youth come from the foster care system (the kids call it foster scare) or a group home. Some come from a psychiatric hospital or juvenile detention. When a child turns eighteen our society opens the door and pushes them into the streets. We don't care that these kids have no safety net. They have little education, no job skills, no medical care, no food and no place to live. Foster care children tend to be the outcasts of the outcasts. In gutter punk society, fostered kids were often avoided by others.

There are the kids from families simply unable to care for them anymore. With the economy collapsing, even middle class Americans are losing their homes. Often, older children strike out on their own allowing more resources for younger siblings.

Then there are "throwaway youth." It's a sad term, but accurate. This describes kids who are kicked out of their homes because of drug habits or personality issues or because their parents can't deal with their sexual orientation. Sometimes kids run away and adults won't let them return. The bottom line is that most of the homeless youth are honestly homeless.

Most larger cities conduct a census of their homeless population in January of every year. Of course, it is hard to be accurate with a population that is always on the move, but the number that comes up most frequently for youth (anybody under 23) is around 1.5 million on any given day in the United States. The youth under 18 are even harder to count since they tend to be particularly evasive.

You write about families a lot. The street punks form an unusual definition of a family.

Street kids do form an unconventional family of sorts, but there can be a lot of conflict between them. They fight over resources and squatting rights and the best spots for panhandling. But there is also a sense of community, a sort of "us against the world" mentality. They understand each other.

Then there is the Bryce family. They are conventional in so many regards.

The parents are money-oriented, they've got bills to pay, a

lifestyle to maintain. Their daughter turns up her nose at their consumerism way of life and chooses a minimalist existence. But like a lot of adult children today, she still relies on her parents for certain things even while she criticizes them.

Then there are the Kimballs. Even though LDS are very family-oriented, these parents can't seem to overcome the inconvenience of having a child with Lorelei's problems. They methodically try various ways of solving the problem, but once they'd gone through all the obvious options they pretty much gave up. They're only interested in fixing the problem, not learning to live an altered life. Some families end up letting go of children like Lorelei in order to preserve the rest of the family.

Emily is against her parents' consumerism, yet she takes gifts from them that she needs but cannot afford, like car tires.

It intrigued me to look at the social issue of young people without direction in life. I have plenty of friends who paid for their children to attend college. Some dropped out, some are indecisive and drag the experience out for years, some graduate and then move right back in with their parents.

Psychologists are now calling the period between eighteen and twenty-five, "emerging adulthood." Many parents are dismayed and frustrated by their grown children's delayed transition from childhood to self-reliant adult. Parents don't know when to cut their children off financially, when helping is no longer truly beneficial. Then there are the kids who suffer overly involved parents who refuse to let go.

There are so many choices now, particularly for kids from supportive, well-off families. Young adults seem overwhelmed by possibilities, thwarted by the competition and resentful of all the expectations. This is probably the first group of children who don't expect to do as well as their parents did financially, so many of them are rejecting the pressure to go out and achieve. The economy is making it harder for them to succeed, and so they are turning away from the consumerism and ambition of their parents' generation.

Barbara is an interesting, complicated person.

Lots of readers love Barbara and her demons. She was fun to write because she allowed me to express opinions and views that are generally not my own. As a writer, one is constantly in the study of human motives. Barbara is based on people I love and respect, but don't necessarily agree with when it comes to politics, economics and society's responsibilities. Perhaps it is my journalism background that compels me to tell both sides of a story.

On the other hand, I'm not exactly like Emily either. She's not driven to accomplish anything, the polar opposite of me. I'm constantly looking for life's next big challenge. Emily is one of those content people who just wants everybody else to chill. These folks don't bother to consider long-term goals or what the future will bring. They're happy to just exist. That was something different for me to explore as a writer, how to make an interesting character out of somebody with very little drive. In the end, we find Emily is complicated and talented.

You seem to like to write about different professions.

I have an artist friend who says she never asks anybody what they do when she meets them. I found this odd, so I decided to try it myself. It was hard for me not having a concrete way to define someone. I had to just take people as human beings and not look at them in a larger social and economic context. It was an interesting exercise, but not one I could adhere to for long. It's too ingrained in me to ask, "So, what do you do?"

I like to give my characters careers and jobs. I have written about bartending, taxidermy, landscape architecture, public relations, social work, philanthropy, drug trafficking, working for a mulch company, sewing underwear in a factory, being a sculptor, a housewife and a security guard. My next book is about a chef and a botanist. Jobs are an easy way to develop a character because as Emily observed, professions are how we define ourselves in society.

What type of research did you do for this novel? How did you get the details of homeless life?

The youth street outreach program in Austin is called LifeWorks.

The fellow in charge of direct contact with the kids was very generous with his time. He took me to locations important to the homeless youth in Austin. He was very open and answered question after question, guiding me in the right direction. He shared studies about the homeless youth population done on both national and local levels. My work is filled with details—locations, language, music, services and attitudes. I try to be as accurate as I can, as long as it benefits the story.

I found a number of lengthy Internet chats about being young and homeless. One conversation, posted by a girl in Australia, continued for a number of years. Her candid explanations of her day-to-day struggles inspired many of Lorelei's thoughts and situations. I came to admire the ingenuity homeless kids possess. Homeless youth are often viewed as only deficient or deviant, but I found them to be resourceful and clever. They possess a lot of coping skills, a lot of street smarts.

Road Dogg is a real person. I met this young man in a studio while I was interviewing a tattoo artist. He had his street name inked across the tops of his fingers. He regaled me with firsthand accounts of the life of a traveler—train hopping, community houses, how to find work on the road. I had to name a character after him.

He helped a lot with my understanding of what it took to cover your body in tattoos. He described how bored homeless kids pierce and tattoo each other for recreation. Some of the kids even do body modifications, like sewing the upper cartilage of their ears together to make elf ears. My teenage daughter thought this was totally cool, while I found it unnerving.

Tattoos are a large part of the plot of your novel. Did you do research into tattoos?

I talked to dozens of people and visited studios to interview tattoo artists. I read a lot and researched the history of the art form. Tattooing is such a rich historical means of human expression. Other cultures admire the art, but in America, excluding the military, tattooing is associated with criminality or being lower class. People with tattoos are thought to be showing open distain for traditional social mores.

Once, a girlfriend and I took our daughters to the beach. We were in a touristy spot where a shop sold transfer tattoos. My daughter was about five and she begged for a butterfly. While I watched our girls get tiny animal designs I thought, *why not?* I had nowhere to go and nothing to do for a couple of weeks. I got a pretty henna scroll on my neck as a social experiment, just to see if the world would treat me any differently. I was amazed by the change in how I was treated. Granted we were in the conservative South, but still, the transformation of my caste in life was immediate and across the board. I suddenly went from an upper middle class mommy to trash. It was shocking.

Perception is the key word when thinking about tattoos. Some cultures see this form of art as a right of passage. Some view tattoos as a way of beautifying the body and still other cultures use it as a means of showing rank. American culture views it as a statement that says, "I don't play by anybody's rules." This frightens the mainstream; but things are changing. People under thirty don't view tattoos the same way their parents do. It is becoming more accepted and I think tattoos will soon be as ubiquitous as coloring one's hair.

Music plays a part in this book. What music did you listen to while you wrote?

I listened to a lot of amazing music while writing *Anonymity*. I love alternative music, so I enjoyed learning what appeals to kids today. The music is rich and filled with emotion, but the lyrics are dark. These kids aren't listening to silly love songs. Music now expresses a lot of genuine angst. Their songs are about real life struggles.

Four artists that stood out as street culture favorites are Green Day, Beck, Radiohead and Everclear. These artists write expressive, narrative-based songs. *Father of Mine*, by Everclear, is a song very representative of the problems many of the street kids face. These lines from the song are most telling:

Daddy gave me his name,
Then he walked away.

Creep, by Radiohead, is a particularly poignant song. I found that homeless youth had sort of adopted it as their anthem. There are so many sad lines in that song that relate to youth street culture, but the one that stands out to me the most is,
I want you to notice when I'm not around.

I think that says it all.

I encourage parents to listen to these songs. They're beautiful and painful and meaningful and honest. They make you think about what type of society we are providing our kids. Our children are crying out for our attention.

Is it your hallmark to leave something unfinished about your stories, a few loose ends?

I do like to leave things for the reader to ponder after they put down one of my books. Life is a long, rambling adventure. Things are constantly shifting; there are always questions. It is realistic and much more interesting to leave something to consider.

I'm often asked what happened to particular characters, or if I'm going to write sequels. I love it that people are involved enough with my characters to care, but I never expound on what I've written. That's one of the most enjoyable parts of writing for me, knowing that I've piqued someone's interest and made them want to know more.

lifew🌀rks

A portion of the proceeds from this novel will be donated to LifeWorks in Austin, Texas.

LifeWorks functions on the belief that everyone possesses the skills to lead a successful life. LifeWorks counselors are fiercely and unconditionally devoted to assisting homeless youth in Austin. Through street outreach, emergency shelter, life skills training, workforce development, educational support and many types of counseling, LifeWorks seeks to help young people transition from the streets to a self-sufficient, better life.

To get involved or contribute contact LifeWorks.

www.lifeworksaustin.org

512-735-2470

CPSIA information can be obtained at www.ICGtesting.com
Printed in the USA
BVOW072150221112

306265BV00002B/2/P